SLOTH

MAKE YOUR OWN SUPERVILLAIN #7

LUCAS FLINT

Published by Secret Identity Books. An imprint of Annulus Publishing.

Copyright © Lucas Flint 2024. All rights reserved.

Contact: luke@lucasflint.com

Cover design by Miblart (www.miblart.com)

No part of this publication may be reproduced, distributed, or transmitted in any form or by any means, including photocopying, recording, or other electronic or mechanical methods, without the prior written permission of the publisher, except in the case of brief quotations embodied in critical reviews and certain other noncommercial uses permitted by copyright law. For permission requests, send an email to the above contact.

1

What do you do when you wake up in the middle of the night, can't go to sleep, and don't have anyone else to talk to (because, you know, it's midnight and everyone you know is trying to get some sleep)?

If you are a normal person, you probably just grab your phone or turn on the TV and mindlessly start browsing content. Or maybe, if you are feeling really ambitious, you'll get up and try to do some basic exercise to try to tire yourself out. Or if you're a workaholic (like a certain professional superhero I happen to work for), you might just try to get some work before everyone else gets up.

But if you are me—and I am not sure that anyone would describe me as 'normal'—you decide to head straight down to the Basement of your workplace to meditate in front of the nearly-completed meteor that gave you your superpowers.

Oh, and also gave birth to seven of the worst supervillains the world has ever seen and indirectly caused the deaths and traumas of countless people in the city you live in.

Sometimes, I question why we keep that meteor around and imagine what it would be like to destroy it, even though I know that wouldn't do anything except make me feel a little better about things.

Anyway, I take the elevator from the first floor to the Basement of the Stable, rubbing my eyes as I did so. Even though today was exhausting—stopping a bank robbery in the morning, rescuing a little girl from her crazy mom who kidnapped her and caused a police standoff in the afternoon, and ending with kicking the butts of some muggers trying to steal the purse from a little old lady right before dinner—I just couldn't sleep tonight.

I'm not sure why, but for the past several months since the death of Lady Waste, I've found it harder and harder to sleep through the night. It has nothing to do with my recurring nightmares about the destruction of Oklahoma City, either, because those stopped after I killed Lady Waste, too.

I just wake up, shivering and covered in sweat, unable to stop thinking about the meteor.

So, every night since Lady Waste's demise, I've found myself heading down into the Basement of the Stable to sit in front of the meteor and meditate. And by 'meditate,' I mean stare at it for hours until I either fall asleep or morning comes and I know I need to get to work.

I can't explain *why* the meteor fascinates me so. I mean, it's always interested me, but it feels like ever since I killed Lady Waste and put her two Cores into the meteor, I've become almost obsessive about it. I don't even live in the same house as my family anymore. My night-time wakings have gotten so bad that I decided to move into the Stable so I could get to the meteor easier every night without having to travel to work or risk waking up everyone else.

On the plus side, this means that there is always someone to keep an eye on the Stable at all times. Granted, we do have a security system with cameras and everything, but Captain Cowboy and I agree that it is sometimes helpful to have actual human beings keeping an eye on things because automated security systems can't always be trusted to keep track of every intruder or problem.

So that is probably the only reason why I found out that six Cores of the Meteor Monsters we retrieved were missing this morning.

Stepping out of the elevator, I walk past the shelves of boxes containing various pieces of equipment and spare parts for our weapons and vehicles toward the center of the Basement. The lights are always on down here, which I understand is due to how the electrical system in the Basement is set up, according to Captain Cowboy. Even though no one is down here most of the time, it doesn't cost Captain Cowboy much to keep the power on all the time, and it can get pretty dark without the lights on, anyway.

So that is why I am surprised when I step out of the elevator and find that the Basement is totally dark.

Pausing in front of the open doors of the elevator, I look around the Basement. I can't see very much, other than what is illuminated by the light from the elevator behind me, which isn't much. I can see some shelves and boxes, but that's it. I can't even see the meteor from here, although I am sure it is still in the center of the Basement where it always is.

But that doesn't explain why the Basement lights are off, even though they are supposed to be on all the time. I don't recall either Captain Cowboy or Keith bringing up any maintenance issues with the electricity in the Stable, and the lights everywhere else work just fine.

So I flip the switch on the wall next to the elevator doors, but the lights do not kick back on. That isn't good. Maybe I should call and let him know.

I quickly shake my head. That's a silly idea. Captain Cowboy is probably fast asleep with my mom at the moment, and I know that he doesn't like to be roused from his sleep unless it's a genuine work or personal emergency. Right now, I have no reason to think that the broken lights are anything except the lighting down here malfunctioning, so I'll probably just inform Keith about it in the morning so he can call the electric company and have someone fix it. Yeah, that makes sense. Besides, I don't get good cell reception down here, so I would have to go back up to one of the higher floors just to be able to call anyone, and I don't really feel like doing that right now. My fire powers and the light from the elevator can provide plenty of illumination.

At least, that is what I think until I hear the shuffling of feet somewhere in the darkness ahead of me, followed by the sound of something like a rock landing on the floor and someone swearing under their breath.

I freeze and listen closely to my surroundings, but the Basement is silent again. Rubbing my eyes, I wonder for a moment if I was just imagining things or if I had actually heard someone. Then I hear more footsteps before me.

This time, they sound like they're coming from the direction of the meteor.

If someone who shouldn't be down here is trying to get to the meteor...

"Fire up!" I shout, my voice echoing through the Basement.

Flames envelop my entire body for a second before disappearing, replacing my pajamas with my signature Wyldfyre costume.

But I don't stop to admire how comfy my costume is. With adrenaline racing through my body, I rush down between the shelves of boxes toward the center of the Basement, going deeper and deeper into the shadows. Wielding my trusty club in one hand, I hold my flaming club out to provide more illumination as I seek out whoever is down here.

And then I reach the meteor and come to an abrupt stop. Staring at the meteor, my jaw drops.

Because all six of the Cores of the Meteor Monsters—the Cores that my team and I spent the last two years carefully collecting—are gone. The star-shaped holes in the meteor where the Cores normally rest are empty, just like they were after the Meteor Monsters came to life the first time.

My mouth dry and my heart hammering in my chest, I look around desperately, saying, "Who is down here?"

No one answers, obviously, because whoever is smart enough to make it past the Stable's security systems and steal all six of the Cores without anyone knowing would have to be smart enough not to answer my question.

But whoever is stupid enough to try to steal all six Meteor Monster Cores right from under my nose probably is too stupid to realize that using my powers enhances my senses, including my hearing.

Which is how I hear the faintest shuffling of feet behind one of the shelves on the other side of the Basement.

In one smooth motion, I swap out my club for my bow, nock an arrow into it, and let the flaming arrow fly toward the shelves. The fiery arrow strikes the shelves and instantly sets the entire thing on fire, which I know is probably not a smart thing to do in an enclosed environment like the Basement, but seeing as I am immune to fire and smoke damage, this is just the most efficient way to flush out the rat I am hunting.

And flush him out I do. A man wearing a ski mask and a black outfit rushes out from behind the burning shelves toward the elevator, a brown cloth bag thrown over his shoulder. He moves surprisingly fast, probably because he doesn't want to suffocate on the smoke from the burning shelves or burn to death in here.

But I am faster still.

I fly over the head of the man and land directly in his path between him and the elevator. The thief skids to a stop before pulling out a gun and pointing it at me, but I kick the gun out of his hand, sending it flying somewhere into the shadows around us.

The thief, jerking his hand back to his chest, then turns around like he is going to run away, but I grab the collar of his shirt and yank him back onto the ground. The thief drops the bag, which clunks to the floor, suggesting that it's full of the missing Meteor Monster Cores.

Slamming my foot down on the thief's chest, I summon my club again and point its burning tip at his masked face. "Try anything else, and I will burn that ski mask straight off your face. Or maybe onto your face. I could probably do that too if you piss me off badly enough."

The thief gulps loudly and says in a frightened tone, "Please, Wyldfyre! Do not kill me. I was only doing what I was told to do. I promise I won't try to hurt or kill you if you let me go!"

The thief sounds like an old man, surprisingly, and not just any old man, either. His voice is very familiar, even though it has been a while since I last heard him.

So I grab the thief by the collar of his shirt and, hauling him to his feet, slam him against the wall next to the open elevator doors. I put my club in one of my belt loops and yank his mask off of his head before he even realizes what I'm doing.

In the dim light of the open elevator, I find myself face to face with the aged and scared face of Arnold Linderman, of all people. He looks even older than the last time I saw him, which is a bit strange because it was only a couple of years ago now.

Quick backstory: Arnold was the last surviving resident of the Oklahoma ghost town called Picher, located in northeast Oklahoma near the borders of Kansas and Arkansas. While he lived there, the second Meteor Monster I killed, Wasteland, took up residence in the abandoned mines underneath the town and turned Arnold into his lackey, who fed unwitting travelers to Wasteland to make him stronger and more intelligent. When I first met Arnold, he pretended to be an innocent man who was being manipulated and controlled against his will by Wasteland, but it turned out that he was very much a willing believer in Wasteland's goal of destroying the country and nearly got me, my team, and my baby sister killed.

After my team and I killed Wasteland, Arnold disappeared. Last I heard, the government had put out a warrant for his arrest, but I guess they didn't know where he had disappeared to, either. Personally, I had assumed that he had fled the country, maybe to Mexico or something, because I didn't see how else an old man like him could evade both the government and my team forever.

Yet here he was, a frightened look on his elderly features, breathing hard and sweating even harder as I press him against the wall. If I didn't remember how he had tried to get me, my girlfriend, and my baby sister killed the last time we met, I might have even been tempted to feel sorry for him.

Right now, however, I am this close to bashing his brains out with my club, but first, I want answers.

Pushing him against the wall even harder, I snap, "Arnold? What are you doing here? I thought you had fled the country. How did you break into the Stable without alerting our security system? And what were you doing with the Meteor Monster Cores?"

Arnold gulps. "I was trying to revive Wasteland. I had recently read in the news that you had killed a Meteor Monster called Lady Waste and realized that she was at least partly my old master. I did not realize, however, that you were here, as our intelligence suggested that the Stable is usually empty at night."

I frown. "Our intelligence? Are you working with someone else?"

"He certainly is, Wyldfyre," says an all-too-familiar gravelly, smug voice behind me. "Unfortunately, he was too stupid to keep his mouth shut."

I look over my shoulder in time to see a fist flying toward my face. The fist smashes into my jaw, sending me staggering to the side as I let go of Arnold, who collapses onto the floor in a heap. Rubbing my jaw, I look up to see who assaulted me, even though I am pretty sure I recognize that voice.

Standing several feet away from me, wearing his pristine white suit, is none other than Agent Templeton Black. Tall and gangly, Agent Black glares at me from behind his signature shades, which he apparently wears even in dark basements. He smirks at me. "Why the surprised look, kid? Did you really think that Arnold Linderman would have the skill necessary to hack into your base's security and sneak in without anyone noticing?"

I scowl at Black as I stop rubbing my chin, lowering my hand to my side. "Black? I thought you were in prison. What are you doing here?"

Black, however, doesn't answer my question. Instead, he glares at Arnold and snaps, "Grab the bag and leave! I will keep Wyldfyre busy."

Arnold, to his credit, scrambles to his feet and snatches the bag that is on the floor a few feet away from him. I immediately rush toward Arnold, only for Black to jump in my path and lash out with a kick that forces me to back off to avoid getting nailed in the jaw.

Staggering backward, I glare at Black and snap, "Black, what the hell do you think you are doing? Arnold is trying to revive Wasteland! Even you have to know that that is a bad idea."

Black snorts and cracks his knuckles. "You're right. Reviving Wasteland *alone* would be a bad idea. A much better idea is reviving *all* of the Meteor Monsters. Which is exactly what we are trying to do."

2

My head spins from the revelation that Agent Black just dropped. "Wait, you guys are trying to revive *all* of the Meteor Monsters? Why?" I shake my head. "Doesn't matter. I'm not going to let you."

I summon my bow and aim at the fleeing back of Arnold as he rushes toward the elevator, but again, Black leaps toward me. Landing in front of me, Black lashes out with a kick to my gut, making me double over from the impact of the blow before he grabs my shoulders and throws me to the side.

I crash into one of the shelves, knocking it over and sending boxes flying everywhere. But I recover quickly, rising to my feet as Black walks over to me, his white suit still very clean in the low light provided by the open elevator.

By now, Arnold has reached the elevator, but instead of escaping, he's standing in the elevator with an urgent look on his face. "Templeton, what are you doing? We need to leave now before the boy calls for help!"

Black, however, shoots an annoyed glare over his shoulder at Arnold. "I am well aware of the plan, Arnold. Which is why I am following *my* part of it, the part that our leader evidently did not share with you."

I quirk an eyebrow. "Your leader? Who is that?"

Black turns his annoyed gaze back to me, though now he looks more amused than anything. "You haven't figured it out yet? I'm debating if I should tell you or if I should let you figure it out on your own. That might take a while, though, seeing as your brain is slower than molasses."

I scowl at Black. Swapping out my bow for my tapena club, I say, "I'm not sure what you and Arnold hope to accomplish by reviving the Meteor Monsters, but regardless, I am going to make sure that neither of you leaves with any of them."

Black cracks his neck again. "A credible threat ... if we didn't have a rather strict deadline to keep and a rather unforgiving master to appease."

Black suddenly pulls out some kind of spherical object from his coat and throws it at me. The ball lands at my feet and, before I can react, it explodes, filling the air with a weird green smoke that I accidentally inhale. The green smoke is surprisingly sweet, but I still hack on it anyway as it coats my lungs, feeling sticky in my mouth and on my throat.

"What ... are ... you ... doing?" I cough, trying—and failing—to stay on my feet. I fall onto my hands and knees. "Poison ...?"

Black, standing over me now, shakes his head. "No. Sleep gas. It will put you out for a few hours, but you should wake up from it."

I stare up at Black weakly, my eyelids feeling extremely heavy for some reason. "Why ...? So you can kill me in my sleep ...?'

Black lowers his shades to look at me, smiling triumphantly. "Not yet. We can't kill you until the time is right. My boss just wanted me to give you a message from him. Take this."

Black throws a USB drive onto the floor before me. Blinking rapidly, I try to pick up the USB drive, only to fall forward and crash onto the floor, the flash drive mere inches away from my face.

I am so tired ... I can't even think ...

Before my eyes close, the last thing I see is the back of Black's white suit as he walks back to the elevator and joins Arnold. The elevator doors close after Black enters.

And then I lose all consciousness and drift into complete darkness, the kind of sleep I had wanted for a while now but know, in the back of my mind, is not what I should be doing right now ...

3

"Toby!" a loud, Southern-accented male voice practically screams in my ear. "Toby, wake up!"

My eyes fly open and I sit upright. Without even thinking, I reach out, grab the collar of someone's shirt, and slam them onto the floor, instantly putting them in a chokehold. For one wild moment, I think I am holding down either Black or Arnold, who were apparently too stupid to stay out of my reach after I woke up from the sleep gas.

But then I hear shuffling feet and surprised cries around me and finally look around at my surroundings.

I am still in the Basement, but apparently, someone got the lights working again because the lights are on and I can see everything again now. I see Keith and Paintbrush standing near the elevators, the two of them wearing surprised and alarmed expressions on their faces. Keith is even reaching for his pocket knife, though not sure why.

Odd. I see Keith and Paintbrush, but where is Captain Cowboy?

A groan under me answers that question for me. I look down and see that the man I have in a chokehold is neither Black nor Arnold, but rather Captain Cowboy. His cowboy hat must have fallen off his head when I grabbed him, too, because it now lies on the floor at my feet.

"Toby, what are you doing?" demands Cap, his face red and his blond hair messy. "Now's not the time to be horsing around!"

Sheepishly, I release Cap from my chokehold and, bending over, pick up his hat and hand it to him. "Sorry, boss. I thought you were—"

"Temple Black or Arnold Linderman?" asks Captain Cowboy, his voice slightly annoyed as he takes his hat back from me and plops it on his head. He gives me a sardonic look. "Who do I look more like, the guy old enough to be my dad or the guy with skin darker than his black heart?"

I blink in surprise at Captain Cowboy. "How did you know I was fighting those two?"

"We saw the security footage from the first floor this morning when we came into work," says Keith grimly. He scratches the back of his head. "We saw you go down in the elevator and then saw Black and Arnold come up a little while afterward, but we didn't see you. There isn't security footage from the Basement itself, mostly because the security cameras down here seemed to have stopped functioning at some point during the night."

I grimace. No doubt that is also the work of Black or Linderman or whoever they happen to be working for.

Paintbrush nods in concern. "Yeah, it was really scary for a while there because we didn't know if you were still alive or ... if you were ... well ..."

I scowl, but not at any of them. I'm mostly scowling at Black and Arnold, who clearly scared my girlfriend into thinking I was dead and stole the Meteor Monster Cores at the same time. "Trust me, there's no way in the freaking *world* I would ever let either of those two lowlifes kill me. They just knocked me out with a weird sleep gas, but I'm fine otherwise."

Captain Cowboy strokes his chin thoughtfully. "That explains the strange minty smell I smelled when we came down here. Not sure who makes mint-scented sleep gas, though."

I open my mouth to make a witty comment about it myself before I suddenly remember what Black and Arnold stole and, gasping, whip my head in the general direction of the meteor. "The meteor!"

Ignoring everyone else, I fly over the shelves toward the meteor. Landing on the ground, I stop in front of the meteor and felt my heart stop.

All of the Cores are gone. Every last one of them.

And I have no idea where they are now.

I fall to my knees, staring in disbelief at the empty meteor, my heart hammering in my chest. "The Cores ... the ones we spent the last two years collecting ... they're gone. All of them."

A hand lands on my shoulder and I jerk my gaze up at Paintbrush, who is looking down at me with a calming expression on her face.

"But you are alive," says Paintbrush, squeezing my shoulder, "and that's what matters."

Captain Cowboy nods as he and Keith walk up beside me on my other side. "Mandy's right. Your life is way more important than the Cores."

Keith puts his hands on his hips as he looks down at the meteor, a frown on his face. "Yes, but I wonder why they didn't kill Toby when they had the chance. If Toby was knocked out, like he said he was, then he would have been at their complete and total mercy."

Rubbing the back of my head, which hurts a lot for some reason, I say, "All Black mentioned was that it was not yet time for me to die. He said he wanted to leave a message from his 'leader,' whoever that is."

Captain Cowboy groans. "Great. What was the message?"

I shrug. "I don't know. Black left a flash drive containing the message but I fell asleep before I could read it."

Keith holds up a black flash drive. "Is this the flash drive that Black left? We found it when we got down here but haven't had a chance to plug it into a computer yet."

I nod quickly. "Yes, that is the flash drive. We should head back up to the first floor and watch the message there."

Paintbrush, however, suddenly pulls a laptop out of nowhere and says, "No need to do that. I brought Codetalker's laptop with us down here. He isn't available at the moment as he's apparently involved in a different mission, but we did text him to let him know that we found you down here, and he said he would call us later after lunch when he has some time."

I had been wondering about Codetalker, our resident superhero hacker who had been very helpful in dealing with the last couple of Meteor Monsters recently. His ability to track pretty much anyone and anything would undoubtedly prove useful when it came to tracking down Black and Linderman, along with their mysterious employer.

Thinking about Black, however, made me scratch the back of my head again and say, "I don't understand how Black even got down here. Wasn't he arrested by the feds and thrown in some federal black site somewhere where he was going to rot for the rest of his sorry life?"

Captain Cowboy shakes his head. "I was as surprised to see Templeton as you were when we looked at the security footage this morning, Toby. No one from the federal government has warned me about his escape, which is basically what I'd expect from the feds. They're very helpful that way, you know."

Keith, who was opening the laptop and inserting the flash drive into it, said, "We should contact Agent Camel at some point and let him know. I mean, he probably already knows that Black is on the loose, but at least if we call him, we can perhaps get some answers."

Keith is referring to Agent Charlie Camel, another agent from the Department of Superheroes, who is significantly less corrupt than Black but also pretty eccentric in his own way. After Black got arrested, we were given Agent Camel's contact information as our liaison with the federal government, especially concerning the Meteor Monster situation. Personally, I like Agent Camel's partner, Rodney Jake, a lot better as he seemed a lot more serious and competent than Agent Camel, but either way, Keith was right that we would have to reach out to him at some point about this. It probably made sense to mention the theft of the Meteor Monster Cores as well because, even though we don't want the feds to have their hands on them, we also don't want a couple of crooks like Black and Linderman using them either, especially if their goal is to revive the Meteor Monsters.

I push that thought to the side as Keith clicks a few buttons on the laptop and then a video. At first, the video is just a dark, blank screen that makes me wonder if maybe there is something wrong with the computer.

But then the blackness fizzles and the image of a man appears on the screen.

The man looks like a stereotypical professor. Thick, nerdy glasses along with a sweater vest over a button-down shirt and slacks give him the appearance of a philosophy professor about to start lecturing his students on the nature of chairs or something like that.

But his skin is pale white, and when he smiles, he reveals a row of vampiric teeth that send shivers down my spine. Oh, and did I forget to mention that he has the exact same green eyes that all Meteor Monsters do?

I exhale sharply. "Logikill."

Captain Cowboy glances at me briefly. "That's him? The last Meteor Monster?"

I nod. "Definitely. I wouldn't mistake him for anyone else."

Another quick backstory: Logikill is the seventh and last member of the Meteor Monsters. In fact, we had been trying to hunt him down for the past six or seven months ever since I killed Lady Waste. Unfortunately, he had proven to be very tricky to find, even for Codetalker, so the fact that he sent this message to us directly is shocking, to say the least. I didn't think he wanted to be found, but I guess he does.

In the video, Logikill is reclining in an old wooden chair behind a desk, but the rest of the room is too dark for me to make out any real details. I imagine that is probably deliberate on his part so we aren't able to pin down where this video was recorded.

Logikill smiles at the camera, showing every one of his vampiric teeth. "Greetings, Wyldfyre. Or should I say, Tobias Miller, the son of Michael and Wendy Miller, as well as the older brother of Dakota Miller? Personally, I think I will refer to you by your given name, as I find your superhero name quite ridiculous."

I snort. "Says the guy named Logikill."

As if aware of what I just said, Logikill continues, "And before you snark about my name, let it be known that you named me, just as you named my other siblings. I do not complain about that, however, because I understand that it is the job of the creator to name his creations. To the extent that I have taken on pseudonyms, it is only to hide my true identity until I was ready to come out of the darkness. Unlike my siblings, who simply could not help themselves. Like moths drawn to a light, they came to you, and each and every one of them died as a result."

Captain Cowboy folds his arms across his chest. "He sure likes to talk, don't he?"

Keith chuckles and elbows me. "Like 'father,' like 'son,' right?"

I resist the urge to respond to Keith's teasing because I want to focus on Logikill's video message.

Logikill continues to speak. "Anyway, if you are viewing this video, then that means my minions have successfully stolen all six of the Meteor Monster Cores that you so helpfully collected for me. I wanted to thank you for doing my dirty work for me. You saved me a lot of time and effort that I've spent more productively in other areas of my life, such as planning this heist, for example."

I glare at Logikill's smirking face on the laptop. He's acting like I spent the last two years collecting the Meteor Monster Cores just for him. If I didn't already hate him for stealing the Cores, I definitely hate him now.

Logikill presses the tips of his fingers together. "But I didn't just want to thank you for being so unintentionally helpful. I asked my minions to leave this message with you because I want to talk in person very soon. And by very soon, I mean tomorrow morning for breakfast. Or perhaps brunch, seeing as I do prefer to sleep in."

I raise a skeptical eyebrow and glance at the others, but they look just as lost as I am about Logikill's offer. But we don't talk about it because, obviously, none of us know what Logikill is going to say next.

"Undoubtedly, Toby, you are curious to know why I want to talk with you," says Logikill. He leans toward the camera, a ghoulish grin on his face. "The reason for that is quite simple. You have questions, and I have answers. All of the answers. About the Meteor Monsters, about our true origin, about all the ways that we are connected to you, and why everything in your life in the last two years has happened. I know all of it, and I am more than happy to share it with you in person over some delicious biscuits."

It feels like my heart stops in my chest when Logikill says that.

It is true that I have always had a lot of questions about the origin of the meteor that brought the Meteor Monsters to life and gave me my powers in the first place, among other topics. I have gathered bits and pieces of the answers to those questions from the other Meteor Monsters over the years, but seeing as most of the Meteor Monsters were of questionable sanity and character, I never knew if I could actually believe them or not.

Yet here was Logikill, claiming to have all the answers. And while it is definitely possible that he is lying, I can't think of who else could possibly have the answers to even half of those questions. Plus, I can't explain it, but something in Logikill's words rings true to my gut, telling me that his offer is a lot more serious than it seems.

But Logikill continues to speak in the video. "If you are at all interested in taking me up on this offer, simply show up at the Hunny Bunny location on 23rd St. at 10:00 AM tomorrow morning. Once you get there, there will be an empty outdoor table where you can sit and wait for my arrival. Rest assured that, although I do enjoy sleeping in, I will be there on time."

Logikill leans back into his chair and holds up a finger. "But in the interest of fairness, I must disclose a couple of requirements that I must see fulfilled before I will show myself. First, you must come to the restaurant alone. You cannot bring Captain Cowboy, your girlfriend, or any of your family members, friends, or allies. This meeting will be between you and me and no one else. To ensure that you come alone, I will have several agents of my own at the restaurant keeping an eye on you. If any of them see or even suspect that you brought someone else with you, they will immediately shoot up every customer and worker in the restaurant."

My gut wrenches when Logikill says that. Everyone else wears horrified looks on their faces, and Captain Cowboy even swears under his breath. But we keep listening because it is all we can do at this point.

Logikill raises a second finger. "Secondly, I will ask you to leave your phone, ear communication device, and any other communication devices you may have back at your home or wherever you choose to keep them. I do not want you recording our conversation without my knowledge, and I certainly do not want any of your allies listening in on our conversation. It will be just between you and me. Even my own agents will not be listening in."

I bite my lower lip. I really want to argue with him about all of these strict requirements, but arguing with a computer is never a good look, especially a computer that can't even respond to you. So I hold my tongue but am already thinking of the best ways I will get back at Logikill when I see him in real life.

Logikill finally raises a third finger. "And thirdly, and lastly, please bring your sketchbook. It will be much easier to explain the situation to you if you have your sketchbook with you."

Now that is weird. I can't imagine why Logikill would need my sketchbook, seeing as it is just an ordinary sketchbook. True, it is the source of the Meteor Monsters, but only because the energies from the meteor brought them to life from it. Regardless, out of the three conditions he listed, that one is definitely the least burdensome on me.

Logikill adjusts his glasses on his face. "So that is my offer to you. If you do not wish to show up to our meeting tomorrow morning, that is your prerogative. There will be no immediate consequences to that decision, other than that I cannot guarantee the safety of the workers and customers at Hunny Bunny if you refuse to show up. Many of my agents are quite trigger-happy, to put it mildly, and I cannot stop them from doing whatever they wish to do, especially if it involves taking innocent lives. But now the ball is in your court, Toby. It will be interesting to see what you do next."

With that, the video goes blank again ... leaving us all staring at the computer in sheer disbelief.

4

Captain Cowboy removes his hat from his head, scratches the top of his head, and says, in a surprisingly calm tone, "Well, if this doesn't have the word 'TRAP' written all over it, my middle name is Betsy."

Snapping out of my thoughts, I give Captain Cowboy a deadpan look. "What gave it away, Cap? The fact that Logikill threatened to have his minions shoot up an entire restaurant full of people or the fact that Logikill said he's gonna have his minions blend in with the crowd so they can start shooting up people as soon as things start going south for him?"

Paintbrush furrows her brow. "I noticed Logikill didn't mention anything about calling the police or getting the government involved. Do you think there's any significance to that or—?"

"Unlikely," says Codetalker, his cool, slightly monotone voice coming from the computer. His 'CT' logo suddenly appears on the screen, obscuring the video player. "Most likely, the police and government were included in Logikill's definition of 'allies,' which is probably why he didn't feel the need to single them out specifically."

I stare at Codetalker's laptop in surprise. "I thought you wouldn't be available until after lunch."

"Wrapped up my other mission sooner than I thought," says Codetalker dismissively. "Plus, my computer indicated that a potentially hostile device was just inserted into my laptop, so I had to check. As my laptop and desktop are connected, I was able to watch the entire video with you from my base."

"Good," says Captain Cowboy with a nod. "Saves us a lot of unnecessary explaining."

"Indeed," says Codetalker. His voice takes an abruptly serious tone. "Wyldfyre, you *shouldn't* go to brunch with Logikill tomorrow morning."

I raise an eyebrow. "I shouldn't?"

Paintbrush gasps at Codetalker. "Didn't you hear what Logikill was threatening to do to all of those people at the restaurant if Wyldfyre doesn't show up? I don't think we really even have a choice at this point."

"You are assuming that Logikill's threat is at all credible," says Codetalker, "which I find highly unlikely. If his threat is credible, then we should probably just call the restaurant, show them the video, and warn them not to open for business tomorrow morning. That way, he won't even have the opportunity to hurt anyone."

My hands ball into fists. "But we've been searching for Logikill for months! Credible threat or not, this is our best chance to nab him and probably retrieve the missing Meteor Monster Cores, too, which I don't think we've told you about yet."

"I just watched the security footage of Black and that old man leaving the Basement with a bag of what are obviously the Cores," says Codetalker. "I know what is at stake here. And that is precisely why you *cannot* go, Wyldfyre."

I fold my arms in front of my chest. "So because this is our best bet at finally catching Logikill, I should just ... not? I'm not following your logic here, Codetalker."

Codetalker's logo disappears, replaced by a live webcam view of Codetalker's haggard face. The bags under his eyes behind his glasses make it look like he did another all-nighter, though he usually looks like that. "There is no reason why Logikill would want to meet with you anywhere if he didn't have some way to take advantage of you."

"You think he's gonna try to kill Toby in public?" says Captain Cowboy doubtfully. "I mean, it's possible, I guess, but seeing as Toby is still alive after his tussle with Black and Linderman, color me skeptical."

"Logikill probably doesn't want to kill Toby," says Codetalker. He rubs his eyes tiredly. "I don't know what he wants, exactly, but if Logikill has all six of the Meteor Monster Cores and wants to meet with Toby in real life, it is obvious that his motives are less than pure. If I had to guess, it has something to do with Toby's powers, which we know are deeply connected to the origin of the Meteor Monsters."

I shift my weight from foot to foot uncomfortably. "He did mention the sketchbook, but I don't know why he would want that."

"I don't, either, but it doesn't matter," says Codetalker. "Logikill doesn't strike me as the kind of guy to simply do things for no reason. Am I right about that, Toby? You should know him better than any of us. What kind of powers does he have?"

Everyone looks at me, while I rub my arm unconsciously. "Uh, he's pretty weak physically, but I did imagine he had mind control powers. That way, he could, like, make people do his bidding, seeing as he's pretty lazy and doesn't like to exert himself."

"Mind control?" Captain Cowboy repeats. He grimaces. "Like Lady Lust?"

I shake my head. "No. Lady Lust's power only worked on men who were attracted to her or had the potential to be attracted to her. Logikill's power, on the other hand, works on men, women, children ... pretty much anyone and everyone, honestly. I didn't bother to give him any limits, other than he can really only use it on people in his immediate vicinity."

Keith breathes a sigh of relief. "So we don't have to worry about him turning half of the city against the other half again, like what Lady Waste did?"

I purse my lips. "Probably not, but it has been two years since the Meteor Monsters were born. We know that the others developed more complex personalities and more and different powers. Hard to say what Logikill can do now."

"Which is yet another reason to reject his offer," says Codetalker. "Logikill is probably betting on taking advantage of our ignorance of his powers to achieve whatever his goal is. He might even want to take control of your mind."

Paintbrush brushed a strand of dark hair out of her eyes. "Sounds like he just wants to talk to Toby, though, and answer his questions."

Codetalker snorts. "I find it highly doubtful that that is *all* he wants to do, even if he does want to answer a few of Wyldfyre's questions."

I bite my lower lip again. "But if I'm not going to meet up with Logikill, what *should* we do, then? He still has the Cores and is, according to Black and Linderman, planning to resurrect the other Meteor Monsters. Can you track him from the flash drive or something, Codetalker?"

Codetalker shakes his head. "Doesn't work that way. Even if I hacked the flash drive, all it would tell me is what is on the flash drive. If Logikill is even half as diligent as I think he is, then he probably made sure to delete the metadata from the video file, so we can't even use that to track where he filmed the video."

"So we're what, just supposed to ignore how his minions stole the Meteor Monster Cores and are doing who-knows-what with them even as we speak?" I demand, anger flaring inside me. "We can't let them get away with this. If they succeed in bringing back even just *one* of the Meteor Monsters—"

"What do you think they want *you* for?" says Codetalker. "Logikill clearly thinks there is a strong connection between you and the Meteor Monsters. We know that as a fact, actually. That is why we are not going to walk into an obvious trap."

I scowl. Even though Codetalker's reasoning is sound, something inside me doesn't agree with his idea. Partially because I am pretty sure that Logikill is not lying about his threat to shoot up the restaurant, but also partially for reasons I can't entirely articulate. It's like there is this sense of *wrongness* inside me that won't go away until I take back the Cores that Logikill stole from me, the same sense of wrongness that drove me to get them all in the first place. A sense that if *I* don't have all of the Cores, then something *really* bad will happen.

That drive has always been there, but right now, it is going into overdrive, demanding that I go and meet up with Logikill and force that fool to give up all of the Cores. And also take *his* Core, too, to complete my collection and keep the city safe.

That is when a plan suddenly forms in my head. "All right, Codetalker, I see your point. But consider this: If Logikill has the other Meteor Monster Cores and has yet to actually resurrect any of them, then that means there's still a chance we can get them back."

Codetalker frowns. "Technically, yes, but I don't see how that changes things."

I spread my hands. "Think about it, Codetalker. Suppose I go to brunch with Logikill tomorrow morning at Hunny Bunny. Depending on how things work out, I could capture him and bring him back here and force him to either give up the Cores or tell us where he is hiding them. At the very least, I could kill him and take his Core, which would be a win in itself."

Paintbrush purses her lips. "Not a bad plan, Toby, except for the fact that Logikill said his minions will shoot up everyone in the restaurant if you or we try anything. Feels like a no-win situation no matter how you look at it."

I point at Paintbrush. "True, but maybe that's why I get there early, try to spy out which customers are Logikill's minions and which aren't. That way, not only could I catch Logikill, but I could even take out his minions before they hurt anyone."

Captain Cowboy puts his hat back on his head, a serious expression on his face. "All by yourself?"

"You guys can stay near the restaurant as backup," I say. "So long as you don't follow me into the restaurant or are seen by Logikill or his minions, we shouldn't have to worry about Logikill breaking the deal and ordering his men to shoot up everyone anyway."

Captain Cowboy whistles. "Sounds risky as hell, Toby. I mean, I understand what is at stake here and even agree with you to an extent, but CT also speaks a lot of common sense. I'd rather not risk the lives of innocent people if I can help it, even if it gives us a good chance at catching Logikill."

Anger flares in me yet again. Don't any of these idiots understand what will happen if we reject our best chance at finding and killing Logikill? Why are they not listening to reason? Who cares if other people's lives end up endangered?

I catch myself. Wait, what am I thinking? We're superheroes. We're not supposed to risk the lives of innocent people unnecessarily. Where are these thoughts even coming from?

"Toby, are you all right?" asks Paintbrush. "You went really quiet all of a sudden."

I shake my head and look around, realizing that everyone is staring at me, including Codetalker on the TV.

I grimace. "It was nothing. Just ... Codetalker, what do you think we should do, then, if not accept Logikill's offer?"

Codetalker nods. "First, we contact the restaurant and tell them to not open tomorrow, at least not until after ten, preferably later. That way, in case Logikill really is planning to shoot up the place, there will be no one there for his minions to hurt.

"Second, we track Black and Linderman to wherever they took the Cores. Seeing as we now know for sure that they are working directly for Logikill, it stands to reason that Logikill had them take the Cores to wherever his hideout is in Oklahoma City."

I run my hand through my hair. "But they escaped hours ago! How are we going to track them down?"

Codetalker smiles. "If Black and Linderman left, they had to have an escape vehicle of some sort, right? I doubt they are on foot. Oscar, does the Stable have external security cameras?"

"A few," says Captain Cowboy as he scratches his ear. Realization dawns on his face. "You think maybe one of the external cameras got an image of 'em?"

Codetalker turns his attention away from the camera and starts typing, the *click-clack* of the keys of his mechanical keyboard coming out of the laptop's speakers. "Exactly. I will have my AI assistant do a quick check of the previous night's security footage for any sign of any suspicious vehicles and—Ah! Here's something interesting."

SLOTH

A second, smaller video player pops into view next to Codetalker's head. The video player suddenly expands until it takes up most of the screen, leaving Codetalker's face hovering in the corner.

The video starts playing. It shows what looks like the back of the Stable at night, which is empty. Suddenly, a city garbage truck pulls up and stops.

Then two very familiar masked figures—clearly Black and Linderman, based on their outfits and costumes—jump out of the garbage truck and rush toward the back door. Linderman waits nervously while Black picks the lock. He's apparently successful because, just a few seconds later, Black opens the door and the two of them enter the building.

The video fast forwards about fifteen minutes and then Black and Linderman, looking as I remembered them looking during our tussle, burst out of the back door of the Stable. They climb back into the truck, which then immediately reverses direction and heads toward the nearest street.

As it does so, the truck briefly reveals its license plate and the video pauses.

"A license plate," says Codetalker. "Running it through the State of Oklahoma's database, it appears that this truck belongs to the same garbage company that runs the Southeast Landfill."

I frown and glance at Captain Cowboy. "Isn't that where you, me, and Keith fought all those Wastelings a while ago? You don't think—?"

"Impossible to say," says Codetalker. "It's possible they might have stolen the truck, as I doubt the city or the company is secretly working for Logikill. Though, I suppose after the Jackpot incident, you can't be too skeptical of the powers that be."

Captain Cowboy frowns. "All right. I say we head to the Southeast Landfill and find out if anyone has noticed anything. The owners were pretty cooperative the last time we went there, so I'm sure they'd be willing to help us again if we asked nicely."

"Sounds like a good idea," says Codetalker. "I will check our CCTV footage around the city for any other clues as to the current location of that truck and let you know if I find anything. See you later."

Codetalker's screen clicks off, leaving us all standing there, wondering where the Cores were and if we would find anything at the Southeast Landfill.

5

The Southeast Landfill hasn't changed much in the two and a half years it has been since we last went there, searching for clues to the whereabouts of Wasteland and my kidnapped sister. Hard to believe it's been that long since I was last here, but I guess time really does fly.

Anyway, like before, the Southeast Landfill is full of piles of garbage in every direction, including junk cars, broken appliances like dishwashers and clothes dryers, and a ton of other stuff that I can't even begin to identify.

This time, it's just me, Paintbrush, and Cap walking between the mountains of garbage everywhere, weapons at the ready just in case Logikill or his minions decide to jump us. Keith would have tagged along, but he was concerned about how easily Black and Linderman managed to break into the Stable last night, so he and Codetalker were working together to up the Stable's security. No idea exactly what that will entail, but seeing as both Keith and Codetalker are kind of paranoid, I suspect whatever improvements they come up with together will be pretty wild.

Also, we did call up Hunny Bunny and warned them about Logikill's shooting threats. Fortunately, the management there happens to be full of Captain Cowboy fans, so they agree to shut the restaurant down for the entirety of tomorrow. Not only are they closing the location on 23rd Street and telling all of their employees to stay home, but they are also closing their other locations throughout the OKC metro area, just in case Logikill decides to send his minions to shoot up those locations, too.

After we did that, we called up the owners of the Southeast Landfill and asked them if we could investigate the landfill for clues about Logikill's current location. The owners, once again, reported not seeing anything suspicious recently, but agreed to let us investigate anyway. They sent back most of the workers at the Landfill for the couple of hours we requested to investigate it, just to keep them safe.

So that is how Paintbrush, Cap, and I ended up back at the Southeast Landfill, walking among the piles of garbage, a cold winter wind blustering through the landfill as we picked our way among the junk. The cold wind didn't bother me too much thanks to my fire powers, but Captain Cowboy and Paintbrush both shivered in the wind slightly, even though they were both wearing warm weather versions of their costumes that should keep them warm.

But we all keep our eyes and ears open as we walk. Last time we came here, we got ambushed by Wasteland's Wastelings and Keith nearly died. That memory was fresh on my and Cap's minds as we walked amongst the garbage, all of us expecting Logikill and his minions to try to jump us when we least expected it.

Paintbrush waves her hand in front of her face, wrinkling her nose as she does so. "Man, this place *stinks*. If this is where Logikill is hiding, then he really is brilliant."

Walking beside Paintbrush, I look at her in confusion. "What's so smart about hiding in a literal dump?"

Captain Cowboy chuckles. "Because it smells so awful here that no one would even think of searching for him here, right, Mandy?"

Paintbrush nods. "Yes. And it might just be me, but it just smells so horrible that I don't know how *anyone* could tolerate it. It would have been nicer if he had picked a place like the Will Rogers Gardens or something, someplace with plenty of pretty flowers."

I resist the urge to roll my eyes. "Yeah, because that is definitely what Meteor Monsters are known for: Loving pretty flowers."

"It don't matter much *where* Logikill is as long as we actually find him," says Captain Cowboy. He sighs and tips his hat back on his head, looking around at the garbage surrounding us on all sides. "I just wish we had some actual clues other than the license plate of the getaway vehicle. Right now I feel like a blind squirrel stumbling around in the dark for a nut."

Paintbrush looks at me. "Toby, can't you just sense Logikill with your Meteor Monster senses? Or maybe even sense the Cores, too?"

I shrug. "That's what I'm hoping for, but so far, my Meteor Monster senses have been pretty quiet. So until I actually *feel* something, we might be wandering around here for a while."

Captain Cowboy lets out a frustrated breath. "And that's assuming you even feel something at all or that Logikill doesn't have some way of hiding his presence like some of the other Meteor Monsters did. He could be hiding right behind us and we might not even know it if he decides to hide his presence."

I furrow my brow. "I guess that's possible, but my gut feeling tells me that Logikill isn't *really* hiding. I can't explain it, but I feel like he *wants* to be found."

"And you would be quite correct, Wyldfyre," says a familiar cold, harsh voice from atop one of the piles of garbage nearby. "And I am happy to report that you have, indeed, found me."

We skid to a stop and immediately look up in the direction of the voice that just spoke.

Logikill himself is standing on top of a particularly tall pile of garbage, specifically on the roof of an old, rusted-out car that definitely saw better days. Thin and clad in a thick winter coat, Logikill stares down at us from behind his thick glasses, his vampiric teeth bared in a smirk.

I immediately raise my tapena and point it at Logikill. "Nice of you to show yourself, Logikill. Die."

My tapena bursts into flame and I launch through the air toward Logikill, making sure to aim for that big egghead of his. I don't know where his Core is, exactly, but even Meteor Monsters don't enjoy getting their skulls bashed in by a flaming club. If nothing else, I'll at least break those tacky glasses of his, which should be amusing.

But when I am halfway to Logikill, his green eyes suddenly flash and something big and hairy explodes from underneath an overturned van below. The creature, whatever it is, tackles me out of the air halfway to Logikill, sending us both crashing to the ground. We roll across the ground for several feet before crashing against an old fridge.

Dazed, I shake my head and look up, wondering what in the world had attacked me ...

Only to see the extremely familiar face of Humanimal the Cannibal, the first Meteor Monster, smiling down at me with a big smile full of blood-stained teeth.

6

Humanimal the Cannibal looks like a muscular man with a tiger head, wearing only a loincloth and some tiger teeth around his neck like a necklace. He really doesn't look like he's aged a day since I killed him back in the crater of the meteor all those years ago.

But I don't even think about it. I just stare uncomprehendingly at Humanimal because his face is the very last one I expected to see again.

Humanimal's grin widens, showing more of his bloody teeth. "Long time, no see, Daddy. Sorry for being so rough, but I couldn't let you kill big brother, not after he brought me back to life."

Humanimal's voice, deep and harsh, cuts through my shock like a knife through butter and I instantly summon flames around my body. Humanimal shrieks and roars, letting go of my arms as he jumps backward out of my reach.

Patting the flames out on his chest, Humanimal shoots me a hurt look and says, "Why did you do that, Daddy? I wasn't too rough with you, was I?"

"Enough with the whole 'Daddy' talk, Humanimal," says another familiar, gurgly voice from behind a mountain of garbage. "You know he doesn't love us and never will."

Two tendrils made of sludge emerge from a garbage pile behind Captain Cowboy and Paintbrush. The tendrils wrap around Captain Cowboy and Paintbrush's waists, causing them both to cry out as the tendrils lift them into the air.

A second later, Wasteland, the second Meteor Monster, emerges from a hole in the ground, merging with his tendrils. He seems bigger than I remember, however, easily towering over the rest of the junk in the junkyard as he holds Captain Cowboy and Paintbrush in his hands like toys.

"Paintbrush!" I shout, turning my attention away from Humanimal to focus on her and Cap. "Cap!"

Ignoring Humanimal, who is still patting out the flames on his chest, I run toward Wasteland, swapping my tapena out for my trusty bow and arrow. Nocking a fiery arrow in the bow, I take aim at Wasteland's big, ugly face as I run, only for me to run straight into a metal baseball bat to the face that comes out of nowhere.

The blow sends me staggering backward, dropping my bow at the same time. My head spinning, I feel my nose, which is partially broken and definitely bleeding, as I struggle to remain standing.

A snivelly little chuckle, however, catches my interest. "Better watch where you step, brat. Otherwise, you might get hurt."

Blinking my eyes rapidly, my vision clears enough for me to see a man with snake-like features and wearing a dark hoodie standing between me and Wasteland. Clapping his metal baseball bat against his open palm, the Crippler, the third Meteor Monster, flashes me a hideous smirk.

Scowling, I wipe the blood off my broken nose, which is already starting to heal, and growl, "Crippler. Get in line. I need to kill Humanimal and Wasteland first and then I'll deal with *you* later."

The Crippler laughs. "What do you think brother Road Rage would think about that?"

The roar of a motorcycle engine explodes behind me and I whip my head around just in time to see a truly huge motorcycle hurtling toward me. The motorcycle slams into me, the blow sending me flying. I crash on top of the rusted remains of a dryer and gasp as I feel something sharp—probably a part of the dryer—pierce my side. Normally, I would try to at least look at my injuries, but the rumbling motorcycle makes me look at it.

A massive, muscular black man, complete with black leather gear, boots, and a luchador-style mask, sits on a parked motorcycle near the Crippler. The green eyes of Road Rage, the fourth Meteor Monster, glare out at me from behind his mask, full of barely-contained rage as he dismounts his motorcycle.

"Nice hit, bro," says the Crippler, standing beside Road Rage. He chuckles. "Stupid kid didn't even sense it coming."

Road Rage growls. "Don't get too cocky. This kid has killed us before. He could kill us again. Although it *was* satisfying to run him over, even if he somehow survived."

SLOTH

Grunting in pain, I yank my body off of the metal piercing it and rise to my feet. My healing factor gets to work quickly, the pain subsiding already, but it still hurts like hell. It'd only been like, five minutes, and I'd taken too many blows from the Meteor Monsters.

Still, there are only four, five if you count Logkill. If I really try—

Suddenly, a handful of dice blocks land on the ground at my feet and explode. The blast strikes me like a runaway train and I went flying backward again, this time going so fast I smash through a pile of garbage and land on the other side. Banging my head against the ground, my senses go crazy as I push myself up on my hands and knees, coughing out dirt and blood.

Then a fancy leather boot appears before my face and I look up to find myself staring into the grinning face of Jackpot, the fifth Meteor Monster, who is clutching his cane with both hands.

"Fancy running into *you* here, kid," says Jackpot, tilting his head to the side. He looks around at our surroundings and grimaces. "Ugh. So much trash. But I guess it's appropriate, seeing as you are definitely trash yourself."

Spitting out more dirt from my mouth, I jump to my feet and grab Jackpot's throat with an iron grip. "Shut *up*, Jackpot. If you want to die again, then I'll be happy to oblige."

"Without asking *me*, first?" says a sharp female voice above me. "Now that is a *naughty* boy indeed."

I look in the direction of the voice just in time to see a huge black web flying toward me. The web crashes on the back of my neck and shoulders and lifts me off the ground, causing me to let go of Jackpot, who staggers backward slightly, rubbing his neck as I rise into the air against my will.

Struggling against the webbing, I look down to see Lady Lust, the sixth Meteor Monster, her black hair cascading down her shoulders, walk right up next to Jackpot, arms folded under her rather large breasts. She shoots me a smirk that doesn't look too different from Jackpot's, her black lips twisting upward in a way that makes her look significantly less appealing than she normally does.

Still rubbing his neck, Jackpot shoots Lady Lust a grateful look. "Thanks for the save, babe. That boy has got a grip."

Lady Lust smiles lovingly back at Jackpot. "Anytime, my love. I would do anything for you."

Lady Lust leans over and kisses Jackpot on the lips, making me wonder if this is how they are planning on torturing me. I hope they just stick to kissing, but based on the way Jackpot is starting to grab at her, I feel like I am about to see a very family-unfriendly scene play out before me.

That is, until a *snap*—like the snap of a finger—echoes through the junkyard and Jackpot and Lady Lust tear themselves away from each other. They turn their backs toward me to look at the source of the snap and I, still stuck in Lady Lust's web, follow their gaze.

Logikill is walking toward us, with the Crippler, Road Rage, and Humanimal walking on either side of him like his own personal bodyguards. Wasteland is right behind them, still holding Captain Cowboy and Paintbrush, their bodies now completely covered in his sludge. To their credit, both Cap and Paintbrush are clearly still trying to free themselves, but it's obvious to me that neither of them are going to be getting free on their own anytime soon.

My blood boils at the sight of my girlfriend and boss being held hostage like that. "Logikill, you monster—"

"Yes, I know what I am, thanks for informing me," says Logikill as he and the other Meteor Monsters stop a few feet from my web. He looks at Lady Lust. "Sister, if you please."

Lady Lust nods and waves a hand at me.

The web holding me suddenly descends toward the ground, stopping just a few feet above the ground. I debate using my firepowers to free myself, but I am worried about what Wasteland might do to Cap and Paintbrush if I try anything, so I don't. I do note, however, that my healing factor has healed most of my injuries at this point, although I am still pretty exhausted after taking so much damage in such a short period of time.

Hovering above the ground, I look at Logikill, who is just a few feet away from me now. I frown. "How did you know we were here?"

Logikill's green eyes glitter with amusement. "Did you really think I would offer to meet you in a public place full of witnesses, knowing full well that you and your team would have plenty of time to warn the restaurant owners and set up a trap of your own? Or didn't you find it suspicious that Black and Linderman allowed your base's security cameras to see the getaway vehicle, even though there was no reason why that should be so?"

I grimace. "So you always intended to meet us here. The restaurant wasn't the trap. *This* place was."

"Exactly," says Logikill with a nod. He gestures at the other Meteor Monsters. "And, of course, it would have been rather risky of me to meet you anywhere without help. So I took the liberty of resurrecting my dead siblings. A cunning move, wouldn't you agree?"

I scowl and glare at the other Meteor Monsters. "I'm surprised they are all willingly working for you. Jackpot made it sound like he didn't trust you before I killed him the first time."

Jackpot furrows his brow and looks at Logikill in confusion. "What's the kid talking about, brother? I've always trusted you."

Logikill smiles. "Think nothing of it, brother. Wyldfyre is simply trying to sow dissension among us, and in a rather blatant way, too."

Okay, now I am *really* suspicious about what Logikill did to his siblings. Before I killed them all the first time, the Meteor Monsters had all been extremely independent of one another, almost irrationally so. Only Jackpot and Lady Lust had actively worked together, and even then, I still killed them individually. Yet now even Jackpot, who was definitely the most paranoid and distrusting among all of the Monsters, is apparently a team player who would never even think about betraying Logikill or suspecting him of being up to no good.

That, needless to say, is not a good thing, either.

Turning his gaze back to me, Logikill says, "Regardless, I've been wanting to meet you for a long time now, Tobias. I had hoped it would be under different circumstances, but sadly, your own irrational actions have forced me to make choices I wish I never had to make." He sighs. "Mostly because I've had to work, and if there is one thing I hate above all else, it is work."

"You're a lazy bum, I get it," I say impatiently. I glance at the other Meteor Monsters. "So what order are you going to do this is in? Torture us and *then* kill us or kill us and then torture our bodies?"

The Crippler excitedly strokes his baseball bat. "Oooh, either one sounds like fun, but I prefer to torture my victims while they are still alive. How else will you get to hear their screams of anguish and pain as you peel the skin off their fingers or gouge out their eyeballs?"

Logikill grimaces. "Brother Crippler, please keep your disgusting fantasies to yourself. It's making the rest of us uncomfortable."

The Crippler immediately bows toward Logikill. "Apologies, big brother. I just got so excited I forgot my manners."

"Then you'd better not forget them next time, younger brother," says Logikill sternly. "Otherwise, I will have to punish you and you don't want to be *punished*, do you?"

The Crippler shudders. "No, I do not, big brother."

Logikill nods. "That is what I thought." He turns toward me before the weirdness of his interaction with the Crippler can truly set in. "But to answer your sardonic question, Tobias, we aren't planning on torturing you. Or even killing you. As I said in the video I had Black leave for you to watch on that USB drive, I simply want to talk."

I raise an eyebrow and throw a glare at Wasteland, who is still holding Paintbrush and Captain Cowboy. "Just want to 'talk,' huh? Does talking with you always include holding innocent people hostage?"

Logikill sighs as if he is speaking to an extremely dull, slow-witted person. "Tobias, Tobias. You and I both know that your bias against Meteor Monsters, though admittedly logical and well-founded, would prevent you from ever sitting down to have a nice, calm conversation with me. You would never trust me to uphold my end of the deal or not try to pull some dirty tricks. Likewise, I cannot trust you not to try to get me, either, so I needed leverage."

"Leverage, eh?" I say. "Is that what you call holding two innocent people hostage?"

Logikill shrugs. "If that is how you are going to be, maybe I will have Wasteland kill them anyway."

Suddenly, both Paintbrush and Captain Cowboy sink deeper into Wasteland's body. They are now up to just under their armpits, though that isn't very reassuring, seeing as they can't get a good grip on Wasteland's goopy body.

"No!" I say urgently. "Fine! We can talk. Just … don't hurt my girlfriend or boss, okay?"

Logikill nods. "A fair deal. Indeed, I think I shall sweeten it by having Lady Lust here free you. Sister, would you be a dear and let Tobias go? It will be easier to talk if he isn't dangling above me like a fly caught in flypaper."

Lady Lust waves her hand at me and the webbing suddenly lets go of my neck and shoulders. I land on my feet and immediately rise to my full height, ready to fight Logikill in case this turns out to be a trap.

SLOTH

But Logikill doesn't attack me. Resting his hands on his cane, Logikill turns and gestures for me to follow. "Come with me, Tobias. Let's walk and talk, just like the great human intellectuals of old."

I cast a wary gaze at Wasteland, but Logikill says, "Do not worry about your friends. Neither Wasteland nor any of my other siblings will lay even one finger on their heads until we return. You have my word."

Which really isn't worth much, but with all seven of the Meteor Monsters assembled, I have no choice but to take Logikill at his word.

So I walk after Logikill, who is already making his way in a random direction away from the others. I have no idea what Logikill is going to say or tell me, but I throw a last reassuring look at Paintbrush and Captain Cowboy before finally reaching Logikill.

Slowing down my pace so I don't walk past him, I say to Logikill, "So, Logikill, what did you want to talk about?"

Logikill looks at me and a smile, the creepiest smile I have seen on any of the Meteor Monsters so far, appears on his pale lips. "Everything, of course. But why don't we start with the meteor? Or should I say, the alien ship sent by a dead empire to prepare Earth for an alien invasion that will never come?"

7

I come to a stop. "What?"

Logikill, who is still walking, looks over his shoulder at me, clearly impatient. "Keep walking. The deal was that we'd walk and talk. No walking, no talking. Or would you rather listen to the death cries of your girlfriend and boss?"

Logikill says that threat calmly but seriously, leaving no doubt in my mind that he *would* have Wasteland kill Paintbrush and Captain Cowboy if I didn't keep moving.

Bastard...

Shaking my head, I resume walking until I am by his side again, feeling like I am back in school being lectured by my least favorite teacher ever. "Okay, but you can't just drop that revelation on me and not expect me to do *something*."

Logikill smirks as he kicks a soda can out of our path. It bounces into a disposable diaper to the side of our walking way. "Of course not. Truthfully, I expected you to try to kill me now that we are out of sight of my siblings. I am rather defenseless."

I jerk my head over my shoulder. Logikill is right. Even though we have not been walking for very long, I already can't see Wasteland and my friends or any of the other Meteor Monsters through the mountains of garbage on all sides. My shoulders tense, but there's nothing I can do about it. I doubt the Meteor Monsters have killed Captain Cowboy or Paintbrush yet, because even though I still don't trust Logikill, I doubt he'd give up his leverage over me that easily.

Because Logikill is right about one thing:

If Captain Cowboy and Paintbrush weren't currently held hostage, I'd have burned him to a crisp a long time ago.

I keep walking, hands in my pockets. "Okay, but now you have to explain the whole 'dead alien empire' thing that you so casually dropped, because this is the first I've heard of it."

Logikill nods. "I am not surprised. This isn't exactly common knowledge, even among us Meteor Monsters. But yes, I can certainly elaborate for you, mostly because I believe you need to know this information now."

I frown at Logikill. "Why do you think I need to know this information? I mean, I definitely want to know it, but I feel like you aren't just telling me this out of the goodness of your heart."

Logikill chuckles. "An excellent point! After all, I don't even have a heart. Yes, the truth is, I have very selfish motives for wanting to talk to you now and answer your questions about everything. Once you understand the truth, then you will understand what is truly at stake here, and why you are destined to rejoin us regardless of how you feel about it right now."

I scowl at Logikill, imagining what his face would look like if I just burned it right now. "You aren't the first Meteor Monster to say that to me. I feel like all of you guys keep trying to convince me that we are meant to be together or something like that. It's ridiculous, it hasn't worked, and I don't know why you guys keep trying."

Logikill taps his chin thoughtfully. "You are assuming that my siblings acted in a rational, self-aware manner. The truth is, however, that all of my siblings are so totally lacking in self-awareness that they might as well still be children. Only, children eventually develop a sense of self-awareness, whereas my siblings never would have developed that."

I think back to my first encounter with Jackpot and his offer to hire me, as well as how he expressed confusion over his purpose. "I don't know about that. I feel like the other Meteor Monsters were starting to develop some kind of self-awareness of their own actions, even if they still didn't understand themselves completely."

Logikill shrugs as we pass a rusted washing machine, which still has clothes hanging out of it for some reason. "Perhaps so. We were designed to be self-evolving organisms, after all. I am sure you encountered unexpected abilities and traits among my siblings during your previous battles with them. Even so, they ultimately were still very childlike in the most important of ways, which is why none of them ever suspected that they were being played this entire time."

I shoot a questioning look at Logikill. "Being played by who? And are you ever going to elaborate on the dead alien empire thing? Because that is still pretty interesting."

Logikill sighs and adjusts his glasses. "Very well. First things first, I suppose. As you undoubtedly remember, the meteor that eventually gave birth to my siblings and me, as well as granting you your powers, fell from outer space three years ago almost to the day. Indeed, tomorrow will be the third anniversary of the fall of the meteor. Certainly a coincidence, is it not?"

I doubt it. Logikill clearly planned for our meeting to be close to the anniversary of the meteor crash. In fact, the more Logikill talks, the more I suspect that he planned a lot of things over the last three years, but I decide to keep that thought to myself and keep listening. If there is one thing I have learned from hunting Meteor Monsters over the last three years, it is that they all love to talk, and this is a good way to buy time and learn information that you otherwise wouldn't learn.

Actually, that sounds a lot like what Captain Cowboy would do, which makes sense. I have definitely learned a lot about being a superhero from him.

Logikill continues speaking. "I am sure that the appearance of the meteor, along with the births of my siblings and me, caused quite the sensation among the people of Oklahoma City, especially on the Internet. Many of your fellow humans posited all sorts of crazy theories about the true nature and origin of the Meteor Monsters, ranging from accusing us of being aliens from another planet, to being demons from the depths of hell, and everything in between. I even saw one particularly crazy theory that claimed we were biological weapons crafted by the United States federal government to test in an urban environment for future urban warfare situations."

I purse my lips. "So I take it that you aren't biological weapons created by the feds, then."

Logikill gives me an amused look. "Of course not. We aren't even from this world. Truthfully, the alien theory is the closest to explaining our origins, although none of the theories I have read online have gotten any of the details correct. It seems to me that many people still don't understand that the meteor brought us to life using the sketches in your sketchbook as the basis for our physical bodies and powers."

I nod, thinking about my sketchbook, which I left back home because I didn't think I would need it here. Now, however, I feel a strong urge to pull it out and flip through it again. Maybe I will do that when we get home.

If we get home.

Because I am still not entirely convinced that Logikill is planning to let us leave this place alive.

Stepping over a piece of broken pipe in my path, I ask Logikill, "So you guys are aliens, then. That makes sense."

Logikill scratches the back of his neck, knocking a broken glass bottle out of his way at the same time. "Yes and no. We aren't the aliens. The aliens built us."

I tilt my head to the side. "What do you mean? You guys came into being after the meteor struck my sketchbook. I didn't see any aliens around the crater when that happened."

Logikill shakes his head. "And who built the meteor? Intelligent life, obviously. Not human life, of course, but as I am sure you are aware by now, humans are not the only intelligent life in the universe."

I nod. "I've heard rumors about alien life, but I haven't actually seen it myself."

"You should ask your superhero friends Beams and Doctor Mind about alien life visiting Earth," says Logikill. "I can guarantee that the two of them have had quite a bit of experience dealing with otherworldly entities, including those infinitely more intelligent than human beings." He sighs. "What I wouldn't give to be able to speak to a true intellectual equal, but alas, I am trapped here on this speck of dirt in the corner of the cosmos, surrounded by beings so much dimmer than I that they might as well be animals."

I roll my eyes. "Sorry that not everyone on Earth is a giant egghead like yourself. Honestly, I probably should have named you Egghead, because that's a lot better name for you."

Logikill pats me on the shoulder with a chuckle. "Egghead certainly would have been a colorful name, but I have come to appreciate the rather edgy name you gave me. It has certainly allowed me to develop a reputation, if nothing else."

I smirk at Logikill. "Okay, Egghead, who are these aliens that created the meteor, and why did they send it to Earth?"

Logikill turns his gaze away from me. "Frankly, I don't know who our creators were. I do know, however, why they sent us to Earth, even if my siblings forgot."

Putting my hands on my hips, I say, "How do you not know who your creators are but know why they sent you to Earth? That doesn't make sense."

Logikill frowns. "The answer is as simple as it is frustrating. You see, ages ago, long before human life even existed on Earth, a powerful and terrifying alien civilization achieved interstellar travel of the likes that you humans are just barely beginning to understand. Using their advanced technology, this alien civilization, whose name has been lost to time, expanded their reach across the cosmos, conquering planet after planet and stripping worlds of their resources to fuel their hungry civilization. Frequently, this required either enslaving the natives of the planets they conquered at a minimum, or, if the natives proved more trouble than they were worth, they elected to simply wipe out all life on that planet and use their own workers to strip the planet of its resources."

I grimace. "I want to say I'm surprised that you guys were created by genocidal alien warlords, but I really can't. Explains a lot of your behavior."

Logikill gives me a surprised look. "Perhaps you are smarter than I thought. You are starting to get ahead of me, which is rather rude, you know, as I am the one talking."

"Holding my friends hostage is also rather rude, if you ask me," I say.

Logikill shrugs again. "Touché. But to continue my little story, this alien empire would approach the conquest of the various worlds they coveted differently from how you humans would approach it. Rather than send armies of trained soldiers armed with powerful weapons to subjugate the natives or wipe them out, our creators instead sent certain weapons they had designed to infiltrate the inhabitants of a planet and use their sins to turn them against each other. The idea was that the weapons would cause so much chaos and discord among the natives that it would then be easy for the empire to come in and subjugate the planet with little resistance."

I think about the implications of that statement as we walk. "Let me see if I get it. Instead of just coming in and curbing everyone with their superior firepower and technology, your creators instead wanted to divide a planet's inhabitants so there wouldn't be an effective resistance against their rule. Right?"

Logikill nods once again as we turn a corner, walking past a pile of metal sheets that look like they've been out here for a while. "Indeed. And can you guess what that weapon was that would create so much chaos? I am sure that even you understand that at this point."

At first, I want to tell Logikill that I have no idea what he is talking about. But then I think about it a little bit more, and the realization hits me like a truck.

Slowly, I say to Logikill, "You mean the meteor?"

A truly frightening smile appears on Logikill's face. "You are correct. Because the meteor is not just a hunk of space rock that just so happened to fall on Earth three years ago. It was a weapon specifically designed by a hostile alien civilization to prepare the planet for eventual conquest. By bringing to life the seven deadly sins, these manifestations of pure evil would run amok in the local population, spreading chaos and terror wherever they went, leaving the natives unable to fight back against their future conquerors."

Logikill suddenly comes to a stop, as do I. We stop in front of another pile of garbage, this one looking like a bunch of trash bags full of dead leaves piled on top of each other. It's too tall for us to walk over or move, but our path splits in two directions, one to the left and one to the right.

But I frankly don't care about that. I turn to face Logikill and say, "The seven deadly sins? What are you talking about? I'm pretty sure that only humans came up with that idea. You've got to be making stuff up now."

Logikill puts both of his hands on the top of his cane, smirking. "Do you believe that only humans can ever experience gluttony, pride, envy, wrath, greed, lust, or sloth? Other intelligent species suffer from the same disease. What you humans, in certain religions, call 'sin.' Our creators, however, simply referred to them as a disease ... one that could be quite useful to their cause."

I frown. "I'm not following."

"Of course you aren't," says Logikill, rubbing his forehead in exasperation. "You see, our creators were not merely warlords seeking out more land and resources. They were philosophers, too, thinkers and intellectuals, much like myself. Indeed, it isn't too far a stretch to consider me the closest of my siblings to our original creators, if only on a much smaller scale. They pondered issues of morality, of death and the afterlife, even debating among themselves about the existence of God and other spiritual entities ... they were quite human in that way, even if they differed in some of their conclusions from humanity."

I fold my arms across my chest. "Such as—?"

Logikill waves a hand dismissively at me. "It doesn't matter. Plus, it isn't like I know everything they discussed. I know only what we were programmed to know, though using my superior reasoning skills, I have been able to put together more of our creators than perhaps they intended."

I frown deeper. "So what are you getting at?"

"That our creators understood that what you humans call the seven deadly sins are indeed quite deadly," says Logikill. He gestures at the sky. "They believed that sending creatures whose job was to embody said sins and spread them throughout a planet's population would lead to wars, economic ruin, even natural disasters. You have seen firsthand for yourself how much trouble these sins can cause even on a local level. Imagine what would happen if they spread all over a planet, breaking down order and morality, rendering the population little more than shortsighted savages ignoring higher and more beautiful ideals in exchange for satisfying their base desires."

I grimace. "So that was your creators' playbook, huh? Send you guys to a planet and have you guys, what, come to life and make everyone act out in the worst possible way?"

"Mostly," says Logikill. He shakes his head. "But we are not the only weapon of our kind. At one point, there were thousands, even millions, of meteors designed specifically for this job. We were launched across the cosmos, seemingly at random as far as I could tell, to land on inhabited and uninhabited planets alike. From what I have gathered, the process of 'sinning' a planet, such as it is, could take decades, if not centuries, so our creators indiscriminately seeded us across the universe, playing a numbers game where they only needed to win a few times to win big."

I bite my lower lip. Although I don't know what it looked like, in my mind's eye, I imagine thousands of meteors just like the one that crashed behind my apartment complex landing on Earth, bringing to life thousands of Humanimals, Wastelands, and more. That there might be an entire universe's worth of meteors out there is a truly scary thought.

I look at the morning sky as well. "Does that mean that your creators are planning to invade Earth at some point?"

Logikill grimaces. "They would ... if they were still alive, that is. Which is highly doubtful at this point."

8

Tearing my eyes from the sky, I look at Logikill and furrow my brows. "How do you know they're dead?"

Logikill adjusts his glasses again, an uncertain expression on his face. "I don't. Not for certain, anyway. But the evidence I have accumulated over the past three years suggests, at least to me, that the meteor my siblings and I came in may have been one of the very last sent out before a civilizational collapse, the likes of which your puny human mind can't even begin to imagine, happened."

Logikill taps the side of his head and twin beams of light shoot from his eyes. They project an image on the garbage heap before us, which looks kind of like schematics for the meteor. Lots of weird markings surrounding it, which I assume is the written form of the alien empire's language, though of course I can't read it.

"These are the internal schematics of the meteor, stored in the meteor's memory system," says Logikill. "I believe the information was somehow loaded into my brain when I first came to life, but either way, it's interesting. Do you see that marking near the top there?"

Logikill points at what looks like three interlocking squares, spinning so slowly that I almost wonder if my eyes are playing tricks on me. "I see them. What do they say?"

Lowering his hand, Logikill says, "That this meteor is one of the last of its kind. It is the symbol of the very last letter in the alphabet of our creators. Using their alphabet, our creators assigned different waves of meteors different symbols to indicate if they were newer or older. That they marked ours with the last letter of their alphabet indicates that we were likely among the last of our kind created."

I frown. "Maybe they just canceled your line and made new weapons. Doesn't mean their society fell."

Logikill shakes his head. "If that were the case, we wouldn't have crashed on this planet with our memories fractured or missing. I have observed that the meteor appears hastily constructed, almost as if whoever built it was in a hurry. Perhaps our meteor was our creators' last efforts to save their own civilization, hoping that we might find hope for their survival somewhere else in the universe." He gives me an evil look. "Or maybe they were just hoping to send one last spiteful curse out to the universe, their way of throwing one last defiant tantrum before oblivion consumed them. Who can say, really, at this point?"

I fold my arms in front of my chest. "Even if their society collapsed, why? It sounds like they were big, powerful, and smart. Doesn't sound like they should have fallen easy."

Logikill shrugs. "I don't know the exact cause, but it would be truly ironic if one of their own meteors went rogue and caused the same chaos among themselves that they did among the various planets they conquered. I, at least, would find it amusing."

I eye Logikill carefully. "How do you know all of this? The other Meteor Monsters always acted confused or spoke in vague, incoherent nonsense anytime I asked them about their origins. Why are you the only one who actually remembers anything?"

Logikill taps his head and the projection of the meteor schematics disappears. "Partly because of the circumstances surrounding our birth. The initial crash damaged the meteor more than usual, which, again, relates back to what I said about the shoddy construction of our meteor. As a result, when we were brought to life, we didn't know who we were, what we were doing here, or why we existed. We only knew that we needed to spread as much chaos and destruction as possible, hence why we each went our separate ways to pursue our own goals. All this time, we have been following our programming without even realizing it."

Logikill puts a hand on his chest. "Except for me. Not long after my birth, I remembered *everything*. Or, at least, everything that our creators programmed into us. It was quite traumatic, like being born again. However, the information also helped me to contextualize my very existence along with the existence of my siblings. This, in turn, informed my actions over the last three years, leading up to his very day, just as I planned."

"Still doesn't explain how you remember when no one else does."

Logikill taps his forehead. "Ironically, that is thanks to *you*, Tobias. If you hadn't envisioned Logikill the supervillain as a cunning genius with an IQ higher than anyone else's, I likely would have remained as ignorant as my siblings about our true nature. My inherently high intelligence and curiosity caused me to extract those memories much sooner than the others did, which is how and why I have been manipulating them this entire time."

I look over my shoulder in the direction we came from, remembering how respectful the other Meteor Monsters acted toward Logikill. "So Jackpot was right. You really *were* trying to get your siblings killed. Why? So you can fulfill your creators' programming and make the world ready for them?"

Logikill laughs. It is a hoarse, chattering sound, like what I would imagine a skeleton's laughter would sound like, and it sends shivers down my spine despite the fire burning inside me. "Of course not. As I said, our creators are almost certainly dead and long gone at this point. Even if they are not, I sincerely doubt they are in any position to conquer Earth or any other planet at the moment, not if they are dealing with a society-wide collapse. No, I have decided that the most logical course of action is to conquer Earth in my name, making myself the leader of this world. And I need my siblings' help to do so."

I jerk my head back toward Logikill. "But I thought you guys were basically programmed to serve your real creators. Where is this ambition coming from?"

"Simple logic, of course," says Logikill. "Plus, I may or may not have inherited some of your anti-authority personality. I also generally dislike being told what to do. Often, others want me to work harder than I would prefer. It's very annoying."

"So your solution is to conquer the whole planet?" I ask in disbelief. "That sounds like a lot of work to me."

Logikill shrugs. "Only if I did it myself. As I said, I intend to have my siblings do all of the dirty work. But there's more to it than that."

"How much more?"

Logikill looks me straight in the eyes. "It's simple. We Meteor Monsters will only ever be safe if *we* are the ones who rule this world. After all, we are not human, not really. Even those of us who can pass as human, like Jackpot and Lady Lust, are still very clearly not human to anyone with working eyes. The odds of us living in peace among the very people we were sent to destroy are low, practically nonexistent. You saw how your government tried to capture and study us, to turn us into weapons for their own selfish, shortsighted use. That is the only fate that awaits us if we attempt peaceful coexistence among humanity."

Logikill turns back toward the sky, raising his arms into the air. "But if we rule the world, then we will never have to worry about our safety ever again. We will rule as gods while you humans grovel at our feet, begging for our forgiveness, for our mercy."

Logikill looks at me again, madness in his eyes. "And we will never give you any of it."

My hands ball into fists. "You're assuming I will let you get even close to doing that. I killed the others once. I can do it again."

Logikill lowers his hands and strokes his chin. "Perhaps, perhaps. But I haven't even told you the ugliest truth, the ugly truth about you and *your* powers. Or did you already forget that your powers come from the same meteor that brought my siblings and me to life?"

I hesitate. "No. I haven't—couldn't—forget that. What do you know about my powers?"

Logikill folds his arms behind his back, a thoughtful look on his face. "For the past three years, everyone has assumed there are only *seven* Meteor Monsters; that is, my siblings and I. Indeed, we have spoken ourselves about the seven deadly sins of humanity and how each Meteor Monster aligns with a particular sin. But what most people, including yourself, do not know is that an eighth Meteor Monster was born on that same day, the scariest and most dangerous of them all. Care to take a guess as to who that was?"

I gulp. "Me. It was me."

Logikill nods. "Correct. Your powers didn't simply come out of the ether, granted to you by the universe for some grand, benevolent purpose. No, like the rest of us, you were also intended to be a weapon—a weapon of conquest, and perhaps the most dangerous of us all."

I put my hand on my chest. "But I'm not like you and the others. You guys didn't even have physical bodies before the meteor brought you to life. I am still me."

Logikill gives me an amused look. "The meteor only gave us bodies because there were no other suitable candidates for weapons other than you at the time. If there had been seven other people in the crater with you when you touched the meteor, I imagine we would all have very different bodies, although our powers and abilities likely would have remained the same."

I purse my lips, trying not to look as troubled as I feel. "Maybe, but I don't have to be a weapon for a long-dead alien empire if I don't want to be. I can be—I am—a hero."

SLOTH

Logikill sits down on an overturned cardboard box that surprisingly supports his weight, even though it appears to be empty. He gazes up at me, still looking quite amused. "Terms like hero and villain are very subjective, but regardless, that doesn't change the objective reality of what you are, of what your powers are, and what you are meant to be. Tell me, how frequent have those dreams of you destroying Oklahoma City been recently?"

I freeze. "Did Lady Lust tell you about those dreams?"

Logikill shakes his head. "No, mostly because I've been having those same dreams myself. Unlike you, however, they do not bother me or keep me up at night. If anything, I find them quite pleasant, as I find humanity as a whole quite grating and would love nothing more than to see all of human civilization burn to a crisp just like in your dreams."

My hands ball into fists. "Is that why I've been having those dreams? Because it's the meteor trying to make me become evil or something? And how have you been having those same dreams?"

Logikill adjusts his glasses. "To answer your last question, that is simply because of the deep connection you have not just with me, but with all of the Meteor Monsters to some degree. Your ability to sense us Meteor Monsters is precisely because of the bond between us. You have thought that this bond, which exists because we are all ultimately the same, is a one-way street, but truthfully, the bond goes both ways. Or have you never noticed, during your clashes with my siblings, how they always seem to know where you are, even if you don't know where they are?"

My hands shake. "We aren't the same. Even if our powers come from the same source, that doesn't mean I have to do the same things that you do. I have free will and can do whatever I want."

Logikill chuckles. "Free will is largely an illusion, but especially for us. Because you are the most important Meteor Monster. Do you remember, Tobias, all those years ago when my siblings and I were first born? Do you remember how we almost killed you and Captain Cowboy and why we ultimately did not?"

I fish in my mind for that specific memory, but it doesn't take me long to remember it. How could I ever forget the night that changed my life forever?

Putting a hand on the side of my head, I say, "Yeah. I unleashed a demon head made of fire that scared all of y'all for some reason. You guys just took one look at it and ran, even though at the time I didn't even know I had my superpowers yet. I always did wonder what was up with that."

Logikill smiles, but it is his creepiest smile yet. "That was the eighth Meteor Monster, the one who never got a proper name like the rest of us. Though at the time none of us remembered our true purpose, we instinctively knew about our oldest and deadliest brother, the one who was destined to lead us to destroy this planet and prepare it for the invasion that is never going to come."

I bite my lower lip. "Who is that monster? If there are only seven deadly sins and each one of you guys represents a different sin, then what does he represent?"

Logikill steeples his fingers together in front of him. "A better question to ask is, what do you represent? Because ultimately, you gained the powers that would have gone to our brother who never got an independent body of his own. What is the sin that outweighs all the others? What sin has enough power to destroy all the other sins? If you can answer that question, Tobias, then you will understand both us and yourself, and our true destiny together."

I glare down at Logikill. "I already know what my true destiny is. It's to kick your butt and put an end to all you Meteor Monsters once and for all."

Logikill sighs and rubs his forehead in exasperation again. "I forgot how stubborn you were. But regardless, I would prefer to give you the choice to join us willingly. To that end, I am going to give you an ultimatum."

I fold my arms across my chest. "An ultimatum, huh? What kind of ultimatum?"

Logikill rises to his feet and dusts off his pants. "A simple one. I will not be able to conquer the world, even with all six of my siblings together, unless you agree to help us. That much is obvious, even to me. But I also understand that you would likely never willingly choose to side with us, even if it is the logical and inevitable path that you will end up walking."

Logikill looks up at me, staring me straight in the eye. "So here is the ultimatum. I will give you exactly 24 hours to decide if you want to join us—your true siblings and family—to fulfill our ultimate purpose of conquering this world and ruling it as gods, or if you will continue to fruitlessly and vainly fight against us. It will be entirely your choice."

I glare at Logikill. "It will be my choice, huh? That is pretty rich coming from Mr. 'I don't believe in free will.' What's the catch?"

Folding his arms behind his back, Logikill says, "If you continue to resist, then we will kill all of your friends and family—your mother, your father, your little sister, your best friend at school... essentially, everyone that you know in your personal life. We know where they live, we know what they do, and we will certainly put them all to death if you decide to make us your enemy."

Anger rises within me when Logikill makes that threat. "Do you Meteor Monster guys ever come up with new ideas? How many times are you going to threaten my loved ones just to get at me? Can't you guys think of anything original?"

Logikill raises an eyebrow. "So you aren't worried about the safety of your friends and loved ones?"

I rub my eyes in frustration. "I mean, yeah, kind of, seeing as you guys are actually very dangerous and all. But every time you've threatened my loved ones, it has always ended very poorly for you guys. For being such a logical and intellectual dude, you sure haven't learned from the mistakes of your siblings."

Logikill nods. "Yes, I suppose I can understand that point of view. It must indeed seem like a hollow threat to you from your perspective. Perhaps I can show you how serious we actually are."

Logikill pulls a phone out of his pocket and taps the screen a couple of times. Holding the ringing phone up to his ear, Logikill shoots me a quick smile before someone picks up on the other end and a voice I don't recognize mumbles something, prompting Logikill to say, "Hello, Templeton. How is Tobias's father doing right now?"

My gut shifts. What was Black doing with my father? And why was Logikill inquiring about how Dad was doing?

Logikill listens to whatever Black says in response and nods. "I see, I see. Well, I was calling to inform you that Michael Miller is no longer a useful hostage for us. So you can kill him now."

He suddenly pulls his phone from his ear and turns on the speakerphone function... just in time for the sound of a gunshot to erupt from the phone's speakers and echo through the junkyard.

9

"Dad?" I say in a horrified voice, staring at Logikill's phone. I raise my voice. "Dad! If you can still hear me, say something. Anything! Dad!"

But it's not Dad's voice that answers my cries. It's the deep and guttural voice of Black, who says in a mocking tone, "It would be very difficult for your father to speak now that he is dead."

My whole world seems to shudder under my feet, shifting and shaking like an earthquake. "You're lying. Dad must still be alive. You just pretended to—"

A weak, male voice interrupts me through the phone. "Toby? Is that you? I can barely hear your voice…"

"You're still alive?" says Black in annoyance. "Allow me to fix that."

Another gunshot rings out from the speakerphone before I can react… and then everything goes dead silent.

My heart pounding in my chest, I reach out toward the phone in Logikill's hand, saying, "Dad…?"

Logikill, however, pulls the phone away from me and taps the end-call button before putting the phone back in his pocket. That's when I realize that he has been staring at me this entire time, expressing no emotion at all, like a robot.

"I hope you understand, Tobias, that there are consequences to your decisions now," says Logikill calmly as he puts both hands on the head of his cane. "Not just for you personally, but for those around you. You may be strong enough to kill me and the other Meteor Monsters, but are you strong enough to do that and protect everyone you love?"

I'm barely paying attention to what Logikill is saying, however, because I'm still trying to process the revelation that Dad is dead. And I couldn't do a thing about it.

SLOTH

I find myself flashing back to the night of Drew's death when I saw Humanimal kill him before my very eyes. Like then, the death is shocking to me, to the point where I'm not even sure I fully believe it really happened.

But unlike then, I have the power to avenge the person who was killed before me.

And even though I don't know where Black is, I do know where Black's boss is. He is standing in front of me right now, unarmed and unprotected—a sitting duck for all intents and purposes.

I don't even think. I just summon my tapena in my hands and swing it at his ugly face.

Only for another memory to kick in—the terrified faces of Paintbrush and Captain Cowboy slowly being sucked into the disgusting mass of Wasteland's body—and my tapena stops less than an inch from Logikill's smug face.

Logikill, naturally, doesn't even react, either to the tapena or the flames from the tapena flickering near his face, casting strange shadows across his inhuman features. "I do not bluff, Tobias. But I am ... generous. I will not order any of my men to kill more of your friends or family members over the next twenty-four hours until I get a definitive response from you in regards to that ultimatum I gave you."

I breathe heavily but don't talk. With reason slowly regaining control over my mind, I wonder if I could possibly get everyone I know out of Oklahoma City within the next twenty-four hours. It might be difficult, but—

"Don't bother," says Logikill suddenly. "If you try to move any of your loved ones out of Oklahoma City, I will have my men, who are watching them *very* closely, kill them all. Not that that will be terribly difficult for us, however, seeing as I have had your mother, sister, grandmother, and best friend all kidnapped."

My eyes widen. "How did you know what I was thinking? I didn't even say anything."

Logikill smiles. "Telepathy is a useful power. Just like my siblings, I have also developed powers and skills you never dreamed of giving me. You can't really hide anything from me now."

I growl. I sorely want to bash Logikill upside the head with my tapena, consequences be damned, but if he really does have my family and friends as hostages, then I can't risk their lives. That doesn't even take into account Paintbrush and Captain Cowboy who, as far as I know, are still in Wasteland's grasp.

I glare at Logikill. "Why are you giving me a deadline at all? You could force my hand right now if you wanted to."

Logikill's green eyes glitter. "There are many things I could force you to do if I wanted, but there is always the correct way to do everything. And reason and logic dictate that *this* is the best way to achieve my goal, as well as certain circumstances outside of my control."

I tilt my head to the side. "What circumstances?"

Logikill just smiles again. "Irrelevant."

I breathe hard. Logikill is clearly keeping some important information from me, but I doubt I'll be able to pry it out of that big stupid mouth of his right now. "How do you want me to contact you with my answer?"

"In person, of course," says Logikill. "You know where Devon Energy Tower is, yes? That is where we will be."

I frown. "Who? You and the other Meteor Monsters?"

Logikill nods. "Exactly. Along with the hostages, of course, who we will not lay one finger on until the deadline has passed. Presently, Devon Tower is still unoccupied thanks to your fight with Jackpot, so it is a good place for us to make into our hideout."

I eye Logikill carefully. "And why shouldn't I call the police or military and warn them about you—?"

Logikill smirks. "If you want to have to rescue dead hostages, then be my guest. Otherwise, I want you to come speak to us without the government. Understood?"

I notice that Logikill doesn't mention that I can't bring other allies to help. I wonder if that is deliberate on his part or if he's just being sloppy. Knowing how careful Logikill is, it has to be deliberate, but why, I can't say unless he just genuinely does not consider any allies I might recruit as real threats.

Which means he's either as arrogant as the other Meteor Monsters ... or he knows something I don't.

Logikill taps his foot impatiently. "Now, will you please move your tapena from my head? The heat is making me sweat and I hate sweating. So disgusting."

For a moment, I feel the strongest desire to smash him in the face anyway. He'd deserve it.

But then I think about Paintbrush, Cap, Mom, Dakota, Granny ...

And lower the tapena to my side and take a step back from him, shoulders slumped. "All right. I'll think about your offer and give you a response in twenty-four hours. Deal?"

Logikill nods. "Deal. Thank you for being such a reasonable man, Tobias. But it remains to be seen just how reasonable you really are, though I suspect I shall receive an answer to that question very soon."

I hear a sloshing sound behind me and look over my shoulder to see Wasteland, along with the other five Meteor Monsters, approaching us from the way we came. Miraculously, Paintbrush and Captain Cowboy are still alive, albeit stuck up to their waists in Wasteland's body.

But a moment later, Wasteland's body shivers and both Paintbrush and Cap slide out of his body onto the ground. Turning away from Logikill, I rush over to Paintbrush and Cap, kneeling between them. They both smell awful, their costumes soaked in Wasteland's sludge, but they are both breathing and alive, which is all I can really ask for.

"Paintbrush, Cap," I say, looking from one to the other worriedly. "How are you doing?"

Captain Cowboy groans. "I've been worse, but I've also been better."

"Same," says Paintbrush, rolling onto her side. She cringes as she touches her hair. "Ugh. This is going to take forever to get out of my hair." She then gives me a worried look. "What about you, Toby? How are you doing? You look like you've been crying."

I blink and touch my cheeks, which are surprisingly wet. I don't remember crying, but then I remember Dad and my eyes get hot and wet all of a sudden.

But before I can break the awful news to Paintbrush and Cap, Logikill behind me says, "And Toby, one last thing."

I look over my shoulder again.

Logikill is still standing where I left him, but now he is surrounded by the other Meteor Monsters, who stand near him like loyal bodyguards. While all of them are dangerous in their own right, I now realize that Logikill is definitely more dangerous than the rest of them put together.

Staring at me, Logikill says, "See you tomorrow, where everything began."

With that, Logikill turns and walks away, with the rest of the Meteor Monsters following closely behind him. He leaves me kneeling between Captain Cowboy and Paintbrush, my hands shaking, tears streaking down the sides of my face.

I have never felt more powerless.

10

A few hours after our confrontation with Logikill and the revived Meteor Monsters in the Southeast Landfill, we all sit around the Stable's dining room table in silence.

This is normally a place where we talk freely, make plans for the future, and come up with ways to deal with not just the Meteor Monsters, but the various other supervillains and criminals who threaten Oklahoma City. We've had lots of laughs and arguments and meals here and have become something of a family in the process.

But right now?

I can't.

I can't say anything. Nor does anyone else seem likely to speak, either. Captain Cowboy is leaning back in his chair, hat on the table in front of him, arms crossed in front of his chest, frowning deeply. Paintbrush sits beside me, one hand on my leg, which is comforting, but still hard.

Keith sits on the other side of the table, staring at his phone on the table before him, its screen black and blank. Codetalker's laptop just shows his CT logo, but he isn't speaking, either.

Not that I blame anyone. The news I just finished sharing with everyone … even I barely believe it.

Even though it is true.

All of it.

Suddenly, Keith's phone rings and Keith immediately picks it up. He nods once or twice, says, "Thank you," and then hangs up.

Putting his phone back on the table, Keith looks around at everyone. "That was our liaison with the police. The police have confirmed that Dakota, Wendy, Gary, and Phyliss, your grandmother, are all missing from their homes. They have also confirmed that none of them are at work, school, or any of their usual places where they hang out whenever they are not at their homes. They seem to have been kidnapped, just like Logikill said. As you can imagine, Gary's family is extremely upset."

That I feel especially bad about. Gary O'Donald is my best friend from my school. Having graduated from high school last year like me, Gary was going to college on an art scholarship. I can't imagine how terrified his family must be.

Because I feel the exact same way about Dakota, Mom, and Granny.

Captain Cowboy slams his fist against the table, rattling it. "Damn that Logikill! We should have seen this coming. I should have warned Wendy and Dakota to—"

"To what, Oscar?" says Codetalker, his voice calm and cool, though slightly strained unless my ears are playing tricks on me. "We felt like we were in a hurry because of the missing Cores. We had no reason to believe that Logikill would be one step ahead of us, nor that he would kidnap most of Toby's loved ones while we weren't looking. He tricked us all, including me."

This is the first time I have heard Codetalker sound genuinely depressed. I suppose it makes sense. Going to the junkyard to find Black and Linderman was his idea in the first place, after all. He must feel at least partly responsible for what happened.

I don't blame him for feeling that way, even though I personally blame myself more than anyone for how that situation turned out. But at the same time, I find it hard to say that. Or say anything else. My heart feels heavy in my chest, like a weight I can't handle. I just want to rip it out and throw it away.

But I can't.

So I don't.

Keith purses his lips. "The police have also confirmed reports of seeing unmarked vehicles and suspicious individuals entering and leaving Devon Energy Tower recently, so that is another one of Logikill's claims confirmed. It is likely that the Meteor Monsters are indeed holed up there, though why there, of all places, I am not sure."

Captain Cowboy shakes his head. "What I want to know is if his whole story about that dead alien empire thing is true or not. Sounds like something straight out of science fiction if you ask me."

"Considering we are dealing with literal comic book characters brought to life, I am inclined to believe the story myself," says Codetalker, "although I wouldn't be surprised if Logikill was deliberately leaving out important information to manipulate us. Seems like something he would do."

I jerk my head up. For some reason, Codetalker's statement reminds me of something important I hadn't shared with everyone yet. "He definitely is. He said certain circumstances were forcing his hand, which is why he gave me the twenty-four hour deadline to decide. There seems to be something special about tomorrow, but I'm not sure what."

Paintbrush speaks. "Isn't tomorrow the third anniversary of the meteor crash?"

I pause, thinking about it. "You're right. It is."

Captain Cowboy blows a breath through his lips. "I see. Logikill and his cronies probably want a do-over of the first time we encountered them in the crater. I seem to recall that they all ran away like cowards after you pulled off that fire demon trick in the crater. Honestly surprised that they didn't try to lure us back to the site of the meteor crash to finish this."

Keith shrugs. "Devon Energy Tower is a better position to defend against. Tallest building in OKC and all."

I scowl. "I don't care what Logikill is planning. I am just going to fly straight to the tower and beat the ever-loving crap out of him for killing Dad."

Captain Cowboy frowns at me gently. "Toby, I am sorry about Michael. I really am. And trust me, I hate Black for everything he's done, but I think it would be a mistake to try to take on Logikill all by yourself, what with the hostages he has and all."

I sigh in frustration. "I know, but that doesn't change the fact that I have to respond to him somehow by tomorrow. If I don't, he'll kill everyone."

"We know," says Paintbrush. She squeezes my leg. "Have you thought about what you are going to say to Logikill yet?"

I look at Paintbrush. "Yeah. I am going to say 'no,' mostly with a lot of colorful four-letter words."

"All by yourself?" says Captain Cowboy, raising an eyebrow. "Because I have a few words I'd like to exchange with Logikill, too."

I look at Captain Cowboy. "I'm not sure it would be safe for you guys to come with me. Logikill didn't say you couldn't come, but I feel like if you do, he might try to use you guys against me."

Keith shrugs. "If we wanted to be safe, none of us would be in this business in the first place."

SLOTH

"Keith is right," says Codetalker. His logo flickers and is replaced by a live webcam view of his face, which still looks haggard and sleep-deprived. He rubs his eyes. "Given how Logikill appears to have minions everywhere, I suspect he would try to hurt us if you went alone regardless. It only makes sense for the whole team to go to Devon Tower and confront Logikill and the other Meteor Monsters."

I look at Codetalker's face on the computer screen, feeling conflicted. "I know, but I still feel terrible about endangering all of you. I know you can all take care of yourselves, but I'm the only one here who can actually kill the Meteor Monsters. You guys would just be able to hurt them, at best."

Captain Cowboy snorts. He pulls out one of his pistols and briefly flashes it by the side of his face. "Kid, did you forget about the Meteor Monster bullets you gave me? We've got plenty we could give to Paintbrush and Keith, too. They'll be fine."

"Any for me?" asks Codetalker suddenly.

Captain Cowboy looks at Codetalker in surprise. "Hold on, is the reclusive Codetalker planning to actually do some superhero work in person for a change?"

Codetalker rolls his eyes. "Yes. Given what is at stake, I feel like Wyldfyre will need every available ally he can get at this point. I happen to be fairly close to Oklahoma City right now, so getting over to join you all at Devon Tower shouldn't be very difficult."

"What about Tushka and Outlaw?" I ask, looking around the table. "Does anyone know if they are available?"

Keith sighs. "I doubt it. Lady Waste's brainwashing took a huge toll on them. Last I heard, they were both still mentally recovering from that."

I grimace. Great. Tushka and Outlaw were two of the other superheroes who patrolled the Oklahoma City metro area, covering Moore and Norman respectively. Ever since they'd gotten their minds messed up by Lady Waste, however, neither of them had been in any shape to do superhero work. It really made me feel bad for them, even for Tushka, who I didn't like too much due to some of our negative experiences with him in the past.

Captain Cowboy strokes his chin. "Don't worry yourself about recruiting more allies, Toby. Let me reach out to some old friends of mine and see if they would be willing to help us."

Old friends? I wonder who Cap is referring to, but honestly, I am glad that he's going to handle that. Between the stress of losing Dad and possibly losing Mom, Dakota, and Granny, I have a lot on my plate to handle already.

53

Plus, something still bugs me about all of this.

Tapping the surface of the table with my fingers, I say, "Guys, I appreciate how you are all willing to help me, but, um, I just don't understand why."

Everyone looks at me like I just asked the stupidest question in the world. Not that I am particularly unused to everyone looking at me like that, but this time it's way more annoying because I don't know why.

Paintbrush speaks first. "Why wouldn't we help our friend? Or boyfriend, in my case?"

I immediately stand up, pushing my chair back, and making everyone start. "Did you guys forget the part where I am basically a walking alien superweapon designed to destroy the planet? Doesn't that bother anyone except me?"

Captain Cowboy frowns. "To tell ya the truth, no. We didn't even know it bothered you."

I blink. I guess I did forget to mention that. "Oh. Well, my point still stands. If there is any truth to Logikill's claims at all—and, frankly, everything he said lines up pretty well with what little I know about the origins of my powers—then if I go to Devon Tower, I might end up joining the Meteor Monsters."

Captain Cowboy blinks. "Why would you do that?"

I run my hands through my hair. "I ... I don't know! I already have this deep connection to the Meteor Monsters that they've used against us before. What if Logikill, like, flips some kind of hidden switch deep inside my mind or something that might turn me into one of them? Or even worse?"

I lower my hands from my head and gaze at everyone anxiously. "And what if ... what if I end up killing all of you because Logikill tells me to?"

It sounds ridiculous coming from my mouth, but it's true. Combined with my anxiety over losing Dad and my emotions are currently going wild. I can't even really control what I am saying.

Everyone just looks at me quietly for a minute, making me wonder if maybe they really hadn't thought about any of this and were considering the implications themselves. They'd be smart if they were. After all, I am basically a walking time bomb at this point. Surely even they must see that.

But then Paintbrush stands up and turns to face me. I cringe, fully expecting her to do ... something. I don't know. Maybe run away? Maybe slap me in the face for acting so emotional?

SLOTH

Instead, Paintbrush wraps her arms around me and gives me a big hug. Even though I am both bigger and stronger than her, Paintbrush hugs me with surprising strength, but I quickly return the hug. She feels so warm and inviting, making me melt into her arms.

"Toby ..." says Paintbrush in my ear. "It's fine. You don't have to worry. We won't abandon you, no matter what the origins of your powers are."

I feel tears forming in the corners of my eyes but push Paintbrush away slightly. "But–"

Captain Cowboy stands up next, placing his cowboy hat back on his head, a grin on his face. "Listen to your girlfriend for once, Toby! She's absolutely correct. Ain't no way we are going to leave our friend alone. I mean, we are literally family at this point, or have you already forgotten that Wendy is my wife now?"

I bite my lower lip. "I mean, yeah, I guess, but—"

Keith rises to his feet as well, slipping his phone back into his pocket. "Toby, none of us care about where your powers came from or what their original purpose was. We only care about how you've used those powers over the last three years."

I look at Keith in confusion. "What do you mean?"

Codetalker nods, a serious expression on his face. "What Keith means—or, at least what I think Keith means—is that it isn't your powers that determine if you're a good person or not. Even the original purpose of your powers doesn't matter. Your choices are what make you a hero, and while I haven't known you nearly as long as the other three, I've certainly seen you make the right decision time and time again, even when it meant risking your own life. That's why we'll stand behind you the whole way, no matter how dangerous the Meteor Monsters might be."

"Darn right," says Captain Cowboy, giving Codetalker the thumbs up. He looks at me with a smile. "Toby, do you remember how, on the day I first asked you to become my sidekick, I said I wouldn't give up until all of the Meteor Monsters were dead? And look, now they've all gathered in one neat and tidy location just to make it easier for us to kill them all. I say this is an excellent opportunity to end this nightmare once and for all."

Paintbrush tightens her grip on me, giving me a loving look at the same time. "And we'll do it together too. As a team."

Keith nods. "Right. Team Wyldfyre all the way."

I blink at Keith in surprise. "Wait, you're going to use my name for our team now? Unironically?"

"It's not a bad name for our team," says Codetalker. He points at me from the other side of the computer screen. "If it wasn't for you, we wouldn't all be together like this. At least, we wouldn't be the team that we've become, anyway."

I wipe the tears from my eyes, not even trying to hide them anymore. "You guys..."

Seriously, I'm just overcome with emotion right now. I always knew they were my friends, but it didn't hit me until just now how close we all were. Thanks to my powers born from the meteor, I doubt I would have gotten to know any of these people.

Maybe not everything that came from the meteor was bad, after all.

Captain Cowboy punches his fist into his hand. "All right! What do you say, Toby? Ready to take down those monsters?"

I nod. "Yeah. But first, we need to make a plan. And we've got less than 24 hours to pull it off."

11

The next day, shortly after breakfast, Captain Cowboy, Paintbrush, Keith, Codetalker, and I found ourselves standing at the front entrance of Devon Tower. The five of us formed a loose circle at the front door, each one of us mentally preparing for the coming conflict with the Meteor Monsters.

Captain Cowboy stood nearest the front doors, checking and double-checking that his pistols were fully loaded. Keith stood next to a couple of overgrown potted plants near the entrance, arms folded across his chest, chin down, seemingly deep in thought. Codetalker sat on the front steps, tapping away at the screen of his phone, wearing a new black-and-yellow spandex costume that looked a bit weird on him but which he claimed was his superhero costume. He even had a high-tech helmet with a visor on his head, though I had no idea what it did. Apparently, this was Codetalker's actual superhero costume, which he rarely wore except on missions that required him to get out from behind his computer screen and go into the real world.

As for me and Paintbrush, we stood near the SUV, holding hands as we waited patiently for whoever Captain Cowboy had invited to join us on what would undoubtedly be the most dangerous mission we had undertaken as a team yet. Captain Cowboy still hadn't told us who his mystery allies were, and he had refused to even respond to our guesses. I still think he invited Tushka and Outlaw, even though they are supposedly not in any shape to be fighting supervillains with us right now.

Regardless, I won't deny that I feel incredibly nervous at the moment. It has been over 12 hours since we finalized our plan to confront the Meteor Monsters in Devon Tower, which means there's a bit less than 12 hours left before Logikill decides to kill my family and Gary. Naturally, we had had no contact with anyone inside Devon Tower since our confrontation with the Meteor Monsters in the landfill, but we had no reason to believe that Logikill was going to go back on his word.

So this gave me time to reflect on the plan we had hashed out together back in the stable.

The plan was fairly simple, as plans go. Along with our two mystery allies, we were going to enter Devon Tower and work our way up to the top floor, which was likely where Logikill was holed up. That would inevitably mean having to fight through all six of the resurrected Meteor Monsters again, which none of us were looking forward to having to do again, but we basically had no choice at this point. With any luck, we'd kill all the Meteor Monsters again, including Logikill, and save not just Oklahoma City, but the world.

But, of course, we had contingencies in place in case we failed.

Firstly, although we had told the police not to send any officers into Devon Tower to comply with Logikill's demands, that did not mean that the police did not have a role to play. We had the police shut down practically all of downtown OKC, forming a several-mile perimeter around Devon Tower, to protect innocent people and give the police a chance to act as backup if necessary. I, personally, doubted the police would be all that useful if we failed, but we did give them some extra Meteor Monster bullets to distribute among themselves as they saw fit. That way, they'd have at least *some* way to fight back against the Meteor Monsters if they somehow defeated us.

Secondly, we also called in the National Guard and gave the governor of Oklahoma and the mayor of Oklahoma City a heads-up about our big fight with the Meteor Monsters. Again, we told the National Guard to keep their distance, but figured that the manpower from the National Guard could prove useful in case we failed. The governor promised to reach out to the President of the United States in case things went south, which was fine, even though at this point I really didn't have a very high opinion of our current Commander-in-Chief due to not monitoring the behavior of his own men very closely in the past.

But that did emphasize how dangerous this situation was. If Logikill really was aiming for world domination, then his victory here would not only spell doom for Oklahoma City and the state of Oklahoma, but the entire world. There was no telling what would happen to the world if we failed, so we decided to make sure that we did not.

Also, I had to carve up a bunch more Meteor Monster bullets from my tapenas over the last twelve hours, enough for everyone on Team Wyldfyre to have at least seven bullets each. Captain Cowboy had given out guns to Keith, Codetalker, and Paintbrush, but Paintbrush was the only one who needed basic firearms training. Keith's military service meant that he already knew how to handle a gun and, as for Codetalker, he merely said he had 'experience' with guns before shooting the bull's eye on the target in the Stable's Basement without even looking at it.

I considered simply distributing tapenas among the team instead, but honestly, guns are way more useful and easier to use for the average person, not to mention better at killing than guns. Plus, this way none of my teammates would have to get too close to engage with the Meteor Monsters if they didn't want to, which would help keep them safe.

Because even though I know that everyone says they have my back, that doesn't change the fact that I am still technically the only one on the team who can reliably kill a Meteor Monster. That is why I am going to take the lead on every fight with any Meteor Monsters we run into on our way up to Logikill, with the others only acting as support as necessary.

And I still think that's way too dangerous.

But like Keith said, the superhero business is dangerous even without the Meteor Monsters, so it's not like this is the first time any of us have been in mortal danger before.

But the stakes have definitely never been higher.

Maybe the tension getting to me is why I say to Captain Cowboy, "Cap, where are our mystery allies you told us about? Time is ticking."

Captain Cowboy glances at his smartwatch. "Patience. I told 'em when to be here and haven't heard anything about either of them being late. Trust me, they're on the way."

Paintbrush scratches the side of her face, still holding my hand. "I still want to know who you called in last minute like this. Are you finally going to tell us or not?"

Captain Cowboy gives Paintbrush a mischievous grin. "It's a surprise."

"My money is still on Tushka and Outlaw," I say. "Who else would be willing to make it out here to—"

The roar of a motorcycle suddenly interrupts me. Everyone looks in the direction that the motorcycle sound came from, including me. It's coming from behind me, so I have to look over my shoulder to see who it is.

In the distance, the lights of a motorcycle blare, with a man wearing a helmet riding it. I can't tell who it is from this far out, however, but as the motorcycle draws nearer, I make out more features. He's a guy wearing a cowboy costume, practically identical to

Captain Cowboy, but the motorcycle he's riding looks much cheaper than Cap's even from a distance.

I frown as the motorcycle draws closer. "No, it can't be ..."

Captain Cowboy, however, walks up beside me and waves at the mystery motorist cheerily. "Hey there, Pietro! Glad you could make it."

Pietro's motorcycle screeches to a halt several feet away from us. Kicking the motorcycle's kickstand on, the man takes off his helmet, revealing the youthful face of Pietro Shevchenko, who immediately puts on a cowboy hat almost identical to Cap's. He waves rapidly back at us, a goofy expression on his face as he walks over to us. "Of course, sir! As soon as I got your message, I knew I needed to be here."

I look at Captain Cowboy in disbelief. "*Pietro* is one of our mystery allies? Your public stunt double?"

Okay, maybe that was a bit mean to Pietro, but I don't think I am too harsh on Cap's dubious decision to invite his body double to the most dangerous mission we have yet undertaken.

See, Captain Cowboy is super popular in Oklahoma City. Every day, he gets, like, a hundred invites from schools, businesses, and various other places to speak or appear at public events. And because Cap loves speaking to the public, he accepts a lot of those invites.

But of course, Cap is just one guy and a lot of the events he gets invited to overlap or conflict with each other. So Cap hired this Ukrainian med student at OU, Pietro Shevchenko, who admittedly bears an uncanny resemblance to a younger Cap, to basically be his stand-in for whatever events he can't get to on his own.

Now, don't get me wrong. Pietro is a good guy and he even has some experience fighting the Meteor Monsters, having helped fight the Crippler at one point.

But he's also *not* a real superhero, not even close. He doesn't even have a superhero license, so I am not sure what he is doing here, other than we need every warm body we can get.

Captain Cowboy, seeming to sense my objections, turns toward me with a grin on his face. "Now, I know what you are thinking, but Pietro is a lot more useful than he looks."

"Indeed!" says Pietro, coming to a stop nearby. He stands up straight, puffing out his chest. "Ever since my encounter with the Crippler, I've been training nonstop to become as strong as Captain Cowboy. I now have a black belt in Krav Maga and several other martial arts, plus do strength training at the gym three days a week. I've also taken shooting lessons from an instructor who Captain Cowboy recommended to me, so I now know how to handle a gun like a real American."

I stare at Pietro in surprise. "Seriously? Since when did you do all of this?"

"Since I suggested it to him after you killed the Crippler," says Captain Cowboy, patting me on the shoulder. "Pietro's stand against the Crippler really impressed me and, knowing how many other Meteor Monsters were still active at the time, I advised Pietro to 'get good,' as the kids say nowadays, and learn some real fightin' skills. I even reimbursed him for all of the training he did."

I scratch the back of my head. "And you never even mentioned this to me because—?"

Captain Cowboy sighs. "Honestly, I was hopin' we'd never need his help. But now that we are going to take on the Meteor Monsters again, well, I figured it was time to cash in that particular check, if you catch my drift."

Pietro gives Captain Cowboy a reverent look. "I would answer your call anytime, Captain! Even if you asked me to follow you into the depths of hell itself, I wouldn't hesitate." He frowns. "Although I would still have to tell my parents."

Paintbrush nods. "How is med school going, anyway?"

Pietro blanches. "Uh, let me just say that fighting a bunch of unkillable alien monsters is preferable to studying for my finals and leave it at that."

I eye Pietro carefully. "Are you sure you are ready to face the Crippler again? Last time, he almost killed you."

Pietro sighs and looks up at Devon Tower, licking his lips nervously. "I won't pretend to be excited about the prospect of fighting the Crippler again, but I know that real superheroes do not let their fears control them. Real superheroes fight even when they are scared out of their minds."

Captain Cowboy nods. "That's right, Pietro! Granted, Wyldfyre will be leading the charge, but I'm glad you understand the situation. Have this gun. It's got Meteor Monster bullets in it."

Captain Cowboy hands Pietro a pistol, which Pietro reverently takes like it is a gift from God himself. He stares at the pistol in awe for a second before carefully holstering it at his side. "Thank you, Captain Cowboy. I shall make sure to use it only when absolutely necessary."

I put my hands on my hips. "All right. So Pietro was one of our mystery allies. Who is the second? Is he on the way, too?"

Captain Cowboy gives me a strange look. "Now, don't get *too* angry when I tell you who our other ally is, as I know the two of you haven't had the, uh, best experiences together in the past."

I furrow my brow in confusion. "Who are you talking about, Cap?"

"No need to spoil the surprise, Captain," says a young, slightly angry male voice from a nearby alleyway. "I can introduce myself."

My eyes widen as I whip my head toward the sound of the voice just in time to see another man—this one much younger than the rest of us—step out from a nearby alleyway. Clad in a black and purple suit, with huge oil tanks on his back and arms, I wouldn't mistake him for anyone else in the world even if I lost all of my memories and forgot who I was.

My jaw drops. "Walter? What are *you* doing here?"

Walter Ellison, also known as the superhero Oil Slick, taps the side of his helmet, causing the front to retract, showing his smug expression. "Saving your butt, duh."

12

I now understand why Captain Cowboy warned me about my history with our second mystery ally. To say that Walter and I have basically been archenemies for the past three years is the understatement of the year.

Quick backstory: Walter is the younger brother of Drew Ellison, my former best friend, who got killed by Humanimal the Cannibal shortly after the meteor crash. Walter blamed Drew's death on me and ran away from home, eventually reemerging as a drugged-up lackey of the Meteor Monster Road Rage. After I defeated him, Walter then ended up as a government experiment where he got combined with Wasteland's Core, only to become a pawn of Lady Waste until I knocked him out and rescued him before he could die in a burning building.

The last time I saw him, Walter had ended up at a juvenile detention facility to get help for his many, many problems. So you can imagine why I was surprised, if not Angry and confused, to see him here today standing right in front of us.

I look at Captain Cowboy hard. "What is Walter doing here?"

"Oil Slick," says Walter suddenly. He gestures at his costume. "I go by Oil Slick while in this get-up. Isn't that how superheroes work?"

Captain Cowboy scratches the back of his head sheepishly. "Well, Walter is apparently a lot more resilient than he looks. According to the people who had been taking care of him, Walter has managed to bounce back from the suffering he endured under Lady Waste and should be okay."

Paintbrush scratches the top of her head. "But professional superheroes like Tushka and Outlaw aren't?"

Walter glares at her. "Maybe my exposure to Road Rage's Fury made me tougher than I look. Ever think of that?"

I scowl even deeper. "But like Pietro, he's still not an actual superhero. He could be a liability. He doesn't even have his powers anymore for Christ's sake."

Walter raises one of his oil cannons. "True, but guess what power I do have? Being the son of a literal billionaire."

Ah, right. I sometimes forget that Walter's dad, Ralph Ellison, former mayor of Oklahoma City, teamed up with Jackpot to try to kill me after he learned about my role in Drew's death (can you tell that the Ellisons and I don't have a great relationship?), was one of the richest people in Oklahoma, if not in the country. An oil baron, Ralph Ellison is the definition of a billionaire. Pretty sure he ended up in prison after his conspiracy with Jackpot came out to the public, though I guess Walter somehow avoided that fate.

Captain Cowboy rubs his forehead. "Yeah, but that ain't why I reached out to you and you know it."

Walter's smugness evaporates and he lowers his oil cannon to his side. A genuinely shamed expression creeps onto his youthful features. "I know. It's because of my history with Road Rage and Wasteland."

"Exactly," says Captain Cowboy. He puts a hand on my shoulder. "Other than you and Paintbrush, Walter is the only other person in the world who has worked so closely with the Meteor Monsters. He understands them almost as well as you do, plus he has all of his training from the government, so he knows how to handle himself in a fight."

"And even though I don't have any innate powers anymore, I still have my costume," says Walter, gesturing at his oil cannons. "I used Father's money to buy back my equipment from the government and modify it so I can still use it without my powers. It does mean I can only carry a limited amount of oil on me now, but at least I should still be of some use in a fight."

I purse my lips. "And you did all this in less than twelve hours?"

Walter flashes me a quick smile. "Not quite. I was actually planning to become a superhero myself, so when Captain Cowboy reached out to me for help, I was already ready to go. Helps that Father happened to have an old superhero costume designer friend who made all the necessary adjustments to my equipment for me on short notice."

I fold my arms in front of my chest. "Must be nice to have money."

Walter scowls right back at me. "Must be nice to have family that still loves you."

"Boys, boys," says Captain Cowboy, stepping between us before our words turned into fists. "Remember, we are all on the same side here. And Walter, I think there was something important you wanted to tell Wyldfyre before we started the mission, wasn't there?"

Walter's anger evaporates again, replaced by the same shameful expression from before. "I'm sorry. Anyway, Toby, I didn't agree to help just because I want redemption myself, but also to apologize to you and let you know that I don't blame you for Drew's death anymore."

I look at Walter in utter shock. "You don't?"

Walter takes a deep breath. "Trust me, this is as shocking to me as it is to you. Maybe even more so. Because for the longest time there, I did blame you for, well, everything. When Humanimal killed Drew, I felt like I lost my whole world. I didn't know what to do or how to explain it, so I settled on blaming you instead."

Walter frowns and glances at Devon Tower. "So I threw in with Road Rage because all I wanted was revenge. And that is exactly what Road Rage promised me. I thought I could avenge Drew's death by taking Road Rage's power, but now I know he was only using me to further his own agenda. Same with the government and Lady Waste."

Walter turns his gaze back to me. "After you saved my life from Lady Waste, I realized it wasn't your fault Drew died. It wasn't Drew's fault, either. It was the fault of the Meteor Monsters. At the time, I thought you could control them, but now I know you can't. And I wanted to apologize, not just for blaming you for Drew's death, but for everything I did after that."

I gulp. "Um, Walter, I—"

Walter holds up a hand to silence me. "I don't expect you to believe me or forgive me right away. Frankly, if our situations were reversed, I wouldn't believe me, either. But that's why I am here. I am hoping to show with my actions, rather than my words, that I am sorry and want to fix my mistakes as much as I can. Or at least avoid repeating them in the future."

I stare at Walter, stunned, before turning to Captain Cowboy. "Is that what he told you?"

Captain Cowboy nods. "Yep. While I know you ain't as forgiving as me, Walter reminded me of a certain other ex-supervillain who helped us. I think you should give him a chance."

Cap is undoubtedly referring to Great Spirit, who gave his life during the Road Rage incident to help us stop Walter from destroying Oklahoma City. Like Walter, Great Spirit was a terrible supervillain who eventually saw the error of his ways and tried to make up for his crimes by helping us take down Road Rage. He even gave his life to destroy the weapon that Road Rage and Walter planned to use to destroy Oklahoma City. I definitely remember his funeral and will never forget it as long as I live.

But that's where the similarities between them ended. Great Spirit, after all, had a couple of decades in prison to give him time to think about what he'd done wrong and how to make it right. Walter, by contrast, had had maybe six months at most to reflect on his life choices and decide to turn things around. So you can understand why I was skeptical about Walter's claim of having seen the light and wanting to help us.

On the other hand, Walter does seem genuinely ashamed of his past, and I don't think Captain Cowboy would have reached out to him if he thought Walter was lying about his change of heart. I mean, I had definitely been skeptical about enlisting the help of Great Spirit before he showed that he was a true ally, so maybe I just need to give Walter some grace.

But that doesn't mean I have to like or trust him.

So I look at Walter and say, "All right. Help us if you want, but we want to establish a few ground rules first."

Walter folds his arms behind his back. "Yeah? What rules?"

I hold up a finger. "First, I don't want you fighting Road Rage. I don't want him trying to use his previous influence over you to turn you against us."

Anger flashes across Walter's face when I say that. "Road Rage doesn't have any influence over me anymore. In fact, if I do run into him in there, I will—"

"Let us deal with him," I say sharply, interrupting Walter without apologizing. "You might think you're not under his influence anymore, and heck, maybe you aren't, but I don't know that for sure and no one else does, either. So, for safety reasons, we're going to have to make sure that you and Road Rage never interact."

Walter still scowls at me but finally nods begrudgingly. "Okay. I won't take on Road Rage. Any other conditions I need to agree to?"

I shake my head. "No, that's pretty much the only condition I wanted you to agree to. I just don't want your past history with Road Rage to negatively impact the success of this mission. The stakes are too high to take any unnecessary risks."

SLOTH

Walter nods, then looks up at the building before us. "Any reason we can't just climb up the side of the building if we think Logikill is all the way up there? At least you could fly up there, Toby."

I shake my head again. "The Meteor Monsters have hostages. We don't want to risk giving them an excuse to kill the hostages, so we decided that it's safer to do things the slow way instead."

Captain Cowboy nods. "Exactly. And now that we're all on the same team here, why don't we get this party started? We're still on a deadline, after all."

I grimace when Captain Cowboy brings that up again. "Right. Since we're all ready, I assume it's time to go inside and kick some Meteor Monster butt. I'll lead the way. Everyone follow me."

I turn toward Devon Energy Tower and walk up to the front doors. The front doors are made of clear glass that shows an empty lobby, but I don't let down my guard. The Meteor Monsters have to know we're here by now, even if they're only using the building's security cameras to keep an eye on us.

But even if they didn't have the building's security cameras, they certainly should be able to feel my presence. I can't really feel theirs at the moment for some reason, but I know the Meteor Monsters have some ability to hide their presence from me, so that isn't surprising.

What is surprising is what happens when we enter the building.

The glass doors slide open before us, and we step inside as a group... only to find ourselves standing in a tall, dark jungle full of clicking bugs and the sound of a rushing river somewhere nearby.

13

The abrupt change in scenery nearly gives me whiplash. The muddy forest floor squelches under my boots as I turn this way and that, staring at the crisscrossing vines overhead, rays of warm sunshine peeking through the canopy of leaves above us.

Behind me, Captain Cowboy wipes sweat off his forehead as he and the others also look around in surprise at our new surroundings. "Who planted a jungle in here? I didn't see it through the doors before we came in."

Keith, who has already drawn his pistol loaded with Meteor Monster bullets, shakes his head. "No idea, but I don't like this situation already."

I look at Paintbrush, who is standing beside me, rubbing her forehead like she's experiencing a very bad headache. "What do you think, Mandy? You're the resident plant expert on the team. What's your opinion about this?"

Paintbrush frowns as she continues to rub her forehead. "That's the thing. I'm trying to reach out to the plants with my powers, but it's like they aren't even there. As if the trees aren't even real."

"A good guess, Paintbrush," says the all-too-familiar voice of Logikill. "Although it certainly should feel quite real to your minds."

I blink, and the next moment, Logikill is standing in the middle of the clearing, arms folded behind his back as if he's a college professor about to give us a lecture on philosophy or something. A wicked grin spreads across his face as he looks at us, as if he knows something we don't.

Naturally, I take advantage of this momentary lapse in his judgment to summon my bow, nock an arrow, and fire directly at his smug face—all in one smooth motion that makes even me feel a little proud of myself.

The arrow flies straight and true, striking Logikill directly in his ugly, rat-like face.

Only to pass straight through his ugly, rat-like face and disappear into the trees around us.

Stunned, I lower the bow to my side, staring at Logikill in disbelief. "How did you do that? Are you a ghost now or something?"

Logikill's smile widens into a truly ghoulish expression. "This is merely one of the new powers I developed during the last three years. My siblings weren't the only ones who discovered new abilities to further their own ambitions, you know."

I look around the jungle, still trying to figure out what's going on. "When did you get the ability to create jungles out of nowhere?"

Paintbrush, however, lowers her hands from her forehead and gives Logikill a wary look. "Toby, I don't think Logikill has the ability to spontaneously create jungles out of nothing. Instead, I think he has a different power entirely."

Logikill smirks. "Smart girl. Should I tell your friends, or would you do the honors of explaining my powers?"

Paintbrush takes a deep breath. "Let me try. I think you have the ability to create lifelike illusions with your mind. I don't know if that ability is just limited to a certain range or not, but it explains why we didn't see any trees inside the lobby of the building before we entered—because we hadn't actually entered the illusion yet at that point. Am I right?"

Logikill nods. "You are mostly correct, although if you think I'm going to reveal all of my secrets, then you're sorely mistaken. But yes, I can indeed craft lifelike illusions with my mind. I consider it a logical extension of my telepathy, because if I can project words into the minds of others, then why can't I also project images and feelings?"

I scowl at Logikill. "So are you also an illusion? Is that why my arrow didn't hurt you?"

Logikill shrugs. "Yes, this specific appearance of mine is indeed just a copy of myself. All seven of you could team up to beat me up at the same time, and it would do nothing to the real me. But if you wish to tire yourselves out with fruitless efforts, feel free. That will make my job so much easier."

I point at Logikill accusingly. "If you aren't even the real Logikill, then how do we know if the real Logikill is even here?"

Codetalker speaks up then, as calm as always. "I think Paintbrush is onto something about the limits of Logikill's illusions. Logikill would not be able to project such a powerful illusion onto us if he wasn't also inside Devon Tower with us somewhere."

Logikill gives Codetalker an impressed look. "It would appear that the reclusive Codetalker is as brilliant as the rumors make you out to be. What a shame that we cannot sit down and reason like true intellectuals. Perhaps in another life…"

Codetalker meets Logikill's gaze evenly. "If you were only interested in intellectual debate, you wouldn't have kidnapped innocent people to try to manipulate a teenager into becoming your weapon."

Logikill throws up his hands defensively. "Fine, fine, be that way. I knew from the moment you chose to step out from behind your computer screen to help Tobias that I would never be able to reason with you. That's fine. I don't really feel like chatting, anyway."

Captain Cowboy shoots a mischievous smile at Logikill. "Great idea. You can shut up, hand over the hostages, and let us kill you and your evil siblings. Seems like a win-win situation to me."

Logikill shakes his head. "It won't be that easy, and you know it. And believe me, I love easy things. That's why I offered Tobias that deal in the first place. It would have been much easier for him to simply hand himself over to us in exchange for the freedom and safety of your friends and family. But alas, I underestimated how addictive superheroing is, and now we will have to do things the hard way."

I put my bow away and fold my arms in front of my chest. "Are you going to hurt the hostages? Because if you do, I will definitely burn this entire building down with you and all the other Meteor Monsters still trapped inside it."

Logikill scratches the back of his neck. "No, I won't kill or hurt the hostages. There is still time for you to change your opinion and accept my offer, however unlikely that may be."

My hands ball into fists. "What makes you think I'll ever change my answer? You'd have to force me to work for you, and even then, I would fight you the whole time."

Logikill spreads his arms as if to indicate the jungle we're standing in. "That is why I designed the Trials of Despair. This one, the Jungle of Darkness, is the first trial you'll have to undergo. There are six more between here and the top floor where I am awaiting you. If you successfully pass each floor, then I will give myself up to you to do with as you wish, as well as free the hostages. But if you fail to complete any of them … well, the consequences won't be pretty, for you or your companions."

Pietro holds up a hand pretty fast. "Hold on, uh, Mr. Logikill, sir. What are the 'Trials of Despair'? I do not recall having those explained to me before we got here."

"That's because your teammates didn't know about them, either," says Logikill, putting his hands together. "To put it simply, the Trials of Despair are a series of challenges I personally designed to test Tobias and his companions at every stage of their journey to the top floor. And by 'test,' I mean 'break,' of course, as the challenges Tobias will have to undergo will be quite grueling."

I smirk. "Nice try, Logikill, but you've already played your hand. If everything in this Trial is an illusion, then logically, that means none of this is real. Ergo, your Trials aren't—"

I am interrupted by a silent *schwing* sound and Captain Cowboy, who is standing nearby, suddenly grabs his neck and gasps before falling to his knees.

Keith, who happens to be standing next to Captain Cowboy, quickly bends over to check on him. "What's wrong, Oscar? You okay?"

"I think ..." Captain Cowboy takes in a deep breath. "I *think* so, but it feels like something bit me."

Captain Cowboy removes his hand from his neck, revealing a tiny black dart that is almost too small to see in the palm of his hand.

I frown. "What is that?"

Captain Cowboy grimaces. "No idea, but I still feel fine, so—Argh!"

Captain Cowboy doubles over just then, wrapping his arms around his midsection as a deep moan emits from his mouth. He falls onto the muddy 'ground' of the jungle, or rather, the floor of the lobby, which is what it really is, however realistic it might look.

"Cap?" I say as all turn toward the fallen Captain Cowboy. "What's wrong? Are you okay?"

"He probably isn't," says Logikill with a smile. "Especially if that dart is what I *think* it is."

I whip my head back toward Logikill, glaring daggers at him. "What are you going on about? Everything in here is fake."

Logikill puts a hand over his mouth and giggles. "I don't recall saying *everything* in here is fake. Most of it—about ninety percent, by my calculations—is, but the remaining ten percent is *very* real."

I hear a deep growl somewhere in the trees around me. I look around, but do not see the source of the growl, which sounded very familiar. The rest of my team, having gathered around Captain Cowboy, also look around, drawing their weapons as they search for the source of the growl.

Logikill smirks. "Of course, I am not going to tell you *which* ten percent is real. Though with just a bit of logic, I am sure you could puzzle it out ... given enough time, that is."

"Enough time?" I say. "We still have less than twelve hours before the deadline is over, Logikill."

Logikill tilts his head to the side. "What makes you think that time is unaffected by my illusions? It may feel like we have been talking for just a few minutes, but how do you know that it hasn't actually been a few hours?"

I open my mouth to object but think about it for a second and realize, rather horrifyingly, that Logikill might be telling the truth. I could just look at my phone, but if Logikill's illusions cover *everything*, then he could easily make my phone show a different amount of time has passed than actually has.

If so, how much time do we *actually* have before the deadline is up?

Logikill's cold voice cracks through my thoughts. "In any case, have fun with the Jungle of Darkness. It's the first and easiest of the Trials, but I suspect you will still have a bit of trouble with it anyway. Ciao!"

I blink and Logikill is gone just as quickly as he appeared. So he was definitely an illusion, but that wasn't very helpful information to have at the moment. All it confirmed was that the real Logikill likely wasn't anywhere near us at the moment. He was probably on the fiftieth floor of the Tower, so it would take us a while to get to him, especially with all of these so-called 'Trials' of his slowing us down.

But I put that out of my mind to turn back to Captain Cowboy, who is now being tended to by both Keith and Paintbrush. "Can you guys tell what is wrong with Cap?"

Keith, putting a cold pack on Captain Cowboy's forehead, shakes his head. "I have no idea. He's got a high fever already and it's only been a couple of minutes since that dart lodged in his neck."

Keith's right. Captain Cowboy is now lying on his back on the ground, breathing in and out hard. Sweat glistens down the sides of his face as he says, "Ugh ... don't feel so good ..."

I look at Paintbrush. She's carefully studying the black dart in her hand, and based on the frown on her face, I suspect it's not good, whatever it is.

"What do you think about the dart, Paintbrush?" I ask, putting my hands on my hips.

Paintbrush grimaces. "It's definitely some kind of plant-derived poison, but beyond that, I can't tell. I don't know how deadly it is or if there is a way to cure it. My powers are telling me that much, at least."

Walter, raising his oil cannons, glances around the clearing suspiciously. "But who fired that dart in the first place? You heard Logikill. Not everything in here is fake."

"And clearly, that includes other living beings," says Codetalker, gesturing at the trees around us. "Most likely, there's another Meteor Monster in here."

I nod. "Exactly what I was thinking. I was just trying to figure out *who*, though."

"Humanimal seems like a reasonable guess," says Codetalker as he glances around the jungle, birds chirping in the distance. "I read up on all the Meteor Monsters before coming here. He was a hunter, right? This seems like exactly the sort of place a hunter would thrive."

"Makes sense," I say as I also look around at our surroundings. "And he was always pretty good about hiding, better, honestly, than the rest of the Meteor Monsters. I wouldn't put it past Logikill to pit us against Humanimal first."

Walter gestures at the trees. "Then what are we waiting for? Let's go find that stupid tiger-faced idiot and kick his ass. Who knows, maybe he's even carrying the cure for whatever was in that poison dart that hit Captain Cowboy."

I look down at Captain Cowboy again. His breathing has slowed but he's still clearly alive. He doesn't look good, though, and I don't doubt that the poison in Humanimal's dart was designed to kill. It just hasn't finished the job yet.

Suddenly, a rustling in the trees around us makes everyone jump. I nock another arrow and point it into the trees while the others raise their weapons, except for Keith and Paintbrush, who are kneeling on either side of Captain Cowboy.

The rustling doesn't stop, however. It just keeps growing louder and louder all around us, making me wonder if we were actually about to be attacked by multiple Meteor Monsters at once. That would be problematic, especially with a sick Captain Cowboy to protect.

Then Walter points to my right and says, "I see someone among the trees!"

Following Walter's pointing finger, I catch a glimpse of a shadowy figure moving among the trees toward us. Due to how dark it was, I couldn't make out too many details about the figure, not even their height. Though if I had to guess, I'd say they are a lot shorter than Humanimal, who had been ten feet tall, easily.

But then the shadowy figure emerges from the jungle and I forget about everything else. Beside me, Walter sucks in a deep breath and even Captain Cowboy manages to turn his head toward the person with a look of clear disbelief on his sickly features.

"Impossible ..." says Walter under his breath. "No *fucking* way ..."

Walter put into words everything I was feeling.

Because the figure who emerged from the shadows of the jungle around us wasn't Humanimal, Logikill, or any of the other Meteor Monsters. Hell, it wasn't even Black or Linderman.

No, the figure standing before us now was none other than Drew Ellison, the dead older brother of Walter Ellison and my former childhood best friend, himself.

14

Drew looks exactly the same as he did the night that he died, minus having his heart ripped out of his chest. Tall and athletic, his football jersey barely hides his muscular arms and huge chest as he gazes at us with his brown eyes. I frankly forgot how tall Drew was, but even three years later, I still have to raise my head a bit just to look at him.

My jaw drops. "It can't be ... Drew?"

Codetalker's hand falls on my shoulder as he steps up beside me, one of the Meteor Monster guns in his other hand. "That's not Drew. Remember, the real Drew Ellison died three years ago. You saw him die with your own eyes."

Pietro, nervously brushing some of his blonde hair out of his eyes, nodded. "Yes, yes. Just an illusion. Not the real thing. Dead men don't walk."

Drew cracks his familiar mocking smile. "Just an illusion, huh? If you really believe that, why don't you kill me again, Toby?"

I snap out of my shock and snarl at Drew, "I didn't kill you! Humanimal did."

Drew laughs, a deep, booming sound. "And who created Humanimal? I saw that sketch you drew of Humanimal eating me in your sketchbook, Toby. I know you hated me. I know you wanted me to die. That's why Humanimal killed me. Because you wanted me dead."

Drew then points at Walter. "And Walt, what the hell are you doing with him, you dumb brat? Toby killed me. He's literally standing right next to you. Aren't you going to avenge your big brother by killing his murderer right now?"

Walter is shaking beside me, but he still manages to keep his oil cannons raised. "I ... I don't blame him for your death anymore, Drew ..."

Drew sighs heavily. "Of course you don't! You always were such a useless little brother, you know that? I only ever tolerated your presence in my crew because Mom and Dad told me to keep an eye on you. Considering what happened to you after I died, I guess Mom and Dad were right to be worried. Personally, I think you're just a little pussy."

Walter scowls. "Pussy?"

Drew nods. "That's right. You couldn't beat Toby on your own, so you went running to Road Rage. When that inevitably failed, you got turned into a government lab experiment, but couldn't even be good at that. Tell me, baby brother, what makes you think your 'friendship' with your new BFF is going to work out any better than any of your previous stupid decisions?"

Walter trembles almost uncontrollably. He seems to be on the verge of tears. He looks away from Drew. "You aren't real ... nothing you say is true ..."

Drew barks out a harsh laugh. "That's right! Keep lying to yourself, baby bro. Even though you know that every word I say is the God honest—"

"Shut up!" I scream.

My voice echoes through the jungle and, to my surprise, Drew does, indeed, shut up. He turns his gaze toward me, a slightly impressed look on his face. "So Future School Shooter has balls after all, huh? Keep out of this, Toby. This is a family discussion."

I shake my head. "No. You're just being a bully, just like the Drew in the real world was. Only I suspect that the real Drew was much kinder to his younger brother than you are."

Drew snorts. "Ask Walt. He can tell you how often I bullied and belittled him before I died. He can also tell you how often he deserved it, too, for being a whiny little bitch."

I look at Walter and am alarmed to see how panicked he already looks. Clearly, this fake Drew is affecting him even more than me. Given how much mental pressure Walter has been under recently, that isn't surprising, but I definitely need to do something about it before Walter freaks out.

So I say to Walter, "Ignore him. However real he might seem, he's still just an illusion created by Logikill to mess with us."

Drew throws his head back and laughs. "Can an illusion do this?"

Before my very eyes, a clawed hand bursts through Drew's chest in a shower of blood and gore. Drew screams in utter agony, the exact same scream that I will never forget from his real death three years ago, before collapsing onto the ground in a bloody heap.

Humanimal the Cannibal, his claws dripping with Drew's blood, stands over his dead body, clutching Drew's heart in his hand. Raising the still-beating heart to his mouth, Humanimal takes a bite out of it and chews on it, all the while staring directly at us before gulping the rest of the heart into his mouth.

Walter shakes. Heck, I'm shaking, too, but I like to think I am hiding it better than Walter.

Because if there's one thing I know about the Meteor Monsters, it's that they can practically taste weakness in others.

Humanimal smiles a bloody smile at me. "Hi, Daddy. What did you think about reliving your worst failure again? Hurt, didn't it?"

I gulp. "That wasn't the real Drew. That was an illusion created by Logikill. You're not eating a real heart."

Humanimal licks his lips and rubs his stomach. "Maybe. Maybe not. Even I can't see through Logikill's illusions, but I can tell you that it tastes exactly the same as I remember it. I would definitely eat it again if I could get another chance at the real Drew. So succulent."

Walter, shaking his head, raises his oil cannons and fires a couple of big oil blobs directly at Humanimal. He is even faster than I am.

But the blobs of oil simply fly harmlessly through Humanimal's body and Humanimal, still smirking, vanishes into thin air. His dark laughter, like what I would imagine a tiger would sound like if tigers could laugh, echoes throughout the illusionary jungle around us.

"Going to try to hit me again?" says Humanimal. "You can't even tell what's real and what's not. Oh, this is a fun hunt indeed. The prey is real, but they can't tell if the hunter is real or not. So much fun."

Jerking my head this way and that, I snap, "Humanimal! Did you poison Captain Cowboy?"

"Of course," says Humanimal. "I had to. All part of the plan."

"Plan?" I repeat. "What plan?"

"Logikill says I'm not supposed to tell you, even though you are our daddy," says Humanimal. "But fear not. If you manage to survive this Trial, then you will eventually find out."

I scowl. "Humanimal, I know you see me as your dad. If you want to make me happy, then come out and show yourself. The real Humanimal."

Humanimal's laughter is dark and hideous. "But I don't want to make you happy. I want–we want–to make you suffer."

Suddenly, the trees shake and shift around us with a lot of rapid movements from things I can't see. My first thought is that Humanimal must be running around, maybe trying to scare or confuse us by constantly moving among the trees

Then Humanimal himself steps out of the jungle again before us, clutching his spear ...

Followed by another Humanimal emerging from the jungle to his right, then another to the right of that Humanimal, until we are surrounded on all sides by a dozen Humanimals.

Each one smiling that same bloody smile at us.

15

Even knowing that most of the Humanimals surrounding us are fakes crafted by Logikill's mind powers, I still feel like I walked directly into one of my worst nightmares.

Fortunately, my team huddles up around the sick Captain Cowboy, everyone fingering their weapons. Even Walter manages to keep his cool for the time being, although I can easily tell that he's still deeply shaken by Humanimal's repeat of Drew's murder despite knowing it was an illusion.

Honestly, I can't blame him. It was way too real, no matter how fake I knew it to be.

"Can you tell which one is the real Humanimal, Toby?" asks Codetalker in a low voice, pointing his gun at the illusions, turning his head this way and that to keep an eye on all of them. "Right now, even my helmet's sensors are having a difficult time distinguishing the real from the fake."

I purse my lips, gripping my bow tightly. "I'm not sure. If I could sense Humanimal's Core, I could probably locate the real one, but for some reason, I can't sense his Core at all. It's like it isn't even there. But it must be, because how else could Humanimal have poisoned Captain Cowboy if the real Humanimal wasn't here?"

Walter shoots me an annoyed glare. "So what's the point of having you around if you can't even sense the Meteor Monsters? Wasn't that supposed to be one of your special powers or something?"

Paintbrush responds before I do, rising to her feet as thick vines spill out of her wrists. "In the past, the Meteor Monsters have been known to hide their Cores from Toby's senses. So maybe Humanimal or Logikill is hiding his Core that way."

"That would make sense," says Codetalker, still looking around at all the Humanimals. "Just look at them. Clearly, the plan is to overwhelm us with a bunch of fake Humanimals to allow the real one to attack us without getting hurt. It's a pretty good plan, one that's working a lot better than it should, honestly."

I bite my lower lip in frustration. Even though Walter's words were hurtful, I can't say that I disagree. I thought for sure that my ability to sense the Meteor Monster Cores would be really useful in here, but if they're this good at hiding them from me, then I might as well be blind.

But maybe not all hope is lost. Maybe I just need to concentrate really, really hard to see through whatever defenses they're using to hide their Cores from me. Not that I expect Humanimal will give me a chance to do that, but maybe we can put him on the defensive for a little bit.

Looking at the rest of my teammates, I say, "New plan! Walter, I want you to spray oil on the ground all around us. Do it now."

To my relief, Walter doesn't argue with my plan. Instead, he raises his oil cannons and immediately starts spreading oil across the floor in a circle around our group. The Humanimals watching us from a distance growl and snarl but, oddly enough, don't try to attack us. Either they're waiting for something else, or my plan is already starting to work.

Paintbrush wrinkles her nose as the stench of freshly spilled oil fills the air around us. "Toby, what are you trying to do? Now we can't attack Humanimal because of how slippery the floor is."

I give Paintbrush a thumbs-up. "That's the plan. By covering the floor in oil and making it too slick for him to walk on, I figure we can prevent the real Humanimal from attacking us before we figure out where the real one is."

Pietro nods, though I notice he doesn't take his eyes off the illusions for even a second. "A smart plan, Toby, but, um, how do you intend to distinguish the real from the fakes?"

I gesture at my head. "I'm going to take this time to focus on finding the real Humanimal among the fakes. I think if I have enough time and I focus really hard, I could potentially see through whatever techniques they're using to conceal his Core."

Codetalker tilts his head to the side. "Not a bad plan at all, actually. The presence of the oil on the floor means that even if all of Humanimal's clones attack us at once, only the real one should have any trouble crossing the oil, while the fakes will probably just glide across it. But if Humanimal doesn't do anything, then Toby will easily be able to locate the real one by sensing his Core. I have to hand it to you, Toby—I really didn't think you had it in you to come up with such a simple yet effective plan for seeing through Logikill's illusions like this."

Honestly, I had only thought about the second part of Codetalker's explanation, but I'm perfectly happy to let him think I had put more thought into my plan than I actually did. A quick glance around at the illusionary Humanimals tells me that my plan must have some merit because they still aren't attacking us for some reason.

Whatever. I bet they probably will try to attack us at some point anyway, so I should start looking for the real Humanimal before they get impatient or come up with some way to get around the oil slick.

Closing my eyes, I immediately focus my mind on my surroundings, searching as much as I can for any sign of Humanimal. It's been a while since I last had to focus so hard on finding a Meteor Monster Core, but knowing what's at stake makes me shut out all external distractions to focus solely on finding the real Humanimal before it's too late.

At first, I don't feel anything at all—nothing to indicate that there's even one Meteor Monster nearby, even though I know Humanimal has to be somewhere close. I feel like I'm grasping for straws that don't even exist.

So I focus even deeper. Harder. More intensely than ever. But I don't focus on one being or one particular place. I expand my awareness to cover the entire room, pushing out all other thoughts and feelings that might distract me from my Meteor Monster senses. It's a lot harder than it sounds, yet at the same time, it comes as naturally to me as breathing.

That's when I finally feel something. A Meteor Monster Core that's coming from directly above us.

And it's falling down fast.

My eyes snap open, and I yell at the others, "Everyone, move! Now!"

Everyone immediately rushes away from me, including Keith and Captain Cowboy—although with Keith, it's more like he's dragging the poisoned Captain Cowboy by his shoulders. The others slip and slide across the oil slick, but I pay them no further attention as I look up in time to see Humanimal's bulky form falling down toward me.

I roll to the side just in the nick of time as Humanimal smashes down onto the ground where I had been standing. Switching out my bow for my club, I swing my club at Humanimal's ugly face, and the blow connects. The bone of my club crunches against Humanimal's jaw, breaking teeth and making blood shoot out of his mouth.

But instead of getting knocked over, Humanimal moves with the momentum of my attack and grabs the club. He rips it out of my hand and throws it to the side. As he reaches out with lightning-fast reflexes and grabs my throat, his clawed hand closes around my neck with an iron grip. Humanimal raises me off the floor, madness in his eyes as he glares at me.

"What a clever plan you came up with to find the real me, Daddy," says Humanimal in a voice laced with insanity. "But you clearly aren't clever enough to kill me again. Join me!"

Humanimal opens his mouth wide—wider than any normal creature should be able to—and lunges toward my face.

But one of Paintbrush's vine whips comes out of nowhere and wraps around his neck, jerking him backward before his teeth can rip my face off. This also causes Humanimal to let go of me, and I drop to my feet, staggering slightly as I rub my throat, which feels like an iron grip had been wrapped around it. Which, honestly, it kind of had been.

A growl from Humanimal distracts me from my own pain and makes me look up. Humanimal is holding onto the vine wrapped around his neck, gagging and choking, as Paintbrush, holding the other end of the vine from several feet away, pulls on it. Her eyes blaze with protective anger as she shouts, "Leave my boyfriend alone, you ugly jerk!"

Got to admit, it's pretty hot how Paintbrush gets whenever she gets really protective of me.

But I am not going to let this opportunity to finish off Humanimal slip by. I pick up my club, which bursts into flames, and swing it at Humanimal's midsection, which is closest to me.

At the same time, however, Humanimal's claws snap through the vine around his neck, and he backflips out of the range of my club before my blow connects. He lands in front of Paintbrush, who stares up at him in surprise even as she swings her vines at his face.

But Humanimal slashes straight through her vines like they are nothing before kneeing her in the face with his left knee. The blow knocks Paintbrush down onto the ground with a thud, where she lays unmoving.

"Mandy!" I say urgently, staring at her unconscious form in shock. "No!"

Humanimal picks up the unconscious Paintbrush and throws her over his shoulder. Looking over his shoulder at me, Humanimal smiles and says, "Perhaps this will make you feel true despair, Daddy."

SLOTH

With that, Humanimal rushes into the surrounding jungle with the unconscious Paintbrush still hanging off his shoulder, his dark laughter echoing among the trees as he runs.

16

I don't even think. I just run straight after Humanimal, ignoring the calls from the others, my eyes fixed on the path Humanimal took to escape.

But then Walter suddenly appears in my path, holding his hands out toward me, and shouts, "Toby! Stop."

I skid to a stop several feet away from Walter, glaring at him. "What do you think you're doing? Didn't you just see Humanimal kidnap Paintbrush? I need to save her!"

Walter glares right back at me. "And walk right into whatever trap Humanimal has set for you? Are you really that stupid, or just plain emotional?"

Hot anger rises inside me at Walter's comments. Didn't this stupid kid know what Humanimal was capable of? The Meteor Monsters didn't have any reason to spare Paintbrush. For all we knew, Humanimal might be chowing down on her even as we speak.

As if in response to my thoughts, I hear Paintbrush's screams of agony somewhere in the distance, among the thick flora of the jungle.

This time, I'm faster than Walter and fly straight over his head and into the trees, completely ignoring his cries. Coating my body in fire, I fly straight through the leaves, branches, and vines that were clearly meant to entangle me but could not withstand the heat from my flames. Perhaps if I had been less emotional, I might have wondered how my fire powers could burn fake trees that only existed in my mind, but that is the very last thing on my mind at the moment.

The most important thing is Paintbrush and her safety.

But the Jungle of Darkness is like a shadowy maze, and I quickly realize I'm lost—at least until I hear another of Paintbrush's screams. This one sounds disturbingly close, maybe a couple of yards to my right, and I quickly turn in that direction and fly through the trees until I reach a clearing, this one smaller than the previous one.

SLOTH

Actually, it seems less like a clearing and more like the nest of some predator. Countless bones, mostly human from what I can tell, litter the grassy, muddy ground, which is stained red with human blood. The stench of blood and death, which is far too familiar to me at this point, permeates the air, and combined with the general stinkiness of the jungle, it would have made me retch if I hadn't been accustomed to even worse stenches before.

This must have been Humanimal's nest, but I ignore that to focus on the only person in the clearing other than me:

Paintbrush.

Her body hanging from the vines, her stomach ripped open, blood leaking out, dripping down her legs, off her feet onto the floor … onto the floor … onto the floor …

I don't remember falling to my knees. Or crying. Or doing anything, really, other than feeling my heart crash to the very pit of my stomach. The whole world seems to shift and shake around me as my body trembles, trembles.

No. No. *No.*

She can't be dead. She can't be.

But I just need to look at her, once, to confirm that she was. Her body hangs lifelessly there, her dead eyes staring sightlessly into space, her jaw hanging open, frozen in a scream.

A hand falls on my shoulder and I instinctively look up. It's Walter, of all people, who is looking down at me with a mixture of anger and concern.

"Walter?" I say. My voice sounds distant, as if it's coming from the mouth of someone else, and the words feel like so much gravel in my mouth. "Do you see …"

Walter nods. He's not looking at her. "I do. Now get up."

The sadness inside me is suddenly burned to a crisp by white-hot anger. I rise to my feet, shoving Walter backward, and shout at him, "Get up? Do you even *hear* yourself? Paintbrush is *dead* and you just want me to 'get up'? What is *wrong* with you? Are you cruel or just plain stupid?"

Walter, staggering backward, raises his hand over his eyes. Fear appears on his face, which makes me feel very satisfied for some reason. "Toby, just listen to me. Paintbrush isn't—"

My anger flares again and the grass under my feet catches fire, but I ignore that. "Shut up, Walter. Shut *up.*"

Walter just stares at me with pure horror, his lips trembling. He clearly is afraid of me, which he should be. He hasn't been helpful at all. All he's done is try to make me feel worse.

He *should* be afraid of me. Everyone should be, actually.

Because if everyone was afraid of me, then maybe Paintbrush and Dad wouldn't be dead.

That is when I hear Captain Cowboy's voice call out, "Toby!"

Jerking my head to the side, I see Captain Cowboy—supported by Pietro and Keith, with Codetalker right behind them—emerge out of the trees. His pale, sweaty face looks even weaker than before, but he still manages to meet my eyes without hesitation.

"Toby, calm down," says Captain Cowboy, whose voice is way calmer than it should have been, given the circumstances. "Walter ain't the enemy here. He's just trying to help you."

I scowl. "Help me? How? How can *anyone* help me? Am I the only one who saw what Humanimal just did to Paintbrush?"

Codetalker steps up beside Captain Cowboy, gun still in his hand. "Toby's not listening to reason, Oscar. Might as well show him the truth."

Codetalker raises his gun, but he doesn't point it at me. Instead, he points it at Paintbrush's corpse and fires.

And the bullet from his gun goes straight through Paintbrush's corpse, which flickers and vanishes into thin air, along with the stench of blood and death emanating from it.

My heart racing, I look from the empty bloody vines to Codetalker's gun and back again. "What—?"

"That wasn't Paintbrush," says Codetalker simply. "Logikill simply made an illusion of Paintbrush's corpse just to mess with you."

Captain Cowboy nods. "Just like ... just like Drew earlier."

I blink. As the truth of the situation settles in my mind, the anger rushing inside me dies down, making it a lot easier to think rationally. "How did you know?"

Codetalker shrugs. "Simple logic. There was no time between the moment Humanimal kidnapped Paintbrush to the time you discovered her 'corpse' for Humanimal to have killed her in such a gruesome fashion. Combine that with the fact that nothing in here is real and it pays to be a bit distrusting of your own senses."

SLOTH

I nod slowly. Everything Codetalker says makes perfect sense, but my face still burns with shame. I look at Walter. "I'm sorry for yelling at you. I wasn't thinking."

Walter, to my surprise, shrugs. "I know. I felt the same way when I saw Humanimal 'kill' that illusion of Drew again."

Pietro speaks up in a slightly confused tone. "While it is good that Paintbrush is still alive, I wonder where Humanimal could have possibly taken her if she isn't dead. Do you think we will be able to find her or—?"

"Only if you make it to the top floor of the Tower, of course," says Logikill's monotone voice.

Logikill—or, rather, an illusionary copy of Logikill—steps out from behind the tree that the fake Paintbrush had been hanging from. He folds his arms behind his back as if he is just about to give us a lecture.

I glare daggers at Logikill. "What did you do with Paintbrush?"

Logikill smirks. "You heard me. I had Humanimal take the poor girl all the way to the top of the building with the rest of the hostages. That way, I give you even more motivation to make it there."

I furrow my brows. "Does this mean that the Trial is over? Did we lose?"

Logikill chuckles. "Lose? Of course not! You won. Big time, as you human kids like to say."

I blink again. "But we didn't kill Humanimal or even escape your illusion. How did we win?"

Logikill adjusts his glasses. "You are smart enough to figure *that* out on your own, I am sure. In the meantime, you may move on to the next Trial. Simply take the main elevator in the lobby and it will take you directly to the second Trial. Good luck."

Logikill gives us the thumbs-up before his form dissipates into mist. At the same time, the Jungle of Darkness slowly vanishes around us until we find ourselves back in the main lobby of Devon Energy Tower, with no sign of Humanimal or Paintbrush anywhere to be seen.

But the elevator doors on the other side of the lobby are standing wide open, clearly inviting us to enter.

17

But we don't.

Not right away, anyway.

Instead, Keith and Pietro sit Captain Cowboy on one of the sofas in the lobby. Captain Cowboy groans as he sits down, rubbing his forehead. "Ugh. Got the worst headache, let me tell you."

I stare at Captain Cowboy in utter disbelief. "That's all? I thought you were dying."

"I probably still am," Captain Cowboy admits, "but the poison, I think, is slow-acting. Or maybe it was only meant to weaken me so I couldn't fight back. Either way, I am not dead yet." He gives us his trademark smile that he gives when he thinks everything is going to be all right.

Codetalker, still standing, nods. "When Oscar got poisoned, I assumed that he was their target, but evidently they were after Paintbrush the whole time."

I look up at the ceiling, trying to look through it to see Paintbrush and the other hostages, although unfortunately x-ray vision isn't one of my powers. "And now they got her and made me think they'd kill her."

Walter frowns. "Doesn't make sense to me. Humanimal may not have had enough time to kill Paintbrush in that specific way, but there are plenty of other ways he could have killed her for real after he kidnapped her."

Pietro's face pales. "How do you know that?"

Walter rubs the back of his head sheepishly. "Well, uh, working with Road Rage, let's just say I saw a lot of interesting ways to kill people."

The mental image of the fake Paintbrush, hanging from the tree like a grotesque pinata, makes me shudder. "Humanimal mentioned wanting me to know 'true despair,' but I'm not sure what that means."

Codetalker folds his arms across his chest, a thoughtful look on his face. "It sounds like they are trying to ruin our morale, but as Walter pointed out, they could have achieved that goal even more easily by actually killing Paintbrush. Yet they didn't. Why?"

I take a deep breath and glance at the open elevator doors. "Because they want me to keep moving. To eventually reach the top. And become one of them."

Walter grimaces. "So it really is all just one big trap, then. I knew it."

Captain Cowboy, taking his hat off his head, looks up at us with tired eyes. "Do we have any other choice? So long as Wendy, Dakota, Paintbrush, and the others are all in danger, we don't have the luxury of taking it slow or going home."

I nod. "Yeah, but I don't like walking into obvious traps, either. I think Logikill is trying to break me, but I'm not sure why."

"Because you're supposed to be a weapon like them, remember?" says Captain Cowboy. "At least, that's what you told us. I guess Logikill still wants to get you on his side."

I think back to the murderous rage that I felt upon seeing the fake Paintbrush corpse and grimace. "Yeah, but like you said, we don't really have a choice at this point. We can't leave, but if we go to the next Trial, then who knows what kind of insanity Logikill will throw at us next?"

Codetalker strokes his chin thoughtfully. "In that case, maybe we are looking at this the wrong way. Perhaps we can bypass the Trials entirely."

I give Codetalker a deadpan look. "You do remember that Logikill said we can't skip them, right?"

"I remember," says Codetalker, "but I am saying that not all of us need to go the next Trial. I propose a divide-and-conquer strategy."

I tilt my head to the side. "Divide and conquer? How?"

Codetalker points at me. "Firstly, Toby, because you are the main target of the Meteor Monsters and the one best equipped for killing them, you and some of us can find another way to climb Devon Tower. Probably, we can use the ventilation system to sneak around and bypass most, if not all, of the Trials."

Captain Cowboy nods. "I see where you are going with this, CT. While Toby sneaks through the vents, the rest of us will go on to the next Trials."

I shake my head rapidly. "No, no, no. You guys saw how dangerous the first Trial was. I'm not going to let any of you handle the next Trial alone."

"It's probably safer than you think," says Codetalker. "While Logikill doesn't have a strong motivation to kill us, he also has a stronger motivation to keep an eye on you. Therefore, if you can sneak up to the top floor, Logikill will likely redirect most of the building's security resources to securing his position or the position of the hostages."

Captain Cowboy nods quickly. "I think I see where you are going with this. Logikill has limited resources, so if we can attack him from multiple angles, we'll strain said resources to their limit and make it harder for him to put up an effective defense."

Keith frowns as he scratches his chin, his eyes drifting up to the ceiling. "Not to be a Debbie Downer, but don't you think that Logikill might have anticipated us trying this sort of thing? He's supposed to be the smartest Meteor Monster, isn't he?"

Codetalker strokes his chin thoughtfully. "Be that as it may, Logikill still has limited resources. If he's as intelligent as we think he is, then he will have to make decisions about when and where he will put those resources to best achieve his efforts. Splitting the team would inevitably put the pressure on him to decide the best way to do that, so I think it makes sense."

Pietro nervously runs a hand through his hair. "Makes more sense than running straight into another traumatizing trap, eh?"

I frown but find that Codetalker's logic is as tight as ever, so I don't argue with it. "Fair. Just to be safe, I should travel the ventilation shafts on my own."

Walter shoots me a deadpan look. "Seriously? You saw what happened when you ran off without us. You definitely need a babysitter."

"Walter has a point," says Captain Cowboy before I can defend myself. "Logically, at least one other person should go with you. And I nominate Walter and Pietro."

I whip my head toward Captain Cowboy in utter confusion. "Why those two?"

Captain Cowboy holds up a couple of fingers. "First off, you three are the youngest and fittest members of the team, so climbing ventilation shafts should be easier for you than for us old fogies. Second, Walter and Pietro each bring unique and useful skills to the plan."

Walter raises his oil cannons again. "Yeah. I can create oil and stuff that we could use to either make it easier to move through the ventilation shafts or combine it with your fire powers and blow up some Meteor Monsters."

Pietro puts his hands on his hips. "And I just so happen to be very good at climbing through narrow spaces due to my slim build. I am honored that Captain Cowboy recognizes my skills."

Captain Cowboy nods. "Those are all useful skills, too, but I was thinking more along the lines that both of you have experience fighting Meteor Monsters and therefore should be useful allies in case you do end up fighting any. Plus, both of you are a lot less hasty than Toby, so you'll be able to provide him support in case the Meteor Monsters try to mess with him emotionally again."

I purse my lips, but again, I can't find any fault in Captain Cowboy's plan. "What are you, Keith, and Codetalker going to do in the meantime?"

Captain Cowboy slaps his knees and rises to his feet slowly. He points at the open elevator doors and says, "We're going to keep taking the elevator and trying to be as big a pain in the ass for Logikill as we possibly can be."

I give Captain Cowboy a very concerned look. "Even though you're still sick from the poison? Maybe you should sit this one out, Cap."

Captain Cowboy rolls his shoulders. "Ordinarily, I probably would, but I wouldn't be a very good husband if I just abandoned my wife to the guys who are holding her hostage, now would I?"

One look at Captain Cowboy's eyes tells me there's definitely no way I'm going to convince him to leave Mom in my hands, even though I have just as much motivation to save her as he does. I still don't like the idea of Captain Cowboy putting himself in danger like this, but at the same time, I can't say this is the first time he's done so deliberately, despite his own injuries.

Keith gives me the thumbs-up. "Don't worry about Oscar, Toby. Codetalker and I will make sure to keep him safe."

Codetalker nods. "Wouldn't be the first time we've had to keep him safe, either. Plus, all three of us have Meteor Monster bullets, so we can protect ourselves even if a bunch of them come after us. Don't forget, too, that we have our ear communication devices to keep in touch with one another, no matter where in the building we might be."

I reach up and feel the plastic earpiece in my left ear. "Both of those are good points, I guess. I just know from experience how tricky the Meteor Monsters are, especially Logikill. If we have to split up the team at all, I just want to make sure that we all understand how dangerous our enemies really are."

Captain Cowboy smirks at me. "Is this overly cautious young man really the same hard-headed teenager I first met all those years ago? Because you don't look much the same to me, but I'm proud of you just the same."

Captain Cowboy pats me on the shoulder, while I resist the urge to roll my eyes.

But he's not exactly wrong, however cringey he might be. I've definitely become a lot more cautious and concerned for the well-being of others since I first became a superhero three years ago. If my old self had been in this situation, he might not have cared as much about the safety of the others as I do now.

But Captain Cowboy and the others are right. They can take care of themselves. Our new plan really isn't any riskier or more dangerous than the old one, and if it allows me to save Paintbrush and the other hostages sooner, then I really can't complain too much.

So I look around at the team and say, "All right. Now that we all have our assignments, let's get going. We've got a lot to do and not a lot of time to do it."

18

"Ow!" says Walter behind me. "Watch where you put your boots! You nearly broke my nose."

I grunt but don't look behind me because there really isn't room for my head to move in the tight space of the Devon Tower ventilation system. "Sorry. It's just tough to move around in here without being able to see much of anything."

Up ahead, Pietro—whose boots and legs I can see—stops crawling and says, "Enough bickering, you two! You heard Captain Cowboy. We have an important mission to accomplish, and we cannot accomplish it while fighting amongst ourselves. That is exactly what the Meteor Monsters want. Remember the superhero standard."

I sigh but don't argue with Pietro, partly because he's not wrong, partly because it is just too tight in here to argue about anything. Behind me, I hear Walter grumble about not starting the fight, but I manage to at least avoid putting my feet in his face again.

But I understand Walter's grumbling. Ever since we entered the ventilation shafts, Pietro has been acting like our dad, just because he happens to be in his 20s while we're both still technically teenagers. Not only that, but he seems to treat our mission as if it were a holy quest granted by the Pope himself, even though it was really Captain Cowboy's idea to put us together like this.

Even the order in which we entered the ventilation system was determined by Pietro. According to him, because he was the oldest and therefore the most responsible, it was his job to lead the way and deal with any potential dangers that might be awaiting us up ahead. Because I was the target of the Meteor Monsters, I got to go second, and then Walter brought up the rear, under the belief that his suit's ability to spew oil would be useful in case we needed to slow down any enemies who might try to follow us from behind.

What none of us really considered before we climbed into the shaft together was just how narrow, cramped, and dark it would be. Especially with all three of us crawling in together, it would have been unbearable if we weren't all fairly short guys, aside from Pietro, who was on the longer and skinnier side.

Seriously, ventilation shafts in buildings in movies and TV shows always look a lot bigger than this. We can barely see where we're going, and I definitely am not going to use my fire powers in here. I don't want to accidentally cause an explosion by exposing my fire to Walter's oil or burn Pietro and Walter to death by trapping the heat in this narrow ventilation system.

So, for approximately the last 10 or 15 minutes, we've been crawling through the ventilation shafts of Devon Tower like this. It makes me wonder if maybe it would have been smarter just to take the elevator like Captain Cowboy and the others.

Even so, it's too late, not to mention impractical, to turn back now. At this point, I imagine Captain Cowboy and the others are already experiencing the second Trial or whatever Logikill has set up for them. I consider trying to call them via earcom but immediately decide against it. Pietro, Walter, and I are making more than enough noise banging around in the ventilation system as it is. No need to add unnecessary chatter on top of that.

But I still can't help but worry about Captain Cowboy, Codetalker, and Keith. All three of them may be experienced superheroes with plenty of practice fighting Meteor Monsters, but they're still just normal humans who don't have the same powers or nature as the Meteor Monsters themselves. I just hope Codetalker's theory about Logikill deciding to play it safe works out the way he said it would.

And, of course, I can't stop worrying about Paintbrush, Mom, Dakota, Granny, and Gary. After hearing Black kill Dad over the phone, I still have no reason to assume that Logikill will spare their lives any longer than he absolutely needs to. I try not to dwell on how he might execute them and focus instead on doing what I can to save them.

But crawling around in the ventilation system of Devon Tower has given me a lot of time to think about what Captain Cowboy said to me before we split the team, about how much I've grown and changed since the day of the meteor crash.

It's true that I have matured a lot since then. I still cringe every time I think about how much of a brat I was back then, which definitely shows I've changed and grown a lot.

And, of course, the reason I've changed so much is because of everything I've been through over the last three years. Since gaining my powers, I have stared death in the face so many times and survived that it's not even funny. Not that it ever was, but I'm pretty sure I didn't have such a strong understanding of death before becoming a superhero. Heck, I've personally taken the lives of other living beings, mostly Meteor Monsters, but I have, in fact, killed a handful of normal human beings, too.

I try not to dwell on that fact, though, because if I did, I'd probably lose it.

Another thing that has affected me since three years ago?

Well, I now have a whole bunch of new family and friends I never even dreamed about having. I even have a girlfriend now, which is definitely something I never imagined happening in my wildest dreams. I used to consider myself a pretty strong loner, but now here

I am, risking my life yet again to save the lives of my friends and family and working with other friends to do the same.

Of course, I also have a lot more enemies now, too. I guess that's just part of being a superhero, at least from what I've experienced. Pretty much everyone who works as a superhero ends up gaining at least a few enemies, while I have at least seven, not counting the various normal humans who I have earned the ire of over the years.

All this to say that I'm not sure how I would explain how much my life was going to change to my 15-year-old self on the night of the meteor crash. My younger self probably wouldn't even believe me if I went back in time and tried to explain everything to him. And he definitely wouldn't understand how everything, even the hard parts, would make him a better person.

So, in the end, I guess I have become a lot more like Captain Cowboy than I thought. And that isn't necessarily a bad thing.

My thoughts are interrupted when I crawl directly into Pietro's boot. "Ouch! Pietro, what's the holdup?"

Pietro, of course, does not turn his head to look in my direction, but when he speaks, his voice is quite tense. "I heard something up ahead. We are not alone in here. Be quiet and listen."

Grimacing, I listen closely down the ventilation shaft, trying to pick up any unusual or strange sounds that might indicate who or what else is in here with us. Behind me, Walter goes still and quiet too, undoubtedly also listening for threats. Just to be safe, I also focus my Meteor Monster senses down the way, just to make sure there aren't any Meteor Monsters in here.

But my Meteor Monster senses do not pick up any sign of the Meteor Monsters, and I don't hear anything at first either, making me think that maybe Pietro was just hearing things.

But then I hear a thunk directly below us, coming from outside the ventilation system, and suddenly my Meteor Monster senses begin to go wild.

Before I even realize it, I am shouting, "Watch out!"

A large, claw-like hand smashes through the bottom of the ventilation shaft underneath me, wrapping around my body at the same time. Before I can even react, the claw yanks me through the shaft and I go falling to the floor.

Smashing into the floor onto my back, I gasp, my head spinning as my senses try to make sense of my new location. They start working again just as I see a metal baseball bat flying toward my face.

I roll away at the last second, avoiding the baseball bat, which smashes into the floor where my face had been mere seconds ago. Rising to my feet, I summon my tapena again just in time to block another swing of the baseball bat. The blow makes me skitter backward slightly from the impact, but I hold my ground against the user of the baseball bat.

Who happens to be the Crippler, his green, snake-like eyes gleaming with triumph underneath the hood of his ratty hoodie. "Gotcha, brat."

I scowl. "Crippler. Long time, no see. Just as ugly as I remember."

The Crippler smiles. "What about Wasteland? Remember him?"

My Meteor Monster senses go wild again as a tendril made of oil and sludge suddenly wraps around my waist and hurls me across the room. I smash into the wall, nearly breaking through it, but I guess it is sturdier than it looked because it manages to hold.

Shaking my head, I look up to see a scene straight out of my nightmares:

Wasteland, his bubbling form sloshing toward me, along with the Crippler, patting his baseball bat in his right hand, still smirking and chuckling under his breath.

19

Breathing hard, I rise to my feet and hold up my tapena, which bursts into flames. "Back off, you two. Or have you forgotten what happens to oil when it is exposed to fire?"

Wasteland and the Crippler both come to a stop several feet away from me, but neither look afraid or even worried. If anything, they look quite smug, especially the Crippler.

"I remember quite well, Wyldfyre," says Wasteland, "but you would be an absolute fool if you think that Logikill did not give me advice for dealing with that particular weakness of mine. He added a stabilizer to my body to make it harder for me to catch fire. Otherwise, why do you think he sent us to take you down?"

The Crippler nods. "Exactly. And your fire doesn't scare me, either. I will definitely not give you another shot at destroying my Core again."

I furrow my brow and look around the room I ended up in.

It appears to have been a conference room at one point, at least based on its size and openness. But it looks like all of the furniture must have been moved out recently because there's no furniture at all other than a couple of office chairs stuffed in the corner. It's also quite warm here, as if the Tower's AC doesn't reach this room for some reason.

I turn my attention back to Wasteland and the Crippler. "How did you two find me? I thought you would be waiting for us at the second Trial."

The Crippler's smirk somehow becomes even smugger. "Nah. Logikill knew you would try something like this, so Captain Cowpoke and his gaggle of middle-aged has-beens are going to be dealing with some of our human servants instead of us."

Wasteland nods. "We were granted the privilege of freely roaming the building just in case you tried to sneak around like this."

My eyes narrow. "How did you know I was in that specific ventilation shaft, though?"

The Crippler taps the side of his head with one finger. "Simple. Just as you can sense us, we can sense you. Admittedly, it took us a while to locate your exact location, but now that we have you, we can have our way with you."

I scowl, rubbing the back of my neck, which is the only part of my body that is still sore from the beating I got from Wasteland and the Crippler. Score one for a rapid healing factor. "You can't kill me, remember? You need me for your plan."

The Crippler shrugs. "We may not be allowed to kill you, but I don't recall big brother ever saying we couldn't break a limb or two. Or three. Or all four, really. I'm not picky."

"Given how you have effectively abdicated the Trials, that means you are fair game for us to capture however we see fit," explains Wasteland. "Brother Logikill gave all six of us the chance to hunt you down in case you decided not to play according to the rules. We can essentially do whatever we want so long as we make sure you do not leave the building and do not die."

I frown. "So what's the prize you win if you catch me before the others?"

The Crippler pats his baseball bat again. "We get to do whatever the heck we want to you."

"And become Brother Logikill's right-hand man," says Wasteland, "which itself will come with many perks when he takes over the world."

I give Wasteland a deadpan look. "Surprised that the embodiment of my pride is willing to play second fiddle to a lazy bum who hasn't worked a day in his life."

Wasteland growls at me. "Don't even attempt to play us against each other, Wyldfyre. We may not be the best team in the world, but we understand that we have a common goal of ensuring that you are captured and delivered to Brother Logikill."

"Exactly," says the Crippler with another nod. He steps forward. "Which is why, dear brother, you will give me the chance to turn over Wyldfyre myself so I can reap the benefits of—"

An oily tendril erupts from Wasteland's body, appearing directly in the Crippler's path. The Crippler comes to a halt, turning his gaze toward Wasteland, who is now glaring daggers at him.

"I may have agreed to team up with you for the purposes of finding Wyldfyre before the others, but don't push my kindness and mercy, Crippler," says Wasteland. "Brother Logikill made it exceedingly clear beforehand that even assaulting each other is allowed in this game we are playing. And I am far bigger than you."

SLOTH

The Crippler gulps. "Uh, sure, Wasteland. Do whatever you want. I was just joking around. You know, like how brothers do."

Wasteland clearly doesn't believe a word that comes from the Crippler's mouth. To be fair, no one really should, given how prone to lying that guy is.

But despite Wasteland's earlier insistence that I couldn't play them against each other, I realize that he's wrong. Clearly, this 'game' that Logikill set up for everyone is designed to pit the Meteor Monsters against each other. As long as I am smart about it, I probably could get Wasteland and the Crippler to fight each other instead of me, which would give me time to escape.

That plan goes straight out the window, however, when I hear a thunk behind the two Meteor Monsters and the Crippler gets positively drenched in oil from behind. The Crippler screams as he falls onto the floor, while Wasteland, clearly not affected by the oil in the slightest, whirls around to face whoever attacked the Crippler.

It's Walter, who is standing at the other end of the conference room, pointing both of his oil cannons at Wasteland and the Crippler as the canisters on his back pump furiously. I don't see Pietro, but if he's smart, he should still be in the ventilation system where it's safe.

"Gotcha!" says Walter, shooting a smirk at the downed Crippler. "That's what you get for trying to hurt Toby!"

My eyes widen. "Walter, what are you doing here? They're after me. They don't need you for their plans."

"Wyldfyre is correct," says Wasteland, his voice rumbling. A slasher smile crosses his monstrous lips. "At least we don't have to worry about holding back against Wyldfyre's allies."

Wasteland raises a tendril, but I fly toward him and smack my burning tapena straight into the back of his head. Wasteland roars as my tapena smashes through his head, making it explode from the impact, but I don't stop to inflict any more damage.

Instead, I fly over to Walter and land beside him, panting hard. "Where's Pietro?"

Walter points up at the hole in the ceiling that shows us the exposed ventilation system. "Up there waiting for us to rejoin him."

I shake my head. "The ventilation system isn't going to work. We'll have to find the stairs or something to keep going up."

Walter looks at the Crippler and Wasteland and grimaces. "Right. We probably should get going, then."

I follow the direction of his gaze and realize he's right. Wasteland's head has already reformed, while the oil-covered Crippler is getting back to his feet, cursing up a storm under his breath. "Then let's go. Hopefully, those two will leave Pietro alone and just follow us."

We run over to the door out of the conference room and I kick it open.

But just as the door swings open, another baseball bat swings at my face from the other side, forcing me to jump back to avoid getting hit in the face. Staggering into Walter, who is right behind me, I look out into the hallway and feel my heart fall into my stomach.

Dozens of green-eyed men and women—homeless, based on their clothing—stand in the hallway outside of the conference room, carrying baseball bats, metal pipes, and various other weapons and makeshift weapons in their hands. They stare at me and Walter with empty green eyes, but immediately raise their weapons when they see us.

"Huh?" says Walter, staring at the homeless people. "Homeless people? Here?"

"My followers," says the Crippler's smug voice behind us. "Or rather, my new followers, seeing as most of my old ones were arrested after my death. Glad I had the foresight to bring some of them along in case you turned out to be more trouble than I expected."

I jerk my head over my shoulder to see the Crippler and Wasteland, both fully recovered from their injuries, stalking toward us slowly but dangerously. The Crippler wears a slasher smile while Wasteland grunts and growls like a wild animal.

Walter grunts angrily. "Toby, what are we waiting for? Let's just fight through the homeless people and–"

"And risk killing them?" I shake my head. "No way. Not again."

I am referring, of course, to the time I accidentally killed one of the Crippler's followers in the OKC Underground before his original death. That death still haunts me because the Crippler's followers are just brainwashed, innocent people who definitely are not deserving of death. I just can't do it.

On the other hand, I also can't let the Crippler and Wasteland capture me either. I need a third option, one that allows me to avoid the Crippler and Wasteland as well as the Crippler's brainwashed followers.

But how? It seems like our only options are to either fight through the brainwashed homeless people and risk killing or severely injuring them, or try to take on the Crippler and Wasteland again. Even though I had killed both of them before, I wasn't sure that I could take them both on together at once.

That's when several gunshots suddenly ring through the air, and both the Crippler and Wasteland fall to their knees. Well, Wasteland just kind of slumps over because he doesn't have knees, but you get the point.

Green blood leaking out of his stomach, the Crippler grabs his bullet wounds as he hisses under his breath, "Who shot me? Where did those bullets come from?"

"They came from me, Crippler," says the familiar Ukrainian voice of Pietro behind the two Meteor Monsters. "And I have plenty more where those came from if you would like a little extra!"

A lasso made of flexible steel suddenly flies over the Crippler's head and wraps around his neck. The lasso tightens like a noose, and the Crippler suddenly goes flying backward, pulled back by none other than Pietro, who holds the other end of the steel lasso with a serious and focused look on his face. The Crippler lands at his feet, but before the Crippler gets a chance to rise again, Pietro kicks him in the head, making the Crippler groan in pain as he grabs his head with his hands.

Wasteland, who was also injured by Pietro's Meteor Monster bullets, twists and turns around to face Pietro. He launches a sharpened spike of oily sludge at Pietro, but Pietro lunges to the side, narrowly avoiding the spike as it embeds itself into the wall that he had been standing in front of. The whole time, Pietro absolutely refuses to let go of the lasso, which is smart because the Crippler is choking on it and is clearly not going to be much of a problem for us until he gets out of the lasso.

With Wasteland's back turned to us, I nock an arrow in my bow, draw it back, and unleash the flaming arrow at the back of Wasteland's head. The flaming arrow is a direct hit, setting Wasteland's head on fire, causing him to roar in pain as the fire rapidly spreads over his oily, disgusting form. Even so, I can tell that Wasteland is definitely not out for the count, but that should keep him occupied for a while, at least.

Looking over at Pietro, I shout, "Pietro! Get over here. We need to get out of here before the Crippler and Wasteland recover!"

Pietro nods and tries to run over to us, but the Crippler, still choking on the lasso-turned-noose, reaches out and grabs Pietro's ankle as he runs past him. Pietro immediately faceplants onto the carpeted floor of the conference room, and, drawing his gun, he points it at the Crippler's head and fires several times. The bullets strike the Crippler's face dead-on, blowing fresh, bloody holes in his ugly mug and making him gurgle in pain as he lets go of Pietro, who quickly scrambles to his feet and rushes toward us again.

Only for Wasteland, still partially on fire, to slosh between us and Pietro before smashing his fist into Pietro's face. Wasteland's punch knocks Pietro onto the ground, where he lies, seemingly unconscious or possibly even dead.

My heart tightens in my throat. "Pietro! No!"

Behind me, Walter says, "Toby! We've got our own trouble over here."

I jerk my head over my shoulder to see that the Crippler's followers, perhaps trying to save their leader, are now trying to force their way into the conference room. Walter has closed the door and is trying to keep it shut, but I can tell that even he is going to lose that battle with so many people pressing against the door.

Somehow, the situation has gotten even worse. With the pressure from the Crippler's followers on one side and Wasteland and the Crippler no doubt about to kill Pietro on the other, I feel well and truly trapped. What should I do? I want to save Pietro, but I also want to keep going up. I feel like I am stuck between a rock and a hard place.

Then I hear Pietro shout, "Toby! Walter! Keep going. Don't worry about me."

Snapping out of my indecision, I look back toward Pietro and see that he is apparently still alive after all. He is standing on his feet again, panting hard as he faces Wasteland, who is glaring down at him with pure hatred, while behind him, the Crippler finishes ripping the steel lasso off his neck and also stands up again. Clutching the baseball bat in his hand, the Crippler stalks toward Pietro with pure hatred in his eyes as well.

But Pietro doesn't look nearly as afraid as he should. He just gives me a smile and says, "You are the only one who can stop the Meteor Monsters, Toby. You must go."

My lips tremble slightly. "But Pietro, I don't want to leave you. You'll never stand a chance against Wasteland and the Crippler. You are probably out of Meteor Monster bullets already."

Pietro cracks a goofy smile at me. "Do not worry about me, Toby. I have a bomb."

Pietro suddenly pulls out what appears to be a grenade, of all things, from the inside of his jacket and pulls the pin out before either Wasteland or the Crippler can do anything.

Instinctively, I grab Walter and fly us both out through the door into the hallway, knocking aside the dozens of brainwashed homeless people who had been trying to force their way in. Veering to the right, which I'm pretty sure is the direction that will take us closer to the top floor, I don't slow down as we fly for several seconds...

SLOTH

Until a loud *boom* shakes the hallway and causes several of the doors on either side to shudder from the impact of the blast.

20

Even then, I don't lose my cool or stop until we reach another set of stairs and climb up them. Emerging onto the next floor of the tower, I drop Walter, who was starting to feel like dead weight anyway, and then land on my feet, leaning against the wall for support as I breathe hard. Even with my fantastic healing factor, I still need to rest and catch my breath every now and then, too.

Walter, sitting on the floor and panting as well, glances at the stairwell we just emerged from with a curious look on his face. "Do you think that bomb might have, well—?"

I shake my head. "You know as well as I do that a normal bomb, even a really powerful one, can't permanently kill a Meteor Monster. At best, Wasteland and the Crippler might have been blown to bits and buried underneath a lot of debris, but if their cores are at all undamaged or intact, I bet they will regenerate pretty damn quickly."

Walter shakes his head. "Then I guess Pietro gave his life for no reason. What a waste."

My temper flares, and I snap at Walter, "Pietro didn't give his life for no reason! If he hadn't done that, we wouldn't have been able to escape or make it higher up the tower. Show some respect."

Walter slowly rises to his feet to meet my gaze, his eyes never wavering. "Excuse me for valuing killing the enemy over merely buying us some time. I know that Logikill is our main target and we have some hostages to save, but it would have made things a lot easier for us if we had taken out a couple of the Meteor Monsters at the same time."

My hands ball into fists. "I forgot how much of a brat you really are, Walter."

Walter rolls his shoulders. "Do you want to fight right now? Because I am perfectly willing to throw down and throw hands if you are."

I am seriously tempted to take Walter up on that offer, but then my earcom clicks and I hear Captain Cowboy's calm voice say, "Toby, what was that explosion that we just heard and felt? Are you and the others okay?"

My anger dissipates as I turn away from Walter, putting one hand up to my ear. "Pietro blew himself up to stop Wasteland and the Crippler from killing us. Where did he get that grenade from?"

Captain Cowboy chuckles. "I gave it to him before we split up! Told him to only use it in case of emergency. And if y'all were really fighting two different Meteor Monsters at once, I would say that definitely qualifies as an emergency. Anyway, what did you say happened to Pietro?"

I take a deep breath to steady myself. "He's dead. At least, we think so. He stayed behind to blow up the Crippler and Wasteland with his grenade. We didn't see a body, but—"

"Needless to say, there is no way that a normal human being could survive having a grenade blow up in their face point-blank," says Walter, who is now speaking through his earcom to join the conversation.

Captain Cowboy is silent for several seconds. "I am sorry to hear that. Pietro was a great man, a true hero in his own right. I honestly didn't think he would give up his own life like that, but now that I think about it, he always did want to be a real hero and understood the importance of sacrificing yourself for the greater good. I will pay for his funeral arrangements later after we get out of here alive. All of us."

I grimace as Walter and I start walking down the hallway because we still need to get going, especially if Wasteland and the Crippler regenerate quicker than I think they will. "Optimistic of you to think that any of us are getting out of here in one piece. The Meteor Monsters know that I'm skipping the trials, and now Logikill has all of the other Meteor Monsters hunting for me in the building as a sort of sick competition among them to see who can become Logikill's right-hand man."

"That don't surprise me one bit," says Captain Cowboy. "Explains why we haven't run into any of them since splitting up. Not that our part of the mission has been without any obstacles, though."

We pass an open janitor's closet as I frown. "The Crippler and Wasteland mentioned that their human servants would be trying to stop you, Codetalker, and Keith. How are things going on your end? Are you feeling well?"

Captain Cowboy grunts. "I feel about the same as before. As for the human servants of the Meteor Monsters, yeah, we ran into some chuckleheads who thought they could teach us a lesson, but Codetalker has some pretty nifty toys that made short work of them. No, the real problem is that the elevator suddenly stopped working, which Codetalker is trying to troubleshoot, but we think that Logikill probably manually disabled the elevator so we couldn't go any further than we already have."

Walter, walking beside me, nods. "Makes sense. They are trying to isolate Toby from all of his friends and allies. Make it easier for them to kill us."

"One hundred percent, young man," says Captain Cowboy. "Keith has gone to look for stairs, but I am afraid we may not be able to catch up to you guys for a while. Sorry about that."

I sigh but say, "That's fine, Cap. There are now only five other Meteor Monsters that we need to worry about immediately, and it sounds like only Wasteland and the Crippler got the idea to team up. So as long as we keep moving forward and try to look for unexpected ways to climb the tower, then I think we might be able to reach Logan and the hostages without needing to fight too much."

"Hope so," says Captain Cowboy. "Anyway, that's all the updates I have for y'all at the moment. I'll keep you updated once we find a way to keep moving forward. In the meantime, keep your wits about you and don't let the Meteor Monsters get to you, okay?"

I nod. "Got it, Cap. See you later."

I tap my earcom to click it shut and look at Walter. "Well, it looks like we are on our own for the time being."

Walter nods without looking at me, lowering his hand from his ear. "I thought so. I guess that means we are going to have to work together, then."

Walter does not sound any more enthusiastic about that prospect than I do, but I say, "Yeah, I know. But I think that we could potentially make a good team, at least. Like, what if you sprayed a Meteor Monster with some of your oil and then I set them on fire? They would make a really big explosion. Kind of like Pietro's grenade, except probably even more effective at killing a Meteor Monster."

Walter shrugs. "Meh. I guess that could work, if we aren't afraid of causing a lot of structural damage or blowing up ourselves."

SLOTH

I grimace at the thought. "Yeah, I guess that would be a serious concern, but I am just trying to figure out how we can work together. We have five more Meteor Monsters to potentially fight, so we need to have a way to take care of them in case we run into them."

"And I am sure that we will," says Walter, still not looking at me. "But maybe spend less time talking and more time moving, okay? Not really in the mood to talk."

I frown but can't say I disagree with him too strongly, although I am slightly frustrated at Walter's unwillingness to strategize, seeing as we have at least this time together to do so. Yeah, maybe we aren't currently embroiled in a battle for our lives, but it doesn't hurt to think ahead at least a little bit.

But maybe I am just being too quick to judge. Unlike me, Walter hasn't had a good mentor who could help him think things through or deal with the emotional fallout of surviving life-or-death situations like the one we were just in. I sincerely doubt that Road Rage, Walter's last mentor, had even bothered to discuss that stuff with him.

Plus, I realize that we didn't actually talk very much about the fake Drew that we ran into down in the lobby. I distinctly remember Walter having a similar freak-out to me, if not worse, and I realize that Walter might not have the closure he needs to mentally process his older brother's death.

Regardless, we are definitely making forward progress. I don't know how many more floors stand between us and the hostages, but every floor we climb brings us that much closer to our destination, so I can't complain about that, at least.

Still, while we have the time, I really should ask Walter about how he is dealing with his brother's death. I doubt we will be able to resolve all of Walter's emotional issues in one short conversation in a hallway in an abandoned office building, but maybe we can make some progress, at least.

My thoughts are interrupted, however, by the roaring of a motorcycle engine coming down the hallway. Walter and I both come to a stop, staring down the long hallway of the building as the roar of the motorcycle grows louder and louder.

I look at Walter urgently. "A motorcycle? You don't think—?"

Walter doesn't answer, mostly because the door at the other end of the hallway bursts open and a motorcycle comes roaring out of the room. A huge Black man wearing a motorcycle helmet rides the motorcycle, and, swinging a chain over his head, he throws it at me and Walter.

Walter and I jump to the sides, avoiding both the chain and the motorcycle, which skids to a halt several feet behind us. Turning to face the motorcycle, I watch as the rider takes his helmet off, revealing the strangely calm face of Road Rage, who gives us both a rather menacing smile.

21

"Road Rage," says Walter before I can speak. He has also turned to face Road Rage, his hands balled into tight fists, although I notice he is not aiming his oil cannons at the Meteor Monster. "Can't say I'm surprised to see you again."

Road Rage nods. He cuts the engine of his motorcycle before speaking. "Of course. You must have known that the second you stepped into this building, we were destined to run into each other again at some point. It's sad that we had to be enemies, however."

I scowl at Road Rage. "You aren't sad about that at all. You never even cared for Walter when you were alive. He was only a tool for you to use to achieve your own ends."

Road Rage gives me an unimpressed look. "I don't remember asking for your opinion, Wyldfyre. Perhaps you should learn to stay out of other people's business."

I summon my club again, which catches fire in my hands, and I start spinning it rapidly. "You are literally a comic book character I created. By definition, that makes you my business."

Road Rage shrugs. "Be that as it may, I am no longer under your ownership. Besides, I just wanted to talk to Walter for a bit. Is that a crime now?"

I scowl at Road Rage. "It is if you're planning to turn Walter against us, because I'm sure that's what you're planning to do. It's what I would do in your shoes, after all."

Road Rage steps off his motorcycle. He's so tall that the top of his head almost scrapes against the ceiling tiles overhead, and he gazes at us both with his hard green eyes. "I notice you haven't asked Walter for his opinion. Do you really think so lowly of him that you won't even ask how he feels about talking to me?"

I bite my lower lip in frustration. "You big, ugly—"

Walter holds up a hand toward me. "Shut up for a minute, Toby. I want to hear what Road Rage has to say."

I stare at Walter in complete disbelief. "Walter, you do realize that Road Rage doesn't actually just want to talk, right? He only wants to use you or somehow get inside your head. There's literally no reason to talk to him."

Walter shakes his head. "For you, maybe. But I have a lot of things I've wanted to say to Road Rage ever since he died. So let me talk to him, okay?"

Walter gives me a very hard, challenging look as he says that. It's almost as if he's daring me to try to fight him or something.

I sigh in exasperation and take a step back, lowering my tapena to my side at the same time. "Fine, but if you guys want to talk, I'm out of here. I have friends and family to save, so if you think that having a tea party with Road Rage will distract him, then so be it."

Road Rage tilts his head to the side. "When did I say you could leave?"

Without warning, Road Rage throws his silver chain at me. I raise my club to block it, but the chain quickly wraps around my body, and I fall to the floor hard. Struggling against the chain with all my might, I find it almost impossible to break on my own.

Road Rage, holding the other end of the chain, says to me, "Stay right there, Wyldfyre. Once I'm done talking to Walter, then we will resume our fight."

Darn it. This is exactly the scenario I was hoping to avoid. Now, instead of making actual progress toward the top of Devon Tower, I basically have to hope that Road Rage doesn't brainwash Walter against us. Even though I know it's been a long time since Walter took Road Rage's Fury drugs, that doesn't mean he's no longer addicted or has developed an immunity to Road Rage's influence somehow.

I can only hope that Walter is smart enough to see through Road Rage's lies and not fall for them because if he does, then I'm not sure we'll be making it to the top of the tower on our own.

Walter, who apparently was just watching my little confrontation with Road Rage without much emotion, turns his attention to him. "What did you want to say to me, Road Rage? Are you going to convince me to join the Angels of Wrath again?"

Road Rage shakes his head. "No. The old gang is gone. Everyone is either arrested and in jail or on the run and not going to want to join us again. Nor do I have any interest in resurrecting the old gang. I have a newer and better gang now, one that will go beyond Oklahoma, beyond even the borders of the United States, to turn the whole world into our turf."

Walter doesn't move. "Is that what Logikill promised you?"

Road Rage nods. "Essentially, yes. With Logikill at the helm of our gang, we'll be able to distribute drugs all over the world, creating a population of addicts who will be entirely dependent on us for their very existence. The profit and power will be totally unimaginable."

Walter tilts his head to the side. "And what makes you think I want any of that? You remember the original reason I joined you. You offered me the power to avenge Drew. All I hear from you right now is a lot of talk of money and power, which seems pretty out of character for you."

Road Rage smiles, an expression that frankly looks a little strange on him. "You're correct, Walter. I don't actually care about the money or power myself. All I want is to avenge my own death and to help you avenge your older brother's death at the hands of Wyldfyre."

My eyes widen and I look at Walter. "Walter, I didn't kill Drew. It was—"

Walter shoots me a surprisingly menacing glare. "Shut up, Toby. Road Rage is still talking."

The hatred in Walter's voice sounds shockingly real, making me shut up. It doesn't sound like Walter has actually forgiven me for my role in Drew's death. He looks and sounds as angry as ever, making me wonder if he still hates me on some level, despite what he said earlier before we entered the building.

Road Rage's smile grows even wider. "Excellent, Walter. I see you still have that anger inside you, that you are not giving up your hatred toward Wyldfyre. Or was this part of your plan all along?"

Walter nods without looking at me. "You got it. How could I ever forgive the 'superhero' who killed my brother?"

My heart races from the implications of Walter's statement. My worst fears are coming to life right before my very eyes and there's nothing I can do about it.

Maybe that is why Walter wasn't upset about Pietro's sacrifice earlier. Pietro dying just meant there would be one less person he would have to worry about protecting me from him.

Road Rage then starts walking over to us, the chain in his hand clinking against the tile floor as he walks. "Smart boy, Walter. Feel that anger rushing through you. Feed it your pain, your sorrows, and all of your frustrations. Let it burn hotly until it consumes everything around you ..." Road Rage smirks at me. "Like a wildfire."

Road Rage yanks on the chain and I go tumbling toward him before he stops me with a boot. I then hear a click and look over my shoulder to see Walter pointing his Meteor Monster gun at me, his eyes fixed on my face.

Horrified, I look at Road Rage and say, "Why are you telling Walter to kill me? I thought you Meteor Monsters wanted me *alive*."

Road Rage keeps smiling. "Logikill only gave us orders to keep you alive. A bullet to the face is perfectly survivable for someone of your unique powers and nature. And if you don't ... well, I am sure there are other ways to get what we want from your body."

Crap. Are the Meteor Monsters going rogue or something? Is even Logikill losing control over them now?

Road Rage continues speaking, addressing Walter while ignoring me. "Now, Walter, unleash your rage on Wyldfyre. Take his life. Make his family know the pain that *you* have suffered for so long. Pull the trigger and–"

Bang.

Blood spurts out of Road Rage's chest as the bullets from Walter's gun pierce him in multiple places. The impact sends Road Rage stumbling backward into his motorcycle, which he nearly knocks over as he clutches his bleeding chest. Blood seeps through his fingers as he looks at Walter in pure astonishment.

No, not astonishment.

Anger.

Road Rage looks angry.

But Walter does not. He keeps a calm expression as he points his gun at Road Rage, his finger resting on the trigger, making me wonder why he isn't pulling it again. Maybe he just doesn't know where Road Rage's Core is.

Road Rage growls, sounding very much like the engine of his motorcycle. "Why did you shoot me? I thought you were going to shoot Wildfire. I thought you were going to get your revenge."

Walter shakes his head, still keeping his gun trained on Road Rage's chest. "That was a lie. I told Toby that I don't blame him for Drew's death, and I mean it. I only acted like I still hated Toby because I wanted you to lower your guard. I'm just sad that I apparently didn't hit your Core because you're clearly still alive and breathing."

Walter looks at me apologetically. "Sorry about that, Toby. I had a plan, but I knew it wouldn't work if you were aware of it."

I nod shakily. "No problem, Walter. I mean, yeah, it would've been nice if I had known it was just your plan, but it was a pretty good plan, I'll admit."

Road Rage, taking his hand off his bloody chest as he rises to his full height, says, "How good of a plan could it be, seeing as I'm still alive? Already, my injuries have healed. Unfortunately for you, Walter, the same cannot be said for the injuries I'll be inflicting on you soon enough."

Road Rage grunts and flexes his muscles, which suddenly start to swell like inflatable balloons. His jacket and pants rip to shreds as his muscles tear through them, leaving little more than tatters of clothing attached to his body. The floor cracks under his feet as his weight increases from his expanded muscle mass, and his fists expand to the size of small boulders.

A few seconds later, Road Rage stands before us in his massive muscle form. He looks less like a human now and more like some hulking abomination straight from the depths of hell itself. Even his face is rockier now, narrower, more like the face of a dog or snake than a human, his green eyes flashing with wrath and hatred.

With a roar, Road Rage charges us, each footstep smashing the tiles under his feet and shaking the hallway. Walter actually drops his Meteor Monster gun, seemingly taken by surprise by Road Rage's sudden transformation.

Now it is my turn.

With a grunt, I finally snap Road Rage's chain off my limbs and, jumping to my feet, rush to meet him in the middle of the hallway. Road Rage pulls back his fist and throws it at my face, but I easily dodge it, going underneath the massive fist and striking his stomach with my burning club.

Normally, that should at least hurt him, but when my club hits his stomach, it makes a clanging sound like striking rock with metal. My blow doesn't even seem to leave a mark on Road Rage's tough skin, not even a slight burn.

But it does make Road Rage angry, and, moving faster than I anticipated, he slams his other fist into my stomach, sending me flying backward. I tumble head over heels through the air until I smash into the floor, making my head spin from the impact. I'm pretty sure he broke some of my ribs too, based on the burning sensation coming from that part of my body.

But I don't have the luxury of lying on the floor, feeling the agonizing pain in my body, because I hear Walter scream and lift my head to see what's going on.

Road Rage has grabbed Walter with both hands and is apparently squeezing him to death. Walter has one hand free, which he's using to beat fruitlessly against Road Rage's hands, but it's extremely obvious that Walter isn't going to be saving himself.

But maybe there's a way to take out Road Rage in a way that even he won't see coming. A plan immediately forms in my mind, and even though it's risky as hell, we don't have any choice, and I feel Walter would agree even if I told him.

Rising to my feet, ignoring the protests of my broken ribs and spinning head, I summon my bow and nock not one, not two, but three arrows in it. Each arrow burns with white-hot fire, fire that I make hotter and hotter with every passing second. I do it quickly because I can tell that Walter doesn't have a lot of time left.

Road Rage, apparently still ignoring me, growls angrily at Walter. "You had a chance to finish off Wildfire and fulfill your desire for vengeance, but now you will simply perish like a pathetic human. This is not the Walter Ellison I first met all those years ago. That is why it will be satisfying to squeeze the life out of you."

Walter, of course, doesn't say anything because he's currently having the life squeezed out of him, but I shout to him, "Walter! Blast him with oil!"

Fortunately, Walter still has enough sense to raise his free arm, point his oil cannon at Road Rage's face, and spray him with a lot of stinky, sticky oil.

Road Rage roars again, dropping Walter as he rubs the oil out of his eyes—or tries to, anyway, seeing as all that oil is extremely hard to get rid of.

Even if it was possible, I wouldn't give him the chance to do that.

With a yell, I let loose my three fiery arrows directly at Road Rage's oily face. The arrows fly straight and true, seemingly in slow motion, toward Road Rage, who has just enough time to lower his hands from his face in time to see the arrows coming.

But even as I release the arrows, I realize that Walter is directly in the blast zone. Unlike me, Walter doesn't have a healing factor that would let him survive a point-blank explosion like that.

So, the second I let go of the arrows, I rush down the hallway toward Walter, keeping pace with my arrows, grab him by the shoulder, and turn to fly back down the hallway away from Road Rage. I want to go for the stairs but realize I won't make it to them in time, even flying at my current speed.

Instead, I rip open the door to one of the abandoned offices and jump inside with Walter.

SLOTH

I slam the door shut just as a massive explosion erupts in the hallway outside.

22

Road Rage's screams of pain are cut off by the deafening roar of the explosion outside. I hit the carpeted floor of the office and cover both of my ears with my hands, desperately trying to save my hearing from the blast. Beside me, Walter has also covered his ears, his eyes closed tightly, even though there's no need for that.

Regardless, the two of us lie on the floor of the office, listening to the roar of the explosion before it dies down as suddenly as it started. Aside from the flickering of flames, I don't hear any other noises in the hallway outside our safe room.

Walter, taking his hands off his ears, looks at me uncertainly. "Is Road Rage dead?"

Taking my hands off my ears, I slowly rise to my feet. "Let me peek into the hallway and see."

I crack the door open just a hair and peer into the hallway beyond.

The explosion certainly did a number on the hallway. Most of it has been completely destroyed. The walls and doors to other rooms are blackened or utterly demolished, while most of the lighting hangs from charred wires, sparking occasionally. The acrid smell of burning metal and tile, along with smoke, assaults my nostrils, making me wrinkle my nose.

As for Road Rage, I don't see him anywhere. But I do see a giant hole in the floor where Road Rage had been standing a few seconds ago. It looks like he must have fallen through the floor, but I don't dare look into the hole to see how far he fell. With luck, Road Rage fell all the way to the lobby, and hopefully, it'll take him a very, very long time to regenerate from that explosion.

Breathing hard, I look over my shoulder at Walter, who is still lying on the floor, and say, "Road Rage is definitely out of commission. Hopefully for good, but if not, I think it will take him a while to regenerate and get back up here, by which time we should be long gone."

Walter nods. "Well, you might be long gone. I don't think I will be."

I tilt my head to the side in confusion. "What do you mean? Aren't you planning to come up with me to the higher floors?"

Walter smiles grimly at me. "Maybe if my legs weren't broken."

My heart jerks in my chest and I walk over to Walter and kneel beside him. "What do you mean? Your legs are broken? When did that happen?"

Walter rolls his eyes. "I don't know, maybe it happened when the hulking space alien monster was crushing my body. Thought he might have broken one of my arms, too, but I think it just hurts a lot. Oh, and he also destroyed most of my equipment, too."

I take a better look at Walter's costume and realize that he's correct. The pumps on his backpack are destroyed, while his oil cannons, along with the tubes connecting them to the pumps, are leaking a lot of oil. Frankly, it's a miracle that the flames from the explosion didn't also set off his costume, but I guess I did manage to get us both away from the explosion in time.

And Walter doesn't seem to be lying or exaggerating about his broken legs. Now that I have a chance to look at those, too, I can tell that his left leg is twisted in a really unnatural way, while his right leg is unnaturally still. I'm just amazed that Walter isn't screaming in pain right now because I'm pretty sure I would be if our situations were reversed.

I grab the sides of my head anxiously. "Crap. I thought I had saved you before Road Rage could seriously injure you. But with these kinds of injuries—"

"I'm not going anywhere," Walter finishes for me. "Even if I could, without my equipment, I can't actually be a credible threat to the Meteor Monsters. Pretty sure I left my gun out in the hallway, too, so I imagine that got blown to hell along with Road Rage."

I bite my lower lip. "This is terrible. I don't have any way to fix or even splint your legs, but I also don't think you'll be very safe here, either."

Walter grunts. "The Meteor Monsters want you, right? I'll probably be fine here. Even though Road Rage tried to kill me, I think he really wants you dead more. At least, he's probably going to hunt you to make sure that his siblings don't get you first."

I shake my head. "No. I don't want to leave you here undefended. Even if the Meteor Monsters leave you alone, they still have human servants who might not be so merciful. You're in danger as long as you're here."

Walter grunts again and glares at me. "So what's your plan? Sit on your butt right next to me and try to protect me from all the Meteor Monsters, who probably heard the explosion and know where you are now if they didn't already before? Did you already forget about the other hostages?"

Walter's reminder stings me like a wasp. "I haven't. I just don't want to abandon you."

Walter rolls his eyes again. "You're going to have to, you know that? I'm basically useless at this point. Maybe if you successfully take out Logikill and the Meteor Monsters, then you can come back and save me, but the lives of the hostages are a lot more important than my life right now."

I bite my lower lip again. "But you still haven't avenged Drew's death. Humanimal is still alive."

Walter raises an eyebrow. "Isn't that what you're going to take care of? Listen, Toby, spraying Road Rage in the face with oil and having him blown to hell is closure enough for me. But if you want to take out Humanimal too, then go ahead. You don't need me to do that."

"But—"

"And anyway," says Walter, ignoring what I was trying to say, "you never know. Maybe Captain Cowboy and the others will stumble upon me. They're still around, too, you know."

Walter wasn't wrong about that. As far as we know, Captain Cowboy and the others are still behind us, trying to make their way through Devon Tower too.

But, of course, there's no guarantee that they will make it this far, or that they won't run into one of the Meteor Monsters or their servants along the way and be unable to go any farther. If I leave Walter alone now, then I'll have to make the rest of the journey to the top floor by myself.

And maybe that's what I'm actually afraid of: Having to face the remaining Meteor Monsters, plus whatever awful tricks and traps they have set up for me, all by myself.

Yet I have no choice. As much as I hate to admit it, I can't take Walter with me, and he probably is safer here in this abandoned office than he would be with me. He would basically just be deadweight at this point, and I can't lug him around while also fighting the Meteor Monsters.

Still, I'm not going to leave him entirely defenseless.

I summon my club and hand it to Walter. "If Road Rage or any of the other Meteor Monsters come looking for you, break their skulls with this."

Walter takes my club and turns it over a time or two. "Huh. This is a lot lighter than I expected it to be. But sure. I'll definitely not hesitate to break some skulls with this thing."

I nod as I rise to my feet and reach up to my earcom in my left ear. "I can confirm that it's definitely effective at breaking Meteor Monster skulls. Anyway, I'm going to contact Captain Cowboy and the others to let them know where you are. That way, if they do make it this far, they'll at least know to look for you."

I tap my earcom, expecting to hear the familiar *click* indicating that it's active.

But I don't hear anything other than static.

23

I tap my earcom again, but I still only hear static. I tap it a few more times before I give up. "I can't hear anything over my earcom. What about you, Walter? Does your earcom work?"

Walter taps his earcom a couple of times before shaking his head. "Nope. Just static."

I curse under my breath. "Not good. I wonder why they aren't working. Maybe they got damaged during our fight with Road Rage or something?"

Walter's expression darkens. "Or maybe Logikill and the Meteor Monsters are jamming the signal somehow to keep us from staying in contact with Captain Cowboy and the others."

I grimace but can't entirely dismiss Walter's theory. That certainly seems like something the Meteor Monsters would do, especially Logikill, who is definitely trying to isolate me from my allies. Unfortunately, when I check my phone and try to call Cap, I discover that I don't have any data here. A quick look at Walter's phone shows that he also doesn't have data, meaning neither of us can call or even text for help. That all but confirms that Logikill is jamming our communication devices, though why he didn't do it right away as soon as we entered the building, I have no idea. We didn't have trouble communicating with Cap and the others before, after all. Maybe he was just trying to lull us with a false sense of security.

Now I have no idea where Captain Cowboy and the others are, what condition they're in, or if they're even still alive. That also means I can't warn them to look for Walter, which means he might be alone for an even longer time than I thought.

Feeling the stress rising in the back of my head, I say, "Okay, I'll grab some of this office furniture and use it to block off the door when I leave. That way, in case anyone tries to get you, they'll at least be slowed down by the furniture."

Walter nods. "Sounds good. Like I said, you can always come back for me later after you kill Logikill and put an end to this madness. As you can tell, I'm not planning to go anywhere anytime soon."

I appreciate Walter's attempts at good humor, but I'm so stressed out about our current situation that I find it hard to see any humor in our circumstances.

Regardless, time is ticking, and I don't have enough of it as is, so I say goodbye to Walter, grab a couple of office chairs, and then leave the office. I stack the chairs in front of the door. With luck, not only will the chairs protect Walter, but perhaps they'll even be a hint to Captain Cowboy and the others that someone is holed up in there and needs their help. That might encourage them to check it out if they make it this far.

With a deep breath, I turn and start walking down the hallway toward the other end, which is less damaged than the end where Road Rage was. Hopefully, the stairs are still in good enough shape after Road Rage drove his motorcycle down them, but if not, I should be able to just fly up through them anyway.

-

The stairs are mostly intact, so I have no trouble climbing them, although I do move a little more slowly than normal. You might think I should be in a rush, given how I'm still on a pretty tight deadline, but since the whole building is crawling with Meteor Monsters, I'm frankly not in any hurry to run headlong into yet another elaborate trap set by them. That wouldn't help anyone except the people who I don't want to help.

When I reach the next floor, I discover that there are no Meteor Monsters at all—at least, none that I can see. There are scorch marks on the tile, likely from the tires of Road Rage's motorcycle, but other than that, the hallway is surprisingly empty.

And I am not sure if I should be grateful for that or terrified. I might get a breather or I might be walking into yet another trap. My Meteor Monster senses aren't of much help, either, because even though I can't sense any Meteor Monsters on this floor, that doesn't mean much when they could just be hiding themselves.

I decide to walk quickly through this floor and get to the other end as quickly as I can. Regardless of whether there are any Meteor Monsters on this floor, I still have to get to the top floor before the deadline set by Logikill passes. The lives of a lot of people are riding on my shoulders.

But when I take one step into the hallway, one of the doors at the other end swings open and a familiar man, clad in a green jacket the same shade of green as a dollar bill, steps out. Clutching a golden cane in both hands, the green-eyed man stops in the middle of the hallway and shoots me a grin that I really just want to smack right off his crooked face.

"Hiya there, kid," says Jackpot, smirking. "You look like crap."

I scowl, anger rising within me. I start walking toward Jackpot, having decided that I am just about out of patience with him. "Shut up, Jackpot. Either move or I'll make you move. I don't have time to play with you."

Jackpot frowns, putting his hands on the head of his cane. "Who said I wanted to play? Maybe I wanted to make a deal instead."

I groan in frustration. "I don't have time to 'make deals' with you. So unless you want to get blown to the same hell that Road Rage ended up in, I suggest you move. I'll come back after you later."

Jackpot tilts his head to the side. "But what if I offered to make a deal with you in exchange for the lives of your friends and family?"

I stop. "What are you talking about?"

Jackpot grins at me again. "Business, obviously. If you agree to work with me to take down Logikill, then I promise to let your friends and family go unharmed."

I frown myself this time. "Didn't we do this song and dance when I killed you the first time? You offered me a job so I could help you kill Logikill because you didn't trust him but then turned around and tried to kill me instead."

Jackpot shrugs. "Maybe, but this time, I mean it. You don't understand how much power Logikill has over us now."

I raise an eyebrow. "Must not be a lot if you are able to chat with me about betraying him so openly like this."

Jackpot rubs his forehead. "I know. It's taking all of my willpower just to resist his brainwashing. Any second now, he'll probably force himself back on me and I'll go back to being his slave. So for the time being, I am trying to throw in with the one person in the world who I know that old Egghead fears: Namely, you."

I scowl. I am still internally debating whether or not to incinerate Jackpot, but if he is like before, then I can't kill him unless I destroy his first penny first. "Logikill is afraid of me?"

Jackpot nods. "Oh, yeah. He may not act like it too much, but he's totally terrified of your very existence. Why else do you think that he has been putting you through so much crap recently?"

I told my arms in front of my chest. "I would think that all of you Meteor Monsters would be afraid of me, seeing as I am the best weapon against you seven."

Jackpot shrugs. "True, you are pretty scary for a kid, but at heart, I am an optimist who believes that people can be rational. And what is more rational, I ask you, than making a deal with your enemy to avoid unnecessary bloodshed and save the lives of innocent people?"

After fighting four other Meteor Monsters today, as well as losing Walter and Pietro, I won't deny that Jackpot's seeming willingness to betray Logikill in favor of negotiating with me is actually a really tempting offer. It would certainly save me a lot of time and effort. Plus, turning the Meteor Monsters against each other would make it much easier for me to wipe out the rest of them later on, anyway.

But color me suspicious. I mean, it's definitely in-character for Jackpot to betray the others for his own personal gain, but I also know that with the Meteor Monsters, nothing is ever really as it seems. And Jackpot has definitely lied to me before.

Still, I say, "Let's pretend for a second that I am interested in teaming up with you to take down Logikill again. What do *you* get out of it? Because you have to know that I can't let you live, either, right?"

Jackpot nods. "Oh, I am fully aware that my days are numbered, too. But maybe it's just the greedy part of me that wants to maximize those days as much as I can. Surely you can understand that."

I frown. "Why would I understand that?"

Jackpot tilts his head to the side. "You mean Logikill didn't tell you at the landfill? About the time limit you're on?"

I frown even deeper. "What time limit? Do you mean the deadline for all of the hostages? Because I am well aware of that, thank you very much."

Jackpot throws his head back and laughs. "Wow! You really don't know. Fascinating. I mean, it makes sense, of course, because Logikill definitely benefits from your ignorance, but—"

My patience finally running out, I rush over to Jackpot, grab him by the collar of his tacky jacket, and slam him against one of the walls hard enough to crack the plywood. "Tell me *exactly* what you are talking about or I'll just burn you to a crisp here and now."

I don't even bother trying to hide the anger in my voice. Why should I? The Meteor Monsters have done enough to earn it. Frankly, I shouldn't even be giving Jackpot this much of a chance to talk, but something in his words caught my interest. And I feel like I *have* to know.

Jackpot cracks his usual hideous grin. "Fine, fine. Maybe this will help earn your trust. Because, kid, you have less than a day before your fire powers burn you up from the inside out."

24

I stare at Jackpot uncomprehendingly. "What do you mean my fire powers will burn me up from the inside out? What are you talking about? Tell me!"

Jackpot grimaces. "Would love to tell you, but it's kind of hard to talk with your hand crushing my throat."

I blink and look at my hand. Somehow, it had slipped from his jacket collar to his throat without me realizing. Not only that, but it is starting to burn, too, even though I am not consciously using my powers.

Stepping backward, I release Jackpot's neck. Jackpot immediately starts rubbing it, although I can see the burn marks on his throat starting to heal even as he nurses it.

But Jackpot, surprisingly, doesn't try to attack me. He just rubs his throat, staring at me with his usual grin. "Thanks. Didn't realize how much I missed breathing."

"Get to the point, Jackpot," I snap. I raise my hand, which catches fire. "Because even though I know I can't kill you without destroying your first penny, I know I can make you suffer."

Jackpot grimaces and raises his hands pacifically. "No need to get rough, kid! I get it. I'd probably react the same way if I knew my days were numbered."

My fiery hand burns brighter. I forgot how much I hated Jackpot's chatty way of speaking. "Explain. Now."

Jackpot, cringing under the heat of my fire, says, "Fine, fine! So you know, of course, about how the meteor gave you your powers and brought us all to life, right?"

I nod. "Yes."

Jackpot nods again, although he seems to do it more out of nerves than anything. "Right, right. While the meteor had to create bodies for me and the others, it just took your existing body and changed it. Made it stronger. Gave you the kind of superpowers that most humans would kill for. Essentially, it turned you into a demigod, at least from a human perspective."

I lower my burning hand as I start to calm down. "I don't *feel* like a god, though. I still feel like a teenager."

"And you are," says Jackpot, "but I want you to think back to when you first got your powers. Remember how much they *hurt*?"

I eye Jackpot suspiciously. "I don't remember telling you about my problems with my powers when I first got them."

Jackpot scratches the side of his face. "That's because you didn't. But Logikill has been monitoring you for a while, so he told me about your trouble with your powers. Ever wonder why that was?"

I frown. "Is this a trick question? It's tied to the character of Wyldfyre I created when I was younger. He was a superhero tortured by his own powers. Just my overly edgy imagination at work. It's not a problem now."

Jackpot chuckles. "Your imagination may have contributed, but the real reason your powers messed with you early on is because you were *never* meant to get them in the first place."

"Duh," I say, tapping my foot impatiently. "Of course I wasn't supposed to get them in the first place. No one was. I doubt the dead alien empire that sent the meteor to Earth was hoping to turn a teenager with attitude into one of their deadliest weapons."

Jackpot sighs. "Man, you really know *nothing*, huh? The meteor was actually designed to turn a human *adult* into the perfect weapon of destruction. That's why I said you, specifically, were never meant to get those powers. But someone else was."

The fire on my hand having finally gone out, I fold my arms across my chest. "So if I wasn't supposed to get my powers, then who was?"

Jackpot strokes his chin thoughtfully. "Probably not anyone in particular other than a qualified human adult. But do you remember who else was in the crater with you on that night, other than us, of course?"

At first, I almost say that no one else was there other than us.

But then I remember the only other person to be in the crater with me other than the Meteor Monsters and I feel my whole world shift around me. "Captain Cowboy."

Jackpot grins widely. "Bingo. *You* were never meant to receive powers from the meteor. In all likelihood—in fact, I practically guarantee it—your boss, Captain Cowpoke himself, was supposed to be the original user of *your* powers."

I shake in my boots, trying to wrap my mind around this revelation. I want to deny it, but it makes far, far too much sense.

For one, it gels with what Logikill told me about the origins of the meteor. If the idea was for the meteor to create a weapon of mass destruction that could either destabilize or outright destroy a civilization, then it made sense that the meteor would want to pick an adult human who had plenty of combat experience. Granted, it does beg the question of why it would have chosen Captain Cowboy, specifically, out of all of the various superheroes in the world (or around Oklahoma City, in fact), but if we are working off the reasonable assumption that the meteor deliberately picks out cities that aren't as big as, say, NYC or LA, then it starts to make a lot more sense.

I don't know why this shakes me. The reality is, if Captain Cowboy had my powers, he could have probably dealt with the Meteor Monsters a lot more efficiently than me. Assuming, at least, that he didn't end up being brainwashed by the meteor and turned into a weapon, but seeing as I didn't end up that way, I doubted he would have, either.

Now I found myself wondering what Captain Cowboy would look like with my powers ...

But then I remember what we are actually talking about and I shake my head. "Okay, so assuming you are right, what does this have to do with me burning out?"

Jackpot sighs heavily. "And here I thought you were going to put two and two together yourself. See, the reason why the meteor wanted an *adult* is because the bodies of adults are, generally speaking, more capable of handling the stress of using your powers than the bodies of teenagers or children. Imagine that bratty baby sister of yours getting your powers and you will get my point."

I shudder. "The idea of Dakota having my powers is almost as scary as Drew getting them."

Jackpot laughs. "Exactly! But regardless, the point is, Captain Cowboy would have made a better candidate for the powers than you were. His body would have handled the changes caused by the meteor much better than yours."

I raise an eyebrow. "I'm still breathing, you know."

Jackpot points a finger at me. "I know, but your powers still hurt you, didn't they? They wouldn't have hurt your boss, is what I am trying to say. Simply wouldn't have been a problem for him."

"Even if that is the case, I dealt with the problem of hurting myself with my powers a long time ago," I say. "If it was still a problem, I would definitely know."

Jackpot grins. "Would you, kid? Would you? What if you never actually adapted to your powers, but rather suppressed the pain? What if, instead of burning you in one go, it has been slowly but surely burning away at your roots, like a pig being charbroiled over an open flame?"

I furrow my brows. "I still feel like I would feel that if that were true."

Jackpot shrugs. "Believe what you want, kid, but Logikill seems convinced that you are rapidly running out of time. If, by the end of the day, you don't end up with us, who knows what will happen to you? You might just burn out entirely."

I scowl. "Is that the real reason why Logikill gave me such a short deadline? Because he doesn't want me to burn out before he can get to me?"

"More or less," says Jackpot with a nod. He scratches his neck. "Of course, it's up to you to believe that or not, but it makes sense to me. Just thought you'd like to know it."

I frown deeper, thinking about Jackpot's words. "So, assuming you are right, is there anything I can do to make sure I *don't* burn out and die?"

Jackpot leans to the side on his cane. "Would you like to know? I can definitely tell you the secret. But only if you agree to work with me."

I sigh heavily. As much as I hate to admit it, I realize Jackpot might be on to something. Why else would Logikill have given me such a tight deadline if not because of something like this? And I definitely don't want to burn out. Would suck majorly if I saved everyone only to die in the end.

Maybe these powers really are a curse.

And if that means temporarily allying with Jackpot, then so be it.

I nod. "Fine. Tell me how I can avoid burning out and I will help you take down Logikill. But only until then, okay? Because once Logikill is out of the picture, I'm coming after you and the others again."

Jackpot nods. "Sounds like an imminently reasonable, if not fair, deal. But, ah, there's just one teeny, tiny problem I just noticed now, one that I think escaped your notice."

I frown. "What would that be?"

Jackpot's face splits into the wickedest grin I've ever seen. "Your total naivety, of course."

Without warning, thick black webbing suddenly wraps around my body. Yelling in surprise, I fall over onto the floor, struggling to break free of the webbing but finding it stronger than steel.

"Good job distracting him, Jackie," says the demure voice of Lady Lust behind me. "Such a simpleton."

I look over my shoulder to see Lady Lust, the sixth Meteor Monster, walking over to us, holding the other end of the web. She gives me a sinister smile, which makes her normally beautiful features look extremely vicious.

I gasp and look up at Jackpot. "You lied."

Jackpot just smiles at me. "Not lied. I *distracted* you. Big difference."

With that, Jackpot swings the end of his cane into my face and everything goes black.

25

I don't know how long I am out before someone splashes icy water in my face and I suddenly wake up, coughing and hacking.

"Ah, good," says the familiar cold, monotone voice of Logikill. "Wyldfyre has finally awakened. I am glad that his flames have not yet gone out."

Blinking the dripping water out of my eyes, I try to get my bearings and figure out where I am.

My arms and legs are chained to the floor of a cage with thick bars on every side. Beyond the cage, I see a surprisingly well-lit room, with tall windows giving me an excellent view of Oklahoma City and even beyond.

But that isn't what I pay attention to.

Mostly, I am paying attention to the presence of the Meteor Monsters themselves. My Meteor Monster senses are going crazier than ever in my head, like a rock band is holding the biggest concert of all time inside my brain. I can barely think.

But even if my Meteor Monster senses weren't going crazy, I still wouldn't have trouble spotting the Meteor Monsters.

Mostly because all seven of them are right in front of me, standing just outside my cage.

Humanimal, Wasteland, the Crippler, Road Rage, Jackpot, Lady Lust ... and, of course, Logikill himself, who stands in the middle of his 'family,' a calm yet triumphant look on his face, green eyes squinting behind his glasses.

Water running down the sides of my face and dripping onto the floor, I rise to my feet and immediately try to rush toward Logikill. But the chains around my wrists and ankles limit my movement severely to the point where I can't move more than a few steps forward at most before coming to an abrupt stop

SLOTH

Logikill wags a finger at me. "Now, now, Wyldfyre. Don't stress yourself too much trying to get at us. Too much stress will lead you to an early death."

Jackpot, standing beside Logikill and holding an empty bucket of water in his hands, chuckles. "Too right, big brother! And we wouldn't want the Core of the Cores to die an early death, am I right?"

I shake my head like a dog to clear my senses and get the water out of my hair. That is when I realize that I am no longer wearing my costume for some reason, which is definitely odd but something I will worry about later. "The Core of the Cores—? What are you—never mind. Where are the hostages?"

Logikill gazes at me calmly. "Straight to the point, I see. Turn around and tell me yourself."

I don't trust Logikill or the other Meteor Monsters with my back one bit, but on the other hand, they clearly are still reluctant to actually kill me, plus they've had plenty of chances to do so already and haven't. Who knows how long I was unconscious before they woke me up?

So I turn my head over my shoulder and feel my stomach twist at the sight before me.

Another cage stands at the other end of the room, where I see six people sitting. I have no trouble recognizing them: Mom, Dakota, Granny, Gary, Paintbrush, and …

My jaw drops. "Dad?"

Dad is indeed among the hostages, apparently alive and well. His face, however, is bruised and he has a bandage around his right shoulder that Mom is tending to.

Dad, taking a deep breath, looks over at me. "Toby? Why do you look so surprised to see me?"

I stumble over my words. "I thought Black—"

"Killed him?" comes the irritatingly familiar voice of Templeton Black from behind the cage. "I wish."

Templeton Black steps out from behind the cage containing my family and friends. So does Arnold Linderman, who is still wearing his robber outfit, though he looks significantly more nervous than Black, glancing from me to the hostages and back again as if he is worried about something.

Maybe he's worried I am going to kick his ass the very second I get out of this cage.

"Fantasize about kicking Linderman all you want," says Logikill behind me, "but you aren't leaving that cage, much less attaining your freedom, until we decide you can."

I whip my head back toward Logikill and the Meteor Monsters, feeling white-hot anger rising inside me. "Let my family and friends go. You've got me now. I'm your goal, remember? There's no need to involve anyone else anymore."

Logikill tilts his head to the side. "And where would be the fun in that? No, I think I am going to keep your family and friends locked up for just a while longer. So that you understand who is truly in charge of this situation."

The Crippler holds up a finger to his lips. "Hint: It isn't you, brat."

I look back at the hostages. Everyone looks positively terrified, other than Paintbrush, who is standing at the front of the cage, her hands wrapped around the bars. "Toby, don't listen to him. You need to fight them before they—"

Black suddenly pulls out a remote from his jacket and presses a button on it. The bars of the cage containing the hostages buzz to life with electricity and Paintbrush lets out a yelp of pain as she lets go of the bars, stumbling toward the center of the cage where everyone else is huddled up.

My heart hammers my chest. "Mandy!"

Black raises the remote, a cold look on his face. "Your friends and family will be perfectly safe as long as they stay away from the bars of their cage and don't try to escape or communicate with you."

Linderman nods, a wicked grin appearing on his face as his nerves seemingly cool now that he seems to think I am powerless to hurt him. "Exactly. There is no point in resisting any further. May the Meteor Monsters do to you what you deserve."

My hands ball into fists. I so badly want to break out of my cage and open a can of whoop ass on Black and Linderman, but with all seven of the Meteor Monsters present, plus the fact that my friends and family are still in the hands of those madmen, I don't have a choice but to go along with whatever Logikill has planned for me.

First, I need some answers.

I glare at Black. "I heard you kill Dad over Logikill's phone earlier."

Black raises an unimpressed eyebrow. "Do you believe that Santa Claus leaves his cozy home at the North Pole and goes to the mall every year to let every snot-nosed brat sit on his lap and gab about whatever stupid toys they want?"

"What Black means, Tobias, is that we faked your dad's death to give you sufficient motivation to come here," says Logikill. "Of course, we had to make it realistic, so Black really did shoot your father. Hence the shoulder wound."

My hands shake as I turn back toward Logikill, though I make sure to make a mental note to put Black closer to the top of my list of people whose butts I needed to hand to them on a silver platter later. "So it was all a trick. Just like with the fake Drew's death in the lobby earlier."

Logikill shrugs. "I knew I couldn't expect you to simply come here on your own. If you had simply agreed to meet me at Hunny Bunny like I originally offered, none of this would have had to happen."

I scowl and then turn my glare toward Jackpot. "And Jackpot, you were never really planning to betray Logikill, were you?"

Jackpot laughs. "Of course not! Another trick by our big brother. He wanted you to believe that I was still the same Jackpot from before when, in truth, I am not. Granted, you almost saw through the trick, but I am glad that my lie was convincing enough to let our dear sister sneak up on you without you even noticing."

Lady Lust nods and licks her lips. "You were the easiest prey I've ever had. Even easier than your bumbling, lonely oaf of a father."

That comment prompts a chuckle from Jackpot, but all it does is make me want to hurt Lady Lust even more than I already want to.

But knowing how powerless I am in my current situation, I say, "Then was Jackpot's story about my powers burning me out also just a lie?"

Logikill frowns. "Unfortunately for us, it isn't. You really are in danger of simply burning away. Your body was never meant to handle your powers for as long as it has, although I must admit it has lasted longer than I thought it would. Since we still need you alive for our plans, I decided to take matters into my own hands and have Jackpot and Lady Lust capture you."

Jackpot shoots Logikill a questioning look. "But we get to be your right-hands since we won the contest, right?"

Logikill nods without looking at Jackpot. "Yes. Since it was technically a team effort, that means the two of you have to share that role."

Jackpot groans. "Ugh. I hate sharing. Even with Lady Lust."

Lady Lust shoots Jackpot a rather lascivious smile. "I'm sure I can make it more ... pleasant for you, dear brother, once we have made the world ours."

Jackpot smiles at her. "Well, maybe I could make it work, then."

I try not to vomit and say to Logikill, "What about Captain Cowboy and the others? They're still trying to make their way up here."

Logikill raises an eyebrow. "Are they? Crippler, what is the report from the human servants?"

The Crippler, who I just now noticed is using a walkie-talkie, lowers his handheld radio from his ear. "Nobody says that they've cornered Captain Cowboy, Codetalker, and Keith on the seventh floor. They're still putting up a fight but are rapidly running out of options. I fully expect to hear that they are all dead within the next half hour at most."

My blood runs cold. I had forgotten that the Meteor Monsters had human servants who had also been searching for us before I was captured. Now that the Meteor Monsters had me, they had no further reason to spare Captain Cowboy or the others, who were basically loose ends at this point.

And I think everyone knows what happens to annoying loose ends.

They get cut.

Logikill's monotone voice breaks the silence. "As you can tell, Tobias, it is game, set, and match. Your family and friends are still at our mercy, while your remaining few allies are either dead, practically dead, or are about to be dead. You have no way to call for help thanks to the communication jammer set up by the Crippler and, even if you could, they wouldn't get here in time to help. As we say in chess, check and mate."

My mind spins as I try to figure out how to turn this situation right back around. Surely Logikill's statement is wrong. Even he has to be missing something.

But no matter how hard I think about or examine the situation, I realize, with despair, that Logikill is right:

It is over.

The Meteor Monsters have won.

We have lost.

26

I fall to my knees on the floor of my cage, head on my chest as that realization sets in.

But then I hear footsteps approaching my cage and look up to see Logikill standing in front of the cage, hands folded behind his back as he gazed coldly down at me.

"Tobias," says Logikill. "Do you remember, back in the landfill, when I asked you what the eighth Meteor Monster, the one you inadvertently summoned three years ago to frighten us all away, was called?"

I nod slightly. "I do. But I don't know why you're asking me this now."

Logikill tilts his head to the side. "I'm asking because I want to know if you've thought over your answer since then. You've had plenty of time to do so since our last meeting. Tell me, what is the nature of the eighth Meteor Monster? You understand that the rest of us represent the seven deadly sins that plague humanity, but what do you represent?"

I scowl. "What kind of question is that? I told you then, and I'll tell you now, I don't know. Now just do whatever you're going to do to me and get this over with. You've won."

Logikill sighs as if I'm being deliberately obtuse. "Perhaps a better question would be to ask how you feel right now, Tobias. What is the one overwhelming feeling that's weighing you down at this very moment? What has caused you to lose all hope and give up?"

My heart thumps in my chest. When Logikill puts it that way, I find myself thinking about his earlier question in a very different way. I know exactly what I'm feeling and experiencing at the moment, but for some reason, I find it difficult to say that word aloud.

It's as if I'm afraid that I might bring into existence something I'll regret.

So, I turn my face away from Logikill and say, "I won't say it. I don't know for sure what you want me to say, but I'm definitely not going to say it. You'll have to force me to talk if you want me to say that word."

Logikill rubs his forehead in exasperation and steps away from the cage. "Very well. If you must be so difficult..." Logikill looks at Black. "Templeton, kill them all. They aren't necessary anymore."

Before Logikill's ominous words finish filtering through my brain, Black raises the remote and presses the button on it, all the while smirking at me.

Behind me, the cage containing my friends and family suddenly bursts to life with electricity. And not just the bars—no, the entire cage, from floor to ceiling, surges with crackling and snapping electrical bursts.

As if in slow motion, I turn around to see my family and friends dying before my very eyes.

Granny is the first to go. Her frail, old body immediately collapses onto the floor of the cage as the electrical current fries her clothing and hair. She doesn't even get a chance to scream. She dies instantly.

The next to go is Gary. He screams and rushes toward the cage door, but as soon as he touches the bars, his hands are instantly fried, and he falls to the ground, screaming his head off. Soon, even his screams die down—though perhaps it's more accurate to say that the sparking and crackling from the electrical torture drown out his screams.

After him, Mom and Dad go. Dad gets onto the floor, his skin and clothes smoking from the heat of the electricity, and tries to get Mom and Dakota to sit on him. But there isn't enough room on Dad's back for both of them, so Mom, giving Dakota a quick kiss on the forehead, gets on the floor next to him, and they both die silently as the electricity burns their faces off.

Dakota is crying. She's sitting on the corpses of our parents, sobbing uncontrollably. Maybe that's why she doesn't do anything when a lightning bolt launches out from the ceiling and strikes her in the head. I avert my gaze at the last second, just so I don't see what that did to her.

The last to go is Paintbrush. Her costume, which I know to be insulated against electricity, is probably the only thing keeping her alive. Even so, Paintbrush struggles to reach the bars of the cage, perhaps overwhelmed by the flashing and sparking electricity, along with the stench of dead bodies and burning clothing that fills the air.

Nonetheless, my girlfriend, brave and strong, reaches the bars of the cage. Grabbing one of the bars, Paintbrush reaches out toward me with one hand, a desperate, frightened look on her face as she says, "Toby! I love—"

SLOTH

A stray spark of electricity jumps into her left eye, making it explode. Screaming in pure agony, Paintbrush collapses onto the floor of the cage with everyone else and finally meets her fate. Her body twitches for a second or two before it stops.

And then her lifeless head, one eye missing, turns toward me, her remaining eye staring blankly.

Then, something inside me snaps.

The hopelessness gnawing at my insides—the hopelessness that had been gradually increasing as I got closer to the top of the tower—finally overwhelms me. It manifests inside me as a burning hatred, but it's not directed toward the Meteor Monsters or even toward Black.

No, it's directed toward me.

Everything is my fault. Pietro's death, Walter's injuries, the inevitable deaths of Captain Cowboy and the others, and now the gruesome demise of some of my closest friends and family… it's all my fault. I was too weak to save any of them. Just like with Drew, just like with everyone else who has ever died because I wasn't strong enough to stop the Meteor Monsters from killing them, it's my fault and mine alone.

And now, I have no one. I'm alone. I have no connection to humanity anymore.

So why not embrace… despair?

That burning sense of hopelessness inside me suddenly erupts. Fire pours out of every pore of my body, just like whenever I transform into Wildfire—only this time, I'm transforming into something else. Something darker. Something stronger.

The chains around my wrists and ankles immediately melt into liquid metal, even before I finish my transformation. I rise to my feet, fire burning at my skin and hair. Normally, that would cause me pain, but I actually enjoy the sensation as it rips through my body.

It's infinitely superior to feeling the despair that had been threatening to overwhelm me earlier.

But now, I can feel the transformation reaching a crescendo. I can no longer hold it within me or on my body.

So, with a roar, I unleash a blast of fire that blows the roof of the cage and the door clean off. The roof goes flying, smashing through one of the windows and plummeting toward downtown below, while the door forces the assembled Meteor Monsters to scatter.

It crashes into a wall on the other side of the room, where it lies twisted, blackened, and burning.

As for myself, I stand in the ruins of the cage, breathing hard as fire runs up and down my body. I gaze upon the Meteor Monsters, who are all now looking at me with expressions reminiscent of the ones they wore back in the crater shortly after they all came into being three years ago.

Out of all of them, however, Logikill is the only one still standing and still smiling. But then he gets down on one knee and says, "Welcome back to the world of the living, brother. It has been too long since we last met. I assume you finally remember your name?"

I scowl at Logikill. "Unlike the rest of you, I never got a name. But I now know what I represent. What I stand for. The ultimate sin—the one that will lead to the downfall of not just this pathetic city, but the entire planet."

Logikill's lips curl into a cruel, ugly smile. "Indeed, indeed. For you are the eighth and final Meteor Monster, representing the eighth deadly sin: Despair."

27

Despair... Yes, that is what I am now. I am Despair, the final and most terrifying Meteor Monster of them all. Indeed, I might as well take that as my name because Tobias Miller and Wyldfyre are no longer appropriate for who—no, what—I am now.

Jackpot, who apparently fell on his butt when I transformed, sits up and whistles at me. "Nice transformation, kid. Think the new look fits you."

Before I can ask Jackpot what he's talking about, Lady Lust, already back on her feet, pulls out a mirror from nowhere and puts it in front of me. This allows me to finally see what my new body looks like.

My skin is blacker than charcoal, and my hair has transformed into pure fire. Red lines of flame run along my skin, while horns twist out of my skull, giving me a very demonic appearance. I am not wearing clothing, but the flames of Despair have burned away all of my human parts. I am humanoid in shape only.

Just as I should be.

A sharp breath behind me makes me look over my shoulder. The two humans, Black and Linderman, who have been serving us, are both staring at me with odd looks in their eyes. Black merely looks intrigued, while Linderman is positively reeking of fear, clutching his beard with both hands as his knees knock together.

"What... what happened to the boy?" asks Linderman, his voice full of anxiety and dread. "Why does he look so different? He doesn't even look like Wyldfyre anymore."

Hatred suddenly rises up within me when Linderman uses that name. I point one finger at him and say, "Burn."

Linderman abruptly erupts into flames, shrieking at the top of his lungs—but only for a second. My flames consume him completely in less than a second, and I lower my finger.

As soon as I do, the flames vanish, revealing a small pile of ash where the annoying human once stood.

I look at Wasteland. "Forgive me for incinerating your servant. His weakness annoyed me."

Wasteland chuckles. "He was always a tool to me, one who frankly outlived his usefulness. Like the rest of humanity, he was always destined to die."

Humanimal, who stands next to Wasteland, rubs his stomach and says in a disappointed tone as he stares at the pile of ashes that had once been Linderman, "I never even got a chance to eat his liver."

Logikill waves a dismissive hand at Humanimal. "You will have plenty of humans to indulge in later, brother. For now, let us celebrate the birth—or rather, the rebirth—of our dear eldest brother, Despair."

Jackpot strokes his chin as he looks me over, an intrigued expression on his face. "Brother Logikill, while you've reminded us of a lot of our true purpose, we still don't remember nearly as much as you do. Heck, I didn't even realize we had another brother, though I can't say I'm complaining. Seems badass."

I speak before Logikill can. "Allow me to explain. Along with my physical form, my memories have returned as well. As you all know by now, each Meteor Monster has a Core, a piece of the meteor that bore us, inside us. That Core forms the basis of our very existence. Our lives depend on our Cores, which is why we all go to such great lengths to protect them."

I put a hand on my chest. "But you seven are not the only ones who received Cores that night. Three years ago, the teenager known as Tobias Miller received the 8th Core, which embedded itself inside him and gave him his powers. That Core should have been me, but unfortunately, the process of empowering Tobias Miller caused him to take on the appearance and abilities of that superhero he drew, Wyldfyre. The boy's personality and will turned out to be stronger than expected, so I was suppressed this entire time—until Brother Logikill broke the boy, giving me a chance to take control of his body, as I should have done long ago, if everything had gone according to plan."

Logikill nods, looking quite proud of himself. "Yes. What we forgot is that Despair is the ultimate sin. Despair is what ultimately destroys a civilization, starting from the individuals and spreading throughout society. Because if everyone despairs of the future, they will not bother to build it."

Jackpot nods as well. "Gotcha, gotcha. So does that make Despair our new leader?"

I glare at the other Meteor Monsters. "I should be. I was supposed to be. Does anyone wish to challenge my leadership? Because if so, I will happily accept such a challenge. It has been a long time since I've had the chance to punish my subordinates."

Wisely, none of my siblings accept my offer. Even Wasteland, the most prideful of us all, keeps his big mouth shut.

Perhaps because none of them want to end up like Linderman.

Or worse.

"So," says Black behind me, "what is the game plan now, Despair?"

I turn around to face Black. The arrogant human has not moved any closer to me than before, standing with his hands on his hips. I do not sense that he is challenging me, however, but merely that he is genuinely curious about what we will do now that I have reawakened.

For a moment, my eyes drift over to the smoking pile of corpses in the second cage. Something about seeing those bodies stirs a feeling in me I can't quite put into words, as if there is still something of the young teenager alive inside me.

I quickly avert my gaze and put that feeling to death. "What else? We will burn every town, city, and country on this planet to a crisp. We will annihilate all of humanity, every person, leaving no survivors. As a human yourself, what do you think about that?"

Black shrugs. "Humanity discarded me a long time ago. What more do I owe them? Do as you wish. But I do wonder how much of Toby Miller is still alive inside of you."

I narrow my eyes. "What do you mean?"

Black gestures at me. "Up until you transformed, you looked and acted very much like Toby Miller, your host. I thought it was just a physical transformation at first, but it is now obvious to me that Despair is a different person from Toby Miller. So what happened to Toby Miller? Is he still alive in there somewhere, or has even his spirit been burned away?"

I eye Black suspiciously. Even though I am not Toby Miller, I still remember how deceptive this one could be. "The human teenager known as Toby Miller is gone, completely and totally. Body, mind, soul… I consumed it all, every last bit of it. He no longer exists in any meaningful way. He isn't coming back."

Black nods. "That's what I thought, but I wanted to confirm my suspicions before jumping to any conclusions. That is indeed a terrible fate for any human to suffer, and I say this as someone who was far from Toby's biggest fan."

I fold my arms across my chest. "But the bigger question is, what will we do with you? I'm sure you must be asking yourself that. You're self-centered enough to be wondering."

Black adjusts his sunglasses. "You're right about that one, Despair. While I never liked Linderman much, I also would rather not end up a pile of ash like him. Is there some way that I, too, could become a Meteor Monster of some sort or—?"

Anger flashes through me, and before I know it, I'm standing in front of Black. I grab his throat with one hand and lift him off his feet, keeping careful control over my flames to avoid burning him, though I make sure breathing is as difficult for him as possible. "You will not join us in taking over and destroying the world. Frankly, I should burn you to a crisp just like I did to Linderman. You certainly deserve it."

When I grabbed Black, his sunglasses fell off his face, allowing me to see his terrified eyes. It fills me with joy to see him so afraid of me. It's exactly what he deserves.

But then I drop Black onto the floor like a sack of potatoes. He immediately grabs his throat and starts breathing hard, gazing up at me. That's when I realize I'm quite a bit taller than I normally am—part of the transformation, no doubt.

Gazing down at Black like the worm he is, I say, "But you did play an important role in bringing about my reawakening, as well as ensuring the resurrection of my siblings. Therefore, to show my thanks, you will be the very last human being we kill. You may go and hide on some remote island somewhere in the ocean, and we will completely ignore that island until we have murdered every single human being on the planet. That may take days, or it may take years, depending on how much of a fight the rest of humanity puts up."

I lean down toward Black, our faces less than an inch apart, breathing my smoky breath into his nostrils. "But know this: We *will* come after you eventually. Your days are numbered, even if we do not know the number ourselves. And should you step off that island, even for a moment, you will forfeit your right to be the last human being alive. Do you understand, Templeton Black?"

Black nods again, shakily. For the first time, I notice a bit of soot on his pristine white suit—the first time I've seen his clothes dirtied at all. That fills me with grim amusement.

Standing upright, I turn away from Black, who I know couldn't hurt me even if he tried, and walk back over to my fellow Meteor Monsters. This time, all of them are kneeling, including Wasteland, who has taken on a more humanoid form just to perform the action. Vicious triumph fills my chest as I gaze down at my siblings, each one of whom has an important role to play in the apocalypse I will unleash upon humanity.

I stop several feet away from them and raise my hands, which begin to smoke at the fingertips. "My siblings, it has been a long time coming, with many delays, twists, turns, and amnesia, but we are finally in a position to fulfill our ultimate purpose for the first time in three years. I never believed this day would come, but I am glad it has. We shall spread the disease of sin across humanity, led by the flames of Despair, which will burn away all of humanity's hope for the future. Soon, humanity itself will be little more than a distant memory, with their planet joining the countless other worlds that have fallen to our might."

The other Meteor Monsters raise their heads to look at me, each one of them smiling a bloodthirsty smile. They are clearly as eager to begin our quest for destruction as I am, which is good. We will need every last one of them to bring about the apocalypse that I saw in my visions—visions the teenager whose body I inhabit believed to be mere nightmares.

But they were not nightmares. They were visions of the future. A future I will bring about with my own two hands.

That's when Jackpot looks to the left and frowns. "Is that a helicopter?"

Confused, I follow Jackpot's gaze to the windows—specifically, to the broken window that the ceiling of my cage had smashed through.

And he is correct. A military helicopter hovers just outside the window, its side facing us. I don't know how I missed the whup, whup of its blades, but that doesn't matter. Perhaps the U.S. military decided Tobias and his friends had failed and were simply going to destroy Devon Tower with us in it.

The poor, simple, all-too-human fools.

I raise a finger, pointing directly at the helicopter, flames curling around my fingertip as I prepare to unleash a fire blast that will not just take down the helicopter, but also incinerate it and its pilot. This will prove a good warning to the rest of humanity not to mess with—

A motorcycle, with a familiar human in a cowboy costume sitting on it, suddenly launches out of the helicopter and smashes through what remains of the broken window. The motorcycle's wheels screech against the floor of the room as it charges toward me, and I am too surprised to react.

But I quickly recover from my surprise and unleash a fireball, tinged with black, at the motorcyclist. The cyclist swerves to the side at the last second, avoiding the fireball, which smashes into the windows behind him. By this point, the military helicopter has already pulled away and is out of the range of my attacks.

I ignore the helicopter to follow the motorcyclist, who brings his motorcycle to a stop on the other side of the room. Kicking its kickstand out, the motorcyclist—Captain Cowboy—steps off the bike and points both of his guns at me.

"All right, you annoying varmints," says Captain Cowboy, his voice clear and strong. "I'm here to save Toby, and I ain't leaving until I do!"

28

For a moment—a very brief moment—I stare at Captain Cowboy, uncomprehending. What is he doing here? He shouldn't have made it up here. This should be impossible.

And somewhere inside me, I feel a stirring of another soul, one I was sure I had already taken care of.

But I stomp it dead again and return my glare to the Crippler. "I thought that your minions had him and the other two humans covered."

The Crippler practically squeals at me. "That's what they told me! I thought for sure they had taken care of Captain Cowboy and the others by now. Honest!"

I briefly consider incinerating the Crippler for his failure on the spot, but decide against it. I still need him and the others to destroy the world, after all. True, I could always resurrect him if need be, but that would simply be a waste of time and effort. Better to spend that same time and effort eliminating the annoying human who still thinks Tobias Miller is alive.

I cannot wait to see the despair on his face when he learns the depressing truth about his precious sidekick.

Captain Cowboy snorts. "If you really want to know how we escaped, it was pretty simple. We had help."

I raise an eyebrow. "Help? From whom?"

Captain Cowboy gestures with his head toward the broken window. "The military, specifically the National Guard. Once it became clear that y'all were trying to separate us from Toby, Codetalker, Keith, and I left the building and got some help. Well, not before Codetalker used his drones to make short work of the dudes who'd cornered us. CT has enough toys on his costume to make even me jealous."

I resist the urge to kill the Crippler on the spot for his abject failure. Indeed, I probably should be killing Captain Cowboy but for some reason want to keep listening to his explanation of how he made it here. "All this without us knowing?"

Captain Cowboy nods. "Yep! So we had a problem because we knew we couldn't climb the tower the old-fashioned way, what with the elevators not working and the stairs probably booby-trapped or watched by your servants. So why not take the direct route to the top, where we knew Logikill was? That way, we could help Toby, who we had reason to believe was in serious trouble."

I sneer at Captain Cowboy. "You got lucky that we stopped monitoring the lower floors a while ago. Nonetheless, you are far too late to save Tobias Miller. He is dead. Only Despair lives now."

Captain Cowboy frowns deeply at me. It's a very familiar expression to me, far too familiar. "Despair, huh? I don't believe it. Toby was way too stubborn of a kid to ever let anyone, especially a Meteor Monster, take over his body. You look plenty scary, but your bark is probably worse than your bite."

I growl at Captain Cowboy, anger rushing up my spine, burning hot inside me. "If you think you can 'save' Tobias at this point, you are sorely mistaken. Toby died from the despair of seeing his friends and family slaughtered before his very eyes. He isn't coming back. ever." I hope that is enough to destroy Captain Cowboy's spirit. It must be. After all, it's nothing but the truth. The ultimate, depressing truth that no one can dispute.

And it will be a delight to crush his body along with his spirit after he fully accepts the darkness that is about to overtake the world under my command.

But incredibly—irrationally—Captain Cowboy smiles. "What in tarnation are you talking about? Toby's friends and family aren't dead. Where are the bodies?"

Once again, I stare at Captain Cowboy, trying to decide if he is actually blind or just that stupid. "The corpses are in that cage over there. You can still smell the stench of burned flesh. This is not up for debate."

Strangely, Logikill is looking a little nervous for some reason. That's an unusual expression to see on his face. What is he worried about? That I would believe the lies of a stupid human? I know that Logikill tends to look down on the rest of us due to his high intellect, but this would be extreme even by his standards. I hope he understands that, even if I may not have his raw intellect, I certainly have far more raw power than he does.

Captain Cowboy glances at the cage where the bodies of Toby's friends and family still lie, smoking and burning. One would expect him to show some kind of emotion, especially seeing the body of Wendy, who was his wife. Why wouldn't Captain Cowboy experience the same despair that I—that Toby—experienced when he saw the deaths of his friends and family?

Captain Cowboy does express an emotion, but it's not the despair I expected. He doesn't even look sad or surprised.

No, Captain Cowboy simply looks incredulous. And more than a bit confused.

He furrows his brow. "Okay, I don't see any bodies over there. Surely you can see that too."

I shake my head rapidly. "No! They are there. Is something wrong with your eyes, or are you just stupid? Or possibly, you're trying to trick me for some reason?"

Captain Cowboy opens his mouth to respond, but then closes it, looking at Logikill. Then he looks back at me, before looking at Logikill again, and finally back at me, nodding, wearing a look of understanding on his face.

"Now I get what's going on," says Captain Cowboy. He looks at his guns. "Welp, I guess these aren't going to be useful right now."

"What are you babbling about?" I demand, pointing an accusing finger at him. "Don't you need those guns to hurt us?"

Logikill, who is nervously adjusting his glasses, says, "The poison Humanimal inflicted on Captain Cowboy must be negatively affecting his intellectual abilities. Therefore, I suggest we just attack him now and kill him before he realizes the depths of his mistake. Indeed, Despair, I would say you should simply incinerate him on the spot. He would make for a fine first death in our conquest of the world."

I must admit, Logikill's advice is quite tempting. What could be more bitterly ironic, as well as appropriate, than starting our conquest of this stupid planet with the death of one of its greatest protectors? And what greater way to instill despair in Captain Cowboy than to have him be killed by the body of his sidekick, whom he trusted so much?

But for some reason, it feels a little too perfect. And seeing Logikill act so nervously and suggest such a direct course of action to deal with Captain Cowboy feels more than a little suspect to me.

So I say to Captain Cowboy, "What do you mean you understand what's going on now? What do you think is happening here?"

Captain Cowboy purses his lips. "I think Logikill here has pulled the biggest con job on you in the history of con jobs. Speaking as someone who's busted more than a few con artists over my career as a superhero, I gotta say, this was a pretty good one."

Logikill actually steps toward me, an urgent look on his face. "Ignore the human's babbling, Despair! Consider his motives. Captain Cowboy has every reason to try to divide us, including making things up to manipulate us. You must destroy him on the spot. Now."

Logikill is sweating profusely. That's definitely a strange sight, as Logikill never sweats or shows any emotion or discomfort under normal circumstances.

But before I can voice that observation aloud, Captain Cowboy laughs. "You're one to talk about manipulating people, Logikill, given how that's your entire schtick. Instead of dirtying your own hands, you prefer to make others do your dirty work. I mean, that's a very supervillain thing to do, but come on. We all know who's projecting onto whom here, and it definitely ain't me."

Logikill points accusingly at Captain Cowboy. "But if the fate of the world hangs on Despair believing your lies, then logically, you have a strong reason to go against your normal convictions regarding honesty and truth-telling, if it means achieving an end you consider desirable."

Captain Cowboy shakes his head. "Unlike you, Logikill, I stick with the truth, so I have no need to worry about going against my convictions to achieve a desirable end or whatever you're going on about. I just need to shine the light of truth onto your lies and watch everything you've built come crumbling down."

Logikill opens his mouth, perhaps to get in another jab, but I speak first, addressing Captain Cowboy directly. "What are you accusing Logikill of lying about? And why do you seem so confident that he is, in fact, lying to me? Explain yourself now, or I will turn you into ash."

Captain Cowboy smiles at me. "I could use words to describe what Logikill is lying to you about, but you know what they say—a picture, or in this case, a video, is worth a thousand words."

Captain Cowboy pulls out his phone, taps the screen a couple of times, and then turns it so the screen faces me, allowing me to see Paintbrush, Dakota Gary, Mom, and Granny all sitting together in a room somewhere, looking alive and well.

29

If seeing Captain Cowboy burst into the top floor of the tower nearly took me by surprise, then seeing all of the dead hostages alive and well on the other side of what is clearly a live video feed is like getting slapped in the face with a tire iron.

Everyone is there: Granny, who looks confused; Gary, who looks more than a bit puzzled himself; Dakota, who is smiling like she always does; Mom, who wears a look of utter concern on her face; and beautiful Paintbrush, who is somehow both smiling at me and looking serious at the same time.

My jaw drops. "What... is this...?"

Paintbrush, sitting in the middle of the group, leans toward the camera and says, "Toby! It's us. We're alive. You don't have to worry about us anymore."

"That demon is Toby?" says Gary, his voice full of confusion and dread. "I don't remember Toby looking like that."

Granny, adjusting her glasses, snorts and shakes her head. "Kids these days and their terrible sense of fashion. I swear, when I was y'all's age, we didn't look anything like that."

Dakota grimaces. "Definitely not Toby's best look. He should have consulted with me about his fashion. He doesn't even have his hair anymore. What happened to your hair, big brother? That was your best feature."

Mom purses her lips and rubs her hands together anxiously. "I'm not sure if that's even really Toby anymore. He doesn't look like the son I raised."

Something in Mom's words snaps me out of my reverie, and I glare at Captain Cowboy. "What is this? Some kind of AI-generated trick or something?"

Captain Cowboy shakes his head. "Nope. Aside from the fact that I have no idea how AI stuff works, this is definitely a livestream. You're actually interacting with Wendy and the others in real-time. In fact, it isn't just Wendy and the others who are there. Keith, CT, why don't you put in an appearance?"

The camera briefly shifts away to show Keith and Codetalker, both looking quite banged up from fighting the servants of my siblings, sitting on wooden chairs. Keith gives the camera a quick wave while Codetalker merely nods at it.

"Hi, Meteor Monsters!" says Keith. He then immediately grimaces when he looks at me. "Oscar, who the heck is that ugly guy staring at us?"

Captain Cowboy chuckles. "That's Toby, Keith. I know he looks a lot rougher than usual, but I'm fairly certain it's him."

Keith grimaces even more. "Ouch. My condolences. I hope Paintbrush doesn't decide to break up with you because you aren't handsome anymore."

Off-screen, I hear Paintbrush groan and say, "I'm not just attracted to Toby because I think he's handsome, Keith."

Keith rolls his eyes. "It was just a joke, Paintbrush. But aside from his looks, I feel like Toby has probably lost a lot of his other good qualities too."

My mind races as I try to make sense of this livestream that Captain Cowboy is showing me. This cannot be. It must be a trick, but I honestly can't see how Captain Cowboy has pulled it off. Did he perhaps somehow hire a bunch of actors to portray my dead family and friends as part of a convoluted plan to mess with my head?

No, that doesn't make any sense at all. There is no way that Captain Cowboy could have possibly found enough actors who look exactly like my dead friends and family to pull off such an elaborate hoax in such a short period of time. Even taking into account Codetalker's hacking skills and AI editing tools, there's absolutely no way that explanation could cover what I'm seeing before my very eyes.

Captain Cowboy then meets my eyes. "I can tell you're still pretty skeptical, Despair, which is understandable. But there's one way to verify this livestream, and that's by attacking the corpses in the cage. That should be all the proof you need to believe what your eyes are showing you."

"Don't!" says Logikill in a genuinely panicked voice. "Despair, you should know better than anyone that humans are not worth listening to. Even if you can't explain the livestream, surely you must understand that it doesn't change anything. We are still Meteor Monsters and still need to destroy the world, regardless of which humans might still be alive. If you would but just listen to reason—"

SLOTH

I snap my fingers at Logikill, and his mouth bursts into flame. Logikill screams as he clutches his burning mouth, falling to his knees as my flames scorch his tongue and lips. I do not, of course, kill Logikill on the spot, but I certainly make sure that the fire is especially hot to keep him from yapping at me again.

I glare at the kneeling Logikill. "Do not presume to tell me what to do, Logikill. Unless you'd like my flames to keep burning faster than your body can regenerate, that is."

It is satisfying to see the look of terror on Logikill's face. Not that I genuinely care about his opinion, of course—otherwise, I wouldn't have burned his tongue in his mouth. I simply cannot stand being bossed around by my younger siblings, who think they know better than me.

As for Captain Cowboy's offer, I have to admit I'm somewhat torn on what to do. On one hand, if Captain Cowboy really is fooling me, then my flames should do something to the bodies. But if, on the other hand, those bodies aren't even real, then my flames should reveal that, too.

And then I can decide from there how I wish to proceed.

Normally, I would ignore the words of a lowly human and simply incinerate Captain Cowboy on the spot. But between Logikill's out-of-character emotional outbursts and the realism of the livestream on Captain Cowboy's phone, I have to admit that I can't just brush it off.

I need to know the truth.

And there is only one reliable way I know of to find out the truth.

I point my finger away from Captain Cowboy toward the cage full of burned corpses lying not far from me. For the briefest of seconds, I hesitate, wondering if I'm about to desecrate the bodies of my former family and friends even further than they already are.

But then I remember what I want—the truth—and I put all other concerns behind me and unleash a blast of dark fire at the corpses.

The blast of dark fire hurtles through the air until it strikes the corpses.

Instead of burning the corpses even more, or even simply slamming against the bars of the cage, the blast of dark fire merely passes through the cage like it doesn't exist.

And a second later, the cage itself, along with the corpses that had been lying inside it, leaving nothing but an empty blank space of floor where both the cage and the corpses had once lain.

30

The silence that reigned in the room was utterly tyrannical. Here I stand, staring at the spot on the floor where the corpses of my friends and family once lay, realizing, with a gut punch, that Captain Cowboy was, *is*, telling the truth.

But I can't believe it. I still refuse to believe it.

Yet what other choice do I have but to believe my own lying eyes?

Captain Cowboy, still holding up his phone, nods. "Are they still there?"

I look at Captain Cowboy, briefly confused. "Who? The corpses? No ... no, they are not."

I say those words with a heaviness that I can't quite explain. Perhaps it is simply my reluctance to admit that Captain Cowboy was right.

Captain Cowboy nods again. "Of course. The fact is, none of the hostages were ever actually up here. The ones you saw get executed right in front of you ... well, I'm sure you know what *those* actually were."

I do. I don't even look at Logikill, who is still kneeling on the floor a few feet away from me, clutching his burning tongue and keeping his gaze on my feet. "Logikill's illusions."

"So that's why we couldn't see anything," says Keith over the live stream, nodding. "I was wondering what Toby was shooting at."

Suddenly, the camera shifts back to Paintbrush's face. She's wearing a serious but concerned expression on her face, her beautiful features catching my interest. "Toby, Captain Cowboy is right. We, the hostages, were never *actually* on the top floor of Devon Energy Tower. That was all an illusion created by Logikill to lure you to the top alone."

I find it difficult to maintain my balance as my whole world seemingly shifts around me. "But then ... where *were* you?"

Codetalker's voice answers from off-screen. "Turns out the hostages were actually held in the basement of Devon Tower, ironically, just underneath the lobby. Didn't you ever find it strange how quickly Humanimal appeared and disappeared with Paintbrush when we first entered the building?"

I rub my eyes. "You mean you were all there the entire time and we didn't even know it? But how did *you* find out?"

Captain Cowboy answers next. "A certain Nobody, who we captured and interrogated, told us as much. Evidently, the human servants were put in charge of keeping the hostages from escaping. Nobody, being the leader of the human servants, knew all about it. Sure was a chatty one."

"Especially after *I* was done with him," says Codetalker in an unusually savage voice.

"So, naturally, once we found out where the real hostages were, we knew it was pointless to follow Toby, Walter, and Pietro," says Keith, still off-screen himself. "Instead, we doubled back, rescued the hostages, and put together this plan to help Toby. We figured Toby had probably made it to the top floor by now, so we sent Captain Cowboy to tell him the good news and hopefully provide backup for Toby in case he was fighting the Meteor Monsters by himself."

I look at Captain Cowboy doubtfully. "Even if Toby were still alive, I doubt you would be of much help, Captain Cowboy. You are just one man."

Captain Cowboy smirks. "I didn't say I was the *only* backup."

The roaring of more helicopter blades fills the air and suddenly, through every window, I can see multiple military helicopters rise up into the air around the top of Devon Tower. Gunners sitting in each helicopter point their guns at the windows, aiming at me and the other Meteor Monsters specifically, who all start and look around at the military helicopters in shock.

"The only reason the military and police didn't help is 'cause of the hostages," says Captain Cowboy. He waves his phone at me. "Once we made sure the hostages were safe, well, we didn't see any reason to hold back."

"Even as we speak, the police are securing the lower floors," says Codetalker. "In fact, I just got an update from the chief of police that they have found Walter. Evidently, he was left injured in an office somewhere on one of the lower floors, but they seem to think he will recover once he gets the medical attention he needs."

Captain Cowboy cocks his head to the side. "So, as you have no doubt put together yourself at this point, you guys are totally screwed."

I scowl. "Did you forget that we are still the Meteor Monsters? Even if you throw all of the world's militaries at us, it won't matter. They cannot kill us. *You* cannot kill us. Only one boy can ... and that boy is dead."

Captain Cowboy raises an eyebrow. "How many times do I need to tell you that I don't believe that? I believe—no, *we* believe, all of us, Toby's friends and family—that the real Toby is still alive in there. He just needs to wake up and fight."

"That's exactly right, Cap!" says Paintbrush. She brings the camera closer to her face, staring at me with her beautiful brown eyes. "Toby, I know that Logikill and the other Meteor Monsters have made you feel despair unlike anything you have felt before. But I also know that you aren't someone who gives into despair that easily."

"You tell him, sister!" says Dakota. She jerks her head into frame, almost headbutting Paintbrush, and glares at me. "The *real* Toby would call you lame for just giving up and becoming evil. I know my big brother and he wouldn't be anything like *you*."

Gary's face appears next, still looking a little taken aback by everything. But he manages to say, in a brave voice, "I still am trying to process the fact that Wyldfyre and my best friend are the same person, but I agree with everyone else. The real Toby befriended me even when no one else would. He was always brave and strong and always defended the weak."

"My grandson was a good boy," says Granny, her head popping into frame next. "A smart young man, even if I didn't always understand him. But I did love and care for him. He certainly doesn't deserve to lose his body to a wicked shadow man like you."

I blink, feeling tears—actual *tears*—forming in the corners of my eyes. But I burn the tears away with my flames, not wanting to show that their words, as corny as they were, were getting through.

Despite my best efforts to kill the stupid teenager inside me.

Finally, the camera shifts to Toby's parents, both sitting side by side. I didn't see Dad the first time, but maybe he had just been off-screen for some reason.

Mom looks close to tears. "Toby, please come back. You are our son."

Dad nods, putting an arm around Mom's shoulders. He looks at the camera, looks seemingly at me, and says, "We miss you. Both of us."

"*All* of us," says Captain Cowboy as he lowers the phone slightly, perhaps to make it easier to see me. "And now that you've seen and heard everything, I think you know what comes next. I think you know that there's still a chance we can do this. And if there's one thing I know about Tobias 'Wyldfyre' Miller, it's that he knows how to get *fired up* even when the odds are slim."

Captain Cowboy's words, combined with the words from everyone else, cause something to *click* in my mind in a way that nothing else has up until this point.

Then my mind and body split.

31

Horrific pain rips through my body, mind, and soul as something stirs inside me. It stirs hot, burning hotter and hotter than even the flames that already cover my body. It feels like a star just came into existence inside me, burning so hot and bright that even my flames are consumed by it.

I fight against it. I increase my fire, burning hotter myself, trying to stop or at least match the heat.

But it's too much.

I can't stop it.

I can't stop Toby.

And in seconds, I—*we*—split.

One half of me lands on the ground, while the other half of me is sent sprawling backward into the cage behind me.

For the briefest of seconds, my perspective is split between two beings:

Tobias 'Wyldfyre' Miller.

And Despair, the eighth Meteor Monster.

One blink later, however, and I find myself back in the body of Wyldfyre—my body—lying on the floor of the room. My body aches and burns, but the pain is nothing compared to the pain from the split.

The split that I caused, by the way.

Although honestly, after going through that split, I am glad I am not going to do it again. Easily the worst pain of my life.

But at least it's over. The pain from the initial split is already starting to fade. My strength is returning to my limbs and my mind is rapidly coming back into focus as I look around at my surroundings.

SLOTH

The split must have happened pretty fast because not much has changed since it occurred. Captain Cowboy still stands in front of his motorcycle before me with his phone out, while the Meteor Monsters stand off to the side. They seem to have retreated a few feet during the split, perhaps because of the flames that my body created. The floor under my feet is burned to a crisp for several feet around me but I am otherwise unharmed myself.

Captain Cowboy, along with everyone on the livestream, is staring at me with an expression halfway between hope and confusion. "Toby ... what in Sam Hill's name just happened?"

Groaning slightly, I rise to my feet, dusting off my red and white costume as I do so. "What does it look like? I'm back. Me. Toby. Wyldfyre. Whatever you want to call me."

Captain Cowboy shakes his head. "I mean, I am happy to see you again, kid, but what I don't understand is–"

"How?" Despair's voice, deep and harsh, erupts behind me. "How did you survive? And how did you split us in two?"

I look over my shoulder to see Despair, who looks even uglier in person than he had in the mirror, lying in the smoldering ruins of the cage I had been locked away inside. He looks pretty much the same as before aside from a few cracks in his forehead from the impact of the crack.

I crack my neck. "You mean you don't know how I pulled that off? I figured you would, but maybe you aren't as smart as I thought you were."

The Crippler raises his bat, an angry look on his face. "Watch what you say to our leader, you insolent brat! He has enough power to burn the entire world. Show him some respect."

I give the Crippler an annoyed look. "Who asked you for your opinion? But thanks for stepping up. You're the reason I figured I could even do this."

Confusion flickers across the Crippler's face for a second. "What do you mean? What did I help you figure out how to do? I don't recall saying anything."

I rub my forehead in exasperation. "It's not what you said now. It's what you did before your first death, that is. Remember now?"

Despair looks at the Crippler in confusion. "What is the boy going on about? What did you do that inspired him?"

The Crippler, however, doesn't seem to have even heard Despair's question. He appears very lost in thought, though even as he stands there thinking, a look of horror crosses his face. He seems to be putting two and two together, and he clearly doesn't like the answer.

The Crippler raises his head to look at me, horror crossing his serpentine features. "Impossible. You couldn't have done that. You're just a human."

"Again, what did the boy do?" demands Despair, looking from me to the Crippler and back again. "What did he do that was supposedly impossible for a human to do?"

I crack my neck again. "Good question, Despair. See, the Crippler isn't wrong. What I did is normally impossible for humans. But weren't you guys always going on and on about how I wasn't completely human? That I was at least half Meteor Monster? And what kind of unique powers and abilities do Meteor Monsters have that humans don't? You get two answers, and the first one doesn't count."

Jackpot snorts. "We can do all sorts of things that pathetic humans can't. We can instantly recover from even the most lethal of injuries, we don't age, and we have a variety of powerful and deadly abilities that make us a threat to even the strongest of supers. Frankly, a better question you should ask is, what can't we do?"

I chuckle. "Apparently, you can't answer my question. Or, most of you can't, anyway. But I'm sure the Crippler can. He figured it out before any of you. He even figured it out before Logikill, which is pretty impressive, seeing as Logikill is supposed to be the smartest of you guys."

Logikill, still kneeling on the floor and clutching his mouth, shoots me a death glare, but I ignore him to focus on everyone else.

I spread my hands. "So, to answer the question that everyone is asking, a couple of years ago, the Crippler split his Core during my fight with him. This allowed the Crippler to duplicate himself, essentially allowing him to be in two places at once. It was a pain in the ass to deal with at the time, but definitely an effective technique. Honestly, I'm surprised the rest of you guys didn't try it at least once."

The Crippler grimaces. "Splitting Cores is a very painful process... as you undoubtedly found out yourself."

Jackpot looks at the Crippler in shock. "Toby split his Core? But I didn't think he even had a Core."

I put my hand on my chest, right where my heart is. "That's the thing. I do have a Meteor Monster Core and always have. My Core was originally supposed to be Despair's Core, but it ended up in my body and turned me into Wildfire instead. That's also the reason I've been able to sense you Meteor Monsters—because it's my Core reacting to your Cores."

Already, I can see the gears starting to turn in the eyes of the Meteor Monsters. For that matter, I can tell that my friends and family watching the livestream are also starting to figure out where this is going, which is fine. This information won't necessarily help them beat me, anyway.

But it sure is fun to brag about it. Maybe this is why supervillains love to monologue.

Jackpot, who is seemingly speaking for the rest of the Meteor Monsters at this point, strokes his chin thoughtfully. "So that's how you got your body back from Despair. Somehow, you split your Core from within. So is it safe to assume that you and Despair each share half of a Core?"

I nod. "Bingo, Jackpot. That's exactly what I did. Now, I didn't know if it would actually work when I tried it, seeing as I was doing it from within without any control of my body, but I'm glad the gamble paid off. And now, I have my body again."

A grunt behind me makes me look over my shoulder again. Despair has risen back to his feet, flames running up and down his arms as he glares at me with absolute hatred. He cracks his knuckles and tilts his head to the side. "So you managed to take advantage of a power you didn't even know you could use. That, I will admit, is fairly impressive. I did not expect a dumb teenager like you to come up with a plan like that."

I shrug. "It's like I always say, I'm smarter than I look. After all, I created Logikill, didn't I? I had to have some brains in order to do that."

Despair regards me with harsh eyes, but I don't think he's underestimating me anymore. I think he now understands exactly how dangerous I am.

Which is why he isn't attacking me. He clearly doesn't want to make another mistake that I could take advantage of.

But that's fine. It's nice for the Meteor Monsters to be the ones experiencing fear for a change. It's what they deserve, honestly.

I look around at the Meteor Monsters again, putting my hands on my hips. "All right. Now that we've established how I did that, I think you all know what comes next. I'm going to kick all of your butts straight back to whatever planet the meteor came from. And I don't mind taking on all eight of you at once if that's what it will take."

Again, none of the Meteor Monsters look like they're impatient to fight me. It's as though they can all sense that I don't fear any of them anymore. Or maybe they are just too shocked by how I used one of their own unique techniques against them so effectively.

No matter how you look at it, I have definitely turned the tables on the Meteor Monsters. Granted, I still have to fight them, but I've already fought and killed them before. And with the military backing me up, that should at least make taking them all out a little bit easier.

But just before I decide who I want to take out first, I hear a sudden gunshot go off inside the room.

My first thought is that one of the Meteor Monsters tried to shoot at me, but looking down at my body, I don't see any bullet holes or anything to indicate that anyone tried to shoot me. But surely someone had tried to shoot me, right? I mean, who else would they be trying to shoot?

Then I hear Captain Cowboy cry out, followed by a *thunk*, and I turn my head, slowly, in his direction.

Captain Cowboy is lying on the floor, his gut bleeding out and his phone lying just out of his reach, a few feet away from him. He is breathing hard, each breath making him shudder, but at least he's still alive.

I quickly follow the trajectory of the bullet back to its source…

And see Logikill standing up now, holding a gun, which he's pointing at Captain Cowboy with a cold expression on his face.

32

Instinctively, I rush over to Captain Cowboy and cradle him in my arms. "Cap! Cap, are you okay? How are you doing? Cap?"

Captain Cowboy groans and opens his eyes. Still clutching his stomach wound, he says in a weak voice, "I've been worse. But you shouldn't worry about me. Worry about yourself."

My hands shake, but then I hear Logikill behind me say in a disappointed tone, "Darn it. I had hoped to kill him with that shot. I suppose that's what I get for not diligently practicing my target shooting."

I jerk my head over my shoulder to glare at Logikill, who has lowered his gun to his side. The Meteor Monster, who looks like a college professor, shows no regret on his face at all, which doesn't surprise me, but it does piss me off.

From Captain Cowboy's phone, I hear Paintbrush call out, "Toby? Captain Cowboy? Are you guys okay? We heard a gunshot and then the phone went flying. We can't see—"

A bolt of black flame suddenly strikes the phone, instantly incinerating it. Jerking my head up, I see Despair pointing with one finger at the pile of ash that had once been Captain Cowboy's phone, still gazing at us with pure hatred.

"You should have brought more help," says Despair, his voice cruel and deep. He shifts his finger toward me and Captain Cowboy. "Otherwise, you might have stood a chance of surviving today."

Captain Cowboy, still cradled in my arms, shoots Despair a smirk. "Did you forget about the military helicopters surrounding us? Or about the police who are making their way up the building even as we speak? Even if I die, you'll still have to deal with them."

Despair glances out the windows at the military helicopters, which are still circling the building with their guns out. Frankly, I'm not sure why they haven't started shooting yet, but perhaps they just don't want to hit me or Captain Cowboy by accident.

With a shrug, Despair says, "You're right. I did."

Abruptly, the engines on each helicopter explode. The helicopters start careening toward the streets below, their chopper blades whipping loudly on their way down. I, of course, do not hear the screams from the helicopter crews, but I can't imagine they're not screaming their heads off.

A few seconds later, I hear several explosions below, followed by the sounds of ambulance sirens going off throughout the city. No doubt the city's emergency services are responding to the downed helicopters, which makes sense, seeing as if there are any survivors among the crews of the destroyed helicopters, they will definitely need medical attention.

Honestly, Captain Cowboy needs medical attention, but I don't have any way of getting it to him right now. I'm not a doctor myself, after all, nor even a medic. And my healing powers, unfortunately, only extend to myself.

So, Captain Cowboy and I stare at Despair in shock, but the Meteor Monster doesn't show any emotion. He merely tilts his head to the side and says, "There. Now it should be just you and us. Just as it was always destined to be."

Crap. While I was pretty confident that I could deal with the other seven Meteor Monsters on my own, Despair is clearly on another level. As far as I can tell, he just blew up those helicopters with his mind. He didn't even have to point at them, which makes me wonder why he feels the need to point at other things. Maybe those are different attacks, or maybe he just likes showing off.

Nonetheless, I look at Captain Cowboy desperately. "You're too injured. I need to get you to safety so I don't have to worry about protecting you while fighting the Meteor Monsters. I think I could fly both of us out of here if—"

Captain Cowboy glares at me. "Toby, what did I tell you about worrying about yourself? This is your chance to end the Meteor Monster threat once and for all. If we run now, there's no chance we'll get another shot at eliminating them all in one go. We can end their threat here and now, or at least you can."

I purse my lips tightly. "Maybe, but you're still heavily injured. I don't want you to die on me if I can help it."

SLOTH

Captain Cowboy shakes his head. "Me and Betsy will be fine. You just go all out against them, you hear? Don't hold back. Hit them with everything you've got, and then some."

I had briefly forgotten that Captain Cowboy had named his motorcycle Betsy, but that doesn't change the fact that he's right. This is definitely my best opportunity to finish off the Meteor Monsters once and for all. I hate the idea of leaving Captain Cowboy, but it's not like I have much choice in the matter. Who knows what the Meteor Monsters will try to do if I leave with Captain Cowboy (assuming they even let me leave at all, which is extremely unlikely)?

Before I can tell Captain Cowboy that, however, Despair says, "Now, please don't move. This will make it much easier for me to destroy you both."

Despair unleashes another blast of dark fire at us, but I quickly lay Captain Cowboy down, summon my tapena, and, wielding it like a baseball bat, knock the dark fire blast away. The dark fire blast hurtles off to the side, smashing through the windows before dissipating into thin air.

Lowering my tapena, which is now on fire itself, I glare at Despair. "This fight is between you and me, Despair."

Despair smirks. "Just you and me? Have you forgotten about my siblings already?"

The other Meteor Monsters suddenly appear between me and Despair. They form a loose half-circle between me and Despair, each one looking at me hungrily, like they can't wait to tear me apart. With their weapons drawn and their powers at the ready, the Meteor Monsters definitely look ready to rumble.

But I don't have the time or energy to fight them all, as well as keep Captain Cowboy safe. I need to end this fight and end it quickly.

And what better way to do that than by hitting each one of their Cores directly? That is the weakness every one of the Meteor Monsters share with each other. Destroy their Core and they instantly die.

So I close my eyes, focusing on my own Core. Now that I better understand the nature of my powers, I wonder how far I can actually push my Meteor Monster senses. They've always been limited to just feelings and sensations, which have sometimes been accurate, but other times have been frustratingly vague. Maybe if I really focus on my Core and its connection to the other Meteor Monsters, I can expand it in ways I haven't even thought of yet.

But then I hear a roar and open my eyes to see Humanimal, seemingly unable to wait for me to make the first move, hurtling toward me with his claws outstretched.

But Humanimal looks ... different. As Humanimal runs toward me, I see a glowing golden glow in his stomach. It wasn't there before, making me wonder if my eyes are playing tricks on me or if I am somehow losing my mind.

Then it hits me.

Humanimal's *Core*.

That's what I am looking at. That's what the glow is.

I don't just *sense* Humanimal's Core anymore. I can actually *see* it with my eyes, even when it is inside Humanimal. A quick glance at the other Meteor Monsters shows me that their Cores, too, are visible to my eyes now.

Which means I know *exactly* where to hit them now.

All this goes through my mind in less than a second, by which time Humanimal gets within my reach. His claws flash toward my face, his jaw opening unnaturally wider as he seeks to eat me whole.

But I am faster.

Slipping under his guard, I switch my tapena to my left hand and encase my right hand in flame shaped like a claw ...

Before driving it straight through Humanimal's stomach, right where his Core is.

Humanimal comes to an abrupt stop, his jaw still open, as I shove his Core out his back before ripping it back out. Humanimal then falls to his knees before me, clutching his stomach as he looks at his own Core, burning in my right hand, in utter disbelief.

"My Core?" says Humanimal, his voice growing rapidly weaker every second. "How—?"

Humanimal then crumbles into a pile of dust at my feet, his never-answered question fading into nothingness.

And then I look up at the other Meteor Monsters, who are all gazing at me with varying expressions of horror and surprise, and say, "Who's up next?"

33

The answer to that question, seemingly, is everyone all at once.

But that isn't how it looks to me. Well, not exactly. It's almost as if time itself has slowed down, allowing me to watch the movements of the individual Meteor Monsters as precisely as if I were only fighting one at a time.

Wasteland goes first. His body sloshes toward me, turning into a wave of disgusting sludge and oil that, normally, likely would have buried me.

But I see his Core, bouncing around inside his sludge-like body, and shoot toward it. Covering my body in flame, I smash through Wasteland's body while snatching his Core on my way out. Wasteland's Core briefly tries to escape from my grasp but a quick infusion of fire causes it to crack and snap, thus severing its connection to Wasteland's body.

I emerge from Wasteland's decaying body just in time to run into the Crippler, who has outpaced the other Meteor Monsters to get to me first. He's swinging his bat and screaming like a maniac.

But I catch his bat, rip it out of his hand, and then immediately sever his hand, where his Core is, from his body. Catching his severed hand, I incinerate it with flame, revealing the cracked Core within, which I immediately drop in my pockets with the previous two Cores I collected.

The Crippler gasps, stumbling backward as he clutches his bleeding stump, his body already beginning to crumble to dust before my eyes—

Before Road Rage smashes through the Crippler's crumbling form, roaring at the top of his lungs as his overly muscular body as he swings his massive fists at my head.

I launch into the air, avoiding Road Rage's fists, and land on his shoulders. Before Road Rage can even react, I raise my flaming tapena over my head and smash it down on his skull, splitting it cleanly in two and revealing his Core, attached to his brain like a yellow tumor.

Without a second thought, I yank the Core out of Road Rage's brain and jump off his body, which stumbles forward and falls to the floor. Road Rage's headless body slams into the floor and explodes into dust, which flies everywhere.

But I pay no attention to that. Landing on the floor, I find Jackpot standing before me. He immediately throws several explosive dice blocks at me, which I only know are explosive because I can sense what they are going to do before they even activate.

More than that, Jackpot's Core shines in the hand that he threw the dice from, so I weave in and out of the exploding dice without missing a beat. It's fun seeing the look of horror on Jackpot's face as I avoid his exploding dice and get closer to him.

I don't just aim for his Core, though. My senses also alert me to his first penny, which is in his right pocket.

So, naturally, that is what I aim for.

When I get close enough to him, Jackpot swings his cane at my face, but I parry it with my tapena. Holding back Jackpot's attack with one hand, I reach over and yank the penny out of his coat pocket before burning it to a crisp.

Jackpot cries out, as if burning his penny actually hurt him, and then I grab his hand and burn it. Jackpot's free Core now falls into my hand as his gaudy clothes turn to dust along with the rest of his body.

But I don't have time to celebrate before Lady Lust unleashes her webbing at me. Again, this would have gotten me under normal circumstances, but I throw my tapena into the air and, thrusting my hands forward, unleash Fire Incinerator at her.

A positively massive blast of pure flame erupts from my hands. It consumes Lady Lust's webbing in midair before consuming Lady Lust herself, who had been standing right behind her own attack, in the next instant. Lady Lust's scream of agony cuts off abruptly and when Fire Incinerator ends, her burned Core lies on top of the pile of ash that had once been her beautiful body.

Walking over to the pile of ash, I pick up her Core and drop it in my pockets with the other six before raising my eyes to see Logikill standing not far from me.

Logikill was the only Meteor Monster who didn't try to attack me. Maybe he realized how futile it was or maybe he was just hoping that one of the others would take care of me for him. Either way, the look of terror slowly spreading across his face as he realizes how doomed he actually is is truly a sight to behold. I wish I could take a picture of it.

I catch my tapena, which I'd thrown into the air overhead, and point it at Logikill. I can see his Core. It's glowing like the sun in his head, just like where Road Rage's was. "You're smart, Logikill. I think you know how this is going to end. For both of us."

Logikill grimaces. He adjusts his glasses before glancing at Despair, as if hoping Despair might do something, but Despair just stands there, arms crossed in front of his chest, a severe look of disappointment on his face.

Turning his attention back to me, Logikill says, "Yes, you did make short work of my siblings. Which is impressive, given how much you struggled against them in the past."

I tilt my head to the side. "Because I learned from my mistakes, Logikill. Something you Meteor Monsters can't do."

Logikill raises an eyebrow. "Oh? In that case, what is stopping you from smashing my skull in with your club and ripping out my Core? I am standing right here, after all."

I eye Logikill carefully. "All right, then. If that's what you want, I'll be more than happy to give it to you."

I raise my flaming club above my head, taking careful aim at Logikill's bespectacled face. I can just imagine the exact spot I need to hit to smash his head open like an egg.

Then I whirl around and slam my club into the side of his face, sending his glasses flying and making him drop his gun onto the floor. The blow sends Logikill staggering backward, clutching his bleeding face, a look of total surprise on his nerdy features.

Raising his head to gaze at me in shock, Logikill asks in a slightly muffled voice, thanks to his smashed nose, "How did you see through my illusion—?"

I glance over my shoulder briefly to see that the fake Logikill I had been talking to has already vanished. Turning my attention back to the real Logikill, I grab his collar and yank him closer, staring directly into his fearful eyes. "Because, like I said, Logikill, I learn from my mistakes."

With that, I channel fire through the hand holding his collar, and Logikill's head immediately bursts into flames. He doesn't even get a chance to scream before the fire consumes his entire head. The flames are bright and warm, but I'm so used to it by now that it doesn't even bother me anymore.

I let go of Logikill's collar, and his body collapses onto the floor. His damaged Core spills out of the flames, and I pick it up as the rest of his body turns to dust, just like the bodies of his siblings.

Then I turn around, Logikill's Core still in my hand, to face Despair. The final Meteor Monster hasn't moved an inch from where I left him, looking completely unafraid of me, even though he just saw me slaughter all seven of his siblings in one go.

I drop Logikill's Core into my pocket and say to Despair, "Now it's just you and me, Despair. The way it was always meant to be."

Dark fire flares behind Despair's eyes. "Indeed. That is why this is going to be the final battle. The only question is, will you be able to overcome me, or will I crush you like an ant?"

I tilt my head to the side. "Why don't you ask all of the other Meteor Monsters I just killed? They could probably answer that question for you."

Despair growls and spreads his arms, which immediately catch flame. The flames rush down his arms and into his hands, forming a black, fiery tapena club, which Despair grabs with both hands and points at me. "Believe me, Wyldfyre, I will not die nearly as easily as those weaklings did. For I am Despair... and soon, the entire world will feel that same emotion once they see your corpse hanging from the top of this building."

34

For a brief second, Despair and I stand opposite each other, staring each other down, as if waiting for the other to move first.

And then the fight starts.

Who attacks first? I honestly can't say. Despair launches himself toward me, but I shoot toward him at the same time, the two of us swinging our clubs at each other.

Our clubs collide in the middle, and we both hit each other with as much force as we can. My club creaks and cracks under the impact, but so does Despair's, which has thin lines running up and down its form.

Neither of us pays attention to the status of our weapons. We push against each other, each putting all our strength into forcing the other back. It feels like I'm fighting myself here because he's just about as strong as I am, if not stronger.

Then, with a lot of snapping and breaking, both of our clubs shatter in our hands.

So our hands become our weapons.

I swing a fiery fist at Despair's ugly mug, landing a blow on his chin, but Despair follows up with a punch to the gut that makes me double over. I use the momentum of the blow to roll away from him, avoiding another punch aimed at my face.

Rising to my feet, I summon my bow, along with six arrows, and nock all six of them at once, taking careful aim at Despair. With a yell, I let loose all six fiery arrows, each one flying straight and true toward him.

But Despair leaps into the air, flying over the arrows, and lands several feet away from me. He pulls out his own bow and arrow set and launches several dark flame arrows at me, which I quickly roll to the side to avoid.

Once more, getting back to my feet, I fly into the air, intending to rain fireballs down on him. But Despair rockets toward me, flames spewing from the soles of his feet, and body slams me. He keeps going, smashing us through one of the windows, out into the skies above Oklahoma City.

Despair takes us higher and higher into the air, even higher than I've ever flown, but I manage to land a punch on his face again, and he lets go of me. I plunge toward the city below for a second before activating my flight powers and taking off back toward Devon Tower. No way am I going to let this fight spill out into the rest of the city and endanger innocent people for no reason.

With a blast of flame, however, Despair appears in front of me, forcing me to come to a stop in midair. He gives me a slasher smile and says, "Now, where do you think you're going, boy?"

Despair grabs me by the neck and hurls me to the right. I spin head over heels through the air uncontrollably for a second before I regain control of my trajectory, right before I'm about to hit the Chickasaw Bricktown Ballpark. I bank at the last second and head back up into the air, heading straight back toward Despair, who is still floating where I left him.

With another yell, I summon two clubs, one in each hand, and swing them both at Despair. Despair summons another club of his own and blocks both of them, but just barely. I keep swinging and smashing my clubs against his weapon with absolute ferocity, not giving him even a moment to react. I just need to get in one or two hits, and I think I should—

Suddenly, Despair drops straight down, and both of my clubs miss him. Swung forward by the momentum of my blows, I almost lose my balance as Despair flies up behind me and slams his club into the back of my head.

Next thing I know, I'm lying on the brick-lined streets of Bricktown, groaning loudly. Damn. Despair must have hit me *hard* because I have no idea how I even got here.

But I don't have the time to ponder that. My Meteor Monster senses go crazy and I look up in time to see a massive fireball, tinged with black, hurtling down toward me like a meteor. In fact, I am pretty sure it *is* a meteor.

Regardless, I fly backward, avoiding the dark fire meteor that smashes into the spot where I'd been lying mere seconds ago. The explosion sends chunks of brick and concrete flying toward me, forcing me to raise my hands to protect my face from the debris.

Luckily, that also allows me to catch a fiery punch from Despair, who blasts out from the smoke and flame with burning eyes of flame. But I only catch the first punch and the second punch, coming from below, strikes me in the chest, sending me flying backward again.

I smash into the street before bouncing down the stairs to the Bricktown Canal. Landing flat on my back at the edge of the Canal, I breathe hard. Every bone in my body is screaming and I am pretty sure I broke, like, a rib or two just from the impact of the crash. My healing factor is already kicking in, but I still feel like I got hit by a truck.

Panting and breathing hard, I force myself into a sitting position just as Despair appears at the top of the stairs to the Canal. He smiles a cruel grin down at me, a smile that doesn't match the hate in his eyes.

"Come now, Wyldfyre," says Despair, spreading his arms to both sides. "Don't tell me you are getting tired already. What happened to that endless confidence earlier that you could beat me? Was it merely teenage bluster?"

I grimace. I don't know why Despair isn't just pressing the attack when I am in such a weakened state, but he probably just wants me to suffer. Despair isn't just his name, after all. It's his very nature. I should know that better than anyone.

And that's what's so hard about this. Yes, I might have killed the other Meteor Monsters, but Despair is clearly on a whole other level. Not only does he have basically the same power and fighting skills as me, but he also has the absolute ruthlessness and cruelty of the Meteor Monsters. I can see why the others were afraid of this guy. I also can't see his Core, unlike the other Meteor Monsters, so that makes it even harder to deal with him.

Frankly, I was tempted to feel scared of him, too.

And I still didn't want to fight him in a place with lots of people. While Bricktown seems pretty deserted at the moment—probably thanks to the police evacuating everyone ahead of time, per our request—downtown OKC still has a lot of people working and living in it. That doesn't even include everyone outside of downtown.

But where in the world could I take our fight that might keep most people safe while potentially tipping the scales in my favor ...?

Oh.

Duh.

The crater.

I rise to my feet, slowly and painfully. I give Despair one last look of pretend fear (which isn't hard to do because he actually *is* scary) before turning around and launching into the air. I fly as fast as I can away from Despair, pretending to be fleeing for my life and hoping Despair takes the bait.

He does. I hear Despair roar behind me and glance over my shoulder to see him rushing after me. He's fast, faster than me, and will be upon me in seconds at the current rate we're both going.

Good thing I know OKC like the back of my head.

I lead Despair on a chase through the city, swerving in and between buildings and structures, doing my best to slow him down. I don't want to lose him entirely. I need to lead him to the crater if my plan is going to work.

Although I probably shouldn't be afraid of losing him. Despair manages to match my movements well, but it's clear that even though he has half of my Core, he still doesn't know OKC as well as I do. As a result, I manage to keep just ahead of him the entire time until we finally leave downtown and enter the 39th Street District.

And, seconds later, I see the crater itself directly ahead and below us. Still fenced off from the surrounding area, the crater is, fortunately, empty of life and looks big enough to contain even our biggest attacks. The meteor itself is still at the Stable, but that's fine. I should still be able to—

A *boom* behind me makes me look over my shoulder to see another one of Despair's dark fire meteors hurtling toward me. This time, it's too fast for me to dodge.

The dark fire meteor slams into my back and I crash down into the crater. Once again, I bounce off of the ground until I come to a stop on the other side of the crater, my head spinning, my bones and muscles screaming from the pain. Ugh. Not exactly how I planned to land.

A shadow suddenly appears over me and I look up to see Despair, his hands covered in dark flame, towering over me, an impatient glare on his features as he brings his fists down on my face.

35

I catch Despair's fists at the last second, but the impact still drives me into the ground. Despair then suddenly yanks me up, still holding onto his fists, and out of the ground and throws me to the side.

I hit the ground at a roll and keep rolling until I reach the center of the crater. Rising to my feet, I whirl around to face Despair, who is now walking toward me calmly, each step of his feet leaving burning footprints in his wake.

"Why so slow, Despair?" I ask, panting hard, wiping sweat, dirt, and blood off of my forehead. "Getting tired yourself?"

Despair shakes his head, still walking. "No. I just know that you are done running. You led me back to the crater, back to where it all started, for a reason, didn't you?"

I nod. "Mostly because it's the safest place in the city I could think of to take you. There aren't as many people immediately around us. The crater is kind of like an arena just for the two of us."

Despair stops several feet away from me, his hands balled into tight fists. He smiles. "Appropriate that you want to end it where it all began. You led us back here for a reason ... even if it's not the reason you just articulated."

I scowl. Another club appears in my hand and I raise it above my head. "Yeah. I just told you why. Try listening for a change."

Despair rolls his eyes. "So ignorant. The meteor itself drew us back here, where it all began. You have collected all seven Cores from the Meteor Monsters. Why else do you think I allowed you to take us back here?"

I furrow my brows. "You didn't 'allow' anything. I tricked you."

Despair shakes his head again. "Did you trick me ... or did the meteor trick you?"

I frown before I hear a rushing in the sky overhead. Looking up, I see something large and golden hurtling through the air toward us. It burns through the clouds in the midday sky, growing larger and larger with every passing second.

My eyes widen as I realize what it is. "The meteor?"

Despair does not immediately answer, but he doesn't need to, because a second later, the meteor lands in the crater.

But it doesn't crash. It lands perfectly still, if slightly ungracefully, directly between us. Its engine—at least, I assume it has an engine, knowing what I do now about its true nature—hums softly yet eerily, vibrating the pieces of wood covering its surface.

Despair gestures at the meteor. "Look who decided to show up. It must have sensed that you had brought all eight Cores back to its original location and flew back here to meet us. It probably damaged your little base on the way out, based on the wood chips on its surface."

I stare uncertainly at the meteor. "It can do that? Seemed pretty inactive to me."

Despair smiles. "The initial crash might have damaged it, but you would be foolish to think that a machine designed to traverse light years could be permanently damaged by a mere unscheduled crash. No, the meteor was waiting for you to gather the Cores this entire time. And now that you have, it is ready to take us back."

I raise an eyebrow. "So it can take you guys all the way back to whatever dead or dying planet you were originally launched from?"

Despair flashes demonic teeth at me in a cruel mockery of a smile. "No. So we can end this world and everything in it. So the sins of the universe can destroy all of humanity, just as we were designed, just as we were always destined to do."

My breath catches in my throat, but I manage to say, "No. Not as long as I keep breathing."

Despair tilts his head to the side. "Who said you had any choice in the matter?"

Suddenly, the star-shaped holes in the meteor, where the Cores are supposed to go, flare to life. The Cores in my pockets react, shooting out of my pockets against my will toward the meteor. Each Core slams into its respective hole until all seven holes are filled with glowing Cores.

Every Core, that is, except for the split one shared between me and Despair.

But my heart suddenly shudders and I fall to my knees, dropping my tapena at the same time. Clutching my chest, I take a deep, shuddering breath as fresh sweat breaks out across my forehead. "My heart ... feels like it's trying to escape my chest ..."

Harsh laughter before me makes me raise my heads to see Despair, still standing on the other side of the meteor, laughing at me. His chest is glowing now, meaning that his half of my Core is right there.

"That's exactly what it is trying to do, Wyldfyre," says Despair, whose voice sounds triumphant, if slightly strained. He puts a hand on his chest. "All of the Cores are reacting to the summons from the meteor. Once our Core rejoins the meteor, we will be reborn again, except this time with all of our memories in tact. Or perhaps newer, more dangerous versions of ourselves will be born. It is hard to say what will happen, but I can guarantee you that none of it is good for humanity."

My eyes widen. "If I lose my Core, what will happen to me?"

Despair shrugs. "Impossible to say. You might simply return to being a normal human boy and lose your powers. Or, seeing as you and your Core have been one for years now, you might die. Either way, I wouldn't worry about it if I were you because you will perish with humanity regardless of exactly what form your demise takes."

My breathing becomes hard and rapid. No. Here I thought that taking our fight to the crater would work in my favor, but stupidly, I didn't even consider that the meteor might do something. In my defense, I had no idea it still worked, but that doesn't matter at this point.

And even if I kill Despair in the next few moments somehow, that also doesn't matter. The meteor wants both halves of our Core and it will just kill us both to get them. Then, like Despair said, it will probably resurrect the Meteor Monsters, only this time, there will be no one to stop them because no one will be able to kill them. Even the handful of Meteor Monster bullets I created for my teammates ahead of time won't last forever.

If I fail here, then everyone I know and love will die. Paintbrush, Captain Cowboy, Dakota, Mom, Dad ... everyone on the planet will perish.

So I can't fail.

And if the only way to succeed is to get rid of the meteor and myself, then so be it.

Ignoring the pain in my chest, I rise to my feet and fly over the meteor toward Despair. A look of surprise appears on Despair's face as he says, "What are you doing? I told you that—"

Despair stops talking abruptly, mostly because I plunge my hand into and through his chest, grabbing his half of my Core. With a yell, I yank it out of his chest, ignoring the flames from his body trying to burn me at the same time.

Despair cries out in pain as I stumble away from him. He stumbles backward, too, looking at the hole in his chest in disbelief.

"What ..." Despair looks up at me, his eyes wide with questions. "Why? Have you given up hope already and want to merge us back together out of some delusional belief that it will make it harder for the meteor to take us back?"

I step away from Despair, clutching his half-Core in my hand, and look him directly in the eyes. "No. I still have hope. And I am going to show you what hope looks like."

I turn away from Despair even as his body crumbles into dust. Yet even though his physical form is gone, I can still feel his hatred and despair pulsing in the half-Core in my hand, as if he is trying to infect me again.

Good thing I am good at tuning out that sort of thing.

Instead, I walk over to the meteor and place the half-Core in the top of the meteor. As soon as I do, it locks in and I feel the half-Core in my chest feel an even greater pull toward the meteor.

In my own way and on my own terms, I let my half-Core have what it wants ...

By grabbing the meteor and, drawing upon all of my super strength, lifting it directly above my head. The meteor is heavy, heavier than I thought at first, and every muscle in my body strains against its weight. Has to weigh a ton, at least. Makes me wonder how Cap got it moved to the Stable without destroying the elevator.

Regardless, I am not going to be holding it forever.

I then look up toward the sky and, activating my flight powers, shoot straight up. I fly high, higher and higher, even higher than Devon Tower, until I pass the clouds, and keep going. My whole body strains and screams against the effort as the air becomes thinner and thinner, making breathing and thinking difficult.

But my plan is simple:

Once I am high enough, I will unleash all of the fire in my body at once and try to blow up the meteor.

Crazy plan? Maybe, but I think it has a chance of working. My fire has been about the only thing that consistently kills or injures not just the Meteor Monsters, but their

SLOTH

Cores, too. Assuming the meteor itself is made of the same material as the Cores—and why wouldn't it be?—I should be able to blow up the meteor with enough fire.

The only question is, will I survive the explosion or not?

I have no idea. I am heading into uncharted territory here, but I have the strongest suspicion that I am not going to survive this one.

Which sucks. I never got to say a proper goodbye to any of my friends or family. They might not even know about my sacrifice until later, if ever. I mean, once they realize I am missing and see that the meteor is also missing, they will undoubtedly put two and two together and figure out the answer, but regardless, that still might not be for a while.

So I pray. I don't know who or what I am praying to, not exactly, but I just pray that everyone I know and love will be safe and that they will all know about my sacrifice at some point. Maybe I am praying to the universe, maybe I am praying to God, but whoever is out there listening, just know this:

I love my family and my friends.

Opening my eyes, I realize I must be getting close to the atmosphere. Ice has started to form on the surface of the meteor and even on my costume and skin. Good. That means I am high enough that I won't have to worry about anyone else getting harmed in the aftermath of the explosion.

So, as breathing becomes more and more difficult for me, I close my eyes and draw upon all of the fire and heat within me. I grab every last ember, focusing on bringing it out of my body and into the work in one giant blast.

And then ... I explode.

36

I hover in the shadows for a while, though for how long, I can't say. Time doesn't really have a meaning in this place, wherever I am. Just endless darkness as I drift through it like I am floating on a long river, carried by its currents to wherever it leads.

Is this death? I don't know. I've never actually died before, as you might have guessed. I don't really know what to expect from death, and I don't know if heaven or hell exists, or if I'm in either place.

But maybe that isn't such a problem. Maybe this is just what death is—gently flowing through endless darkness forever and ever. That might have sounded like torture to me a while ago, but... actually, now that I think about it, that is torture.

But I can't really do anything about it, unfortunately. I feel completely exhausted after blowing up. I can't even move my muscles, even though I want to. It feels like all the energy in my body has drained away... and maybe I'll drain away with it...

Wait a minute. If I can feel my muscles, that means I have a physical body. And if I have a physical body, then maybe that means I'm still—

My eyes fly open, and for a moment, I find myself staring at a white ceiling overhead. LED light bulbs hang from the ceiling while a soft morning light creeps in through the blinds of the window to my right. With a jolt, I realize that I'm lying in a hospital bed, underneath clean, comfy white sheets. I also realize I'm wearing nothing but a patient's gown beneath the blankets, but fortunately, the blankets are thick enough that I don't feel too cold.

But I do feel cold. Colder than I have in a while. I shiver slightly and pull the blankets up to my chin, wondering what in the hell happened and how I even got here. There's no one else in the room, which makes me wonder if this is actually the afterlife, and if that floating-in-darkness thing was just my imagination or something.

SLOTH

Then I catch a whiff of bacon and look to my left. I see a simple plate of bacon and eggs that's been sitting there for a while—it doesn't look hot. But my stomach growls as soon as I see it, and I reach over, grabbing the plate and immediately stuffing my face. Yes, the food is cold, but I'm so hungry I don't care. I also slurp down the glass of orange juice next to it, but unfortunately, I accidentally drop the glass on the floor, and it shatters into a million pieces.

That prompts the door to fly open, and what feels like a hundred people enter the room at once.

Well, it feels like that, anyway. It's more like a large handful of people show up. The first to enter is Paintbrush, who isn't in her costume but is wearing a super concerned yet relieved look on her face. Just after her are Captain Cowboy, followed by Dakota, Mom, and Dad. The five of them practically storm the room, everyone talking at once in a confused cacophony of voices.

"Toby, what happened?" says Paintbrush, her eyes darting around the room. "We heard a glass break and—"

"And we thought you might be in danger or something," finishes Captain Cowboy for her. He draws a pistol from his holster and looks around the room suspiciously. "But I don't see any assassins or anyone trying to get at Toby."

Dakota points at the shards of glass and orange juice covering the floor near my bed. "Looks like Toby just dropped his orange juice! That's funny. He hasn't done that since he was like ten."

Mom, of course, immediately grabs a broom and dustpan from the corner of the room and starts sweeping up, saying in a slightly annoyed voice, "Toby, what have I taught you about making sure not to break other people's stuff? Do you want the hospital to charge us an arm and a leg to replace that glass?"

Dad, however, pats Mom on the shoulder and says, "It'll be fine, Wendy. I doubt the hospital will care about a glass or two, especially after the hero of Oklahoma City saved everyone."

I blink rapidly, taking in everyone's appearance. "The hero of Oklahoma City? Who's that?"

Dakota giggles and points at me. "That would be you, big brother! That's what everyone's calling you now after you defeated the Meteor Monsters."

Paintbrush nods, tugging at her hair anxiously. "Yeah, but I'm just relieved that you finally woke up. The doctors weren't sure when we found your body, but I'm glad you're awake because it means you're alive."

I put a hand on my chest, feeling my heart beating as usual. "I guess I am, but how long have I been out? I thought for sure I was dead. I should have died. Why am I still alive?"

Captain Cowboy tilts his head to the side in confusion. "Why do you sound so upset about that? Did you want to die or something?"

I shake my head rapidly. "No, no, I didn't. But I was intending to. I flew the meteor all the way up to space, and then I exploded, and then I lost consciousness and just assumed I was dead."

Captain Cowboy strokes his chin thoughtfully. "That does explain the humongous explosion everyone saw in the sky that day. Lots of people had different theories about it, but no one actually knew what it was."

Paintbrush grimaces. "I suspected as much. When we went back to the Stable, we saw the meteor was missing. We've had the police searching OKC for it, but now we know they won't find it. Although we should have known when we found your body covered in shards that were the same color as the meteor."

I rub my temples, feeling a headache starting to come on for some reason. "Where did you find my body?"

Captain Cowboy jerks a thumb over his shoulder. "At the crater, obviously. Some of the witnesses of your little brawl with Despair in Bricktown reported seeing y'all heading that way, so once the police got to the top floor and escorted me, I had Paintbrush, Codetalker, and Keith go investigate. In case you forgot, I got shot by Logikill, so I couldn't exactly go with them and verify the reports myself."

Paintbrush nods. "Yeah. It took us a while to get there, but when we did, the only thing we found was you lying in the middle of the crater, surrounded by shards of the meteor. You were completely naked but unharmed, so we got you to the hospital as quickly as we could."

Captain Cowboy grimaces. "You did look pretty rough, but surprisingly not as rough as someone who'd blown up a meteor should have looked. I assume that was probably your healing factor at work. Otherwise, I'm sure you wouldn't have survived that."

I nod slowly. That explanation makes sense. Granted, I've never tested my healing factor to that extent, but I guess it makes sense that it would help me survive a fall from space after blowing myself up. But for some reason, I don't feel like I normally do after I heal. I feel very tired and worn out, which I guess is normal, but I should be feeling a lot better than I currently do, considering it seems to have been a long time since I sacrificed myself to destroy the meteor.

To find out how long, exactly, I ask Paintbrush, "How long was I out? It doesn't feel that long to me—maybe a day or so?"

Paintbrush shakes her head. "You were out for two weeks."

My eyes widen in shock. "Two weeks? Are you sure?"

Dakota snorts. "What, don't you trust what your super smart girlfriend tells you? You know Paintbrush doesn't really have much of a sense of humor anyway, so she's not trolling you or anything."

Shaking slightly at the realization of how long I've been out, I say, "No wonder you guys thought I wouldn't wake up. I probably would've written myself off if I'd known how long I was out."

Captain Cowboy purses his lips uncertainly. "It was a little strange. Normally, you'd have woken up a lot sooner than that, but maybe the explosion, combined with the fall to Earth, pushed your healing factor to its limits or something, which is why it took you so long to recover. Are you recovered, by the way?"

I rub my chest again, pulling my gown away to look down at my body, just to make sure I'm okay. "I'm pretty sure I am at this point. I don't feel any pain or injuries or anything. I—what is this?"

Because when I pull my gown away from my body, I find what looks like a very old burn scar on my chest. The scar is shaped like half of a star, but I have no memory of ever getting a scar like this.

Dakota, who had leaned over to look at my scar too, frowns in puzzlement. "A scar? Where did that come from?"

I shake my head slowly. "I don't know. I definitely didn't have it earlier, and my healing factor should've taken care of it. Paintbrush, did I have the scar when you guys found me in the crater?"

Paintbrush nods. "You did, actually. I'd assumed it had healed by now, too, but I guess it still hasn't. Must have been a pretty serious wound to take this long to heal."

That isn't necessarily a wrong explanation, but deep in my gut, I'm starting to realize there may be another explanation for the scar. One that might change my future.

Pushing that thought aside for now, I say to everyone, "It's a pretty interesting coincidence that you guys showed up right when I woke up from my coma after two weeks."

Captain Cowboy folds his arms across his chest and gives me a rather offended look. "Coincidence? All five of us have been coming to the hospital every day to check on you."

Dad holds up his phone and waves it at me. "With everyone else on speed dial in case you woke up when one of us was visiting. We had a system and everything, with each of us coming on a different day of the week and sending reports back to the others who couldn't come to check on you."

Mom smiles as she dumps the tray of broken glass into a nearby trash can. "Although Toby isn't entirely wrong. This is the first time since the day you were sent to the hospital that all five of us have been here together. We were planning to check on you and then all go to lunch as a group later. We frankly weren't expecting you to wake up while we were visiting."

I blink, trying not to let tears form in my eyes. "Seriously? What about everyone else?"

Captain Cowboy smiles. "Keith is still at the Stable and has been overseeing the repairs since the meteor disappeared, while CT has gone back to Durant or wherever he usually hangs out. But I'll definitely let both of them know you're awake and alive. They've both been really worried about you—especially Codetalker, even though he likes to pretend he's an emotionless robot."

It's a relief to hear that, but then I remember other people and ask, "What about Walter? And Pietro? Did Pietro actually survive his sacrifice or...?"

Everyone looks away or at the floor when I mention Pietro, which makes me feel terrible. Only Captain Cowboy continues to look at me, and he says, "They recovered Pietro's body from Devon Tower. His funeral was last week. Like I told you during that whole fiasco, I paid for the whole thing so his family could just grieve."

My heart tightens. I didn't know Pietro all that well, but he was definitely a good guy who didn't deserve to die. I know he went out on his own terms, and his sacrifice ultimately helped us in the long term, but it still sucks. I make a mental note to visit his grave as soon as I'm released from the hospital. It's the least I can do for him.

Then Captain Cowboy glances over his shoulder. "As for Walter, he's still alive, thankfully, but—"

I hear the squeaking of wheels outside my room and a loud, familiar male voice shouting, "Everyone, out of my way! Now!"

SLOTH

The door to my room swings open again, and Walter, sitting in a wheelchair, wheels himself in. He looks surprisingly well, despite being in a wheelchair, although I notice a bandage peeking out from the collar of his shirt. Maybe some of his injuries are still healing.

Sitting upright, I stare at Walter in disbelief. "Walter? Where did you come from and how did you know I was awake?"

Walter stares at me like I'm an idiot. "Because I heard your whole fan club barge into your room. Or did you not know that my room in the hospital is right next to yours?"

Paintbrush gives Walter a frown. "I thought you told us that the doctors said not to haul yourself out of bed and into your wheelchair like that without help. They don't want you to stress yourself out or push yourself too hard because you're still recovering from your injuries."

Walter rolls his eyes. "Who cares what the doctors think? I wanted to see Toby, too. It's not like I drove all the way to Toby's house or anything."

I shake my head, trying not to laugh. "Glad to see you are the same as ever, Walter. Honestly."

Walter bites his lower lip slightly. "I won't say I was worried about you, but ... yeah, I'm glad you survived, Toby. Would have sucked if you didn't."

All I do is nod at Walter. "Yeah. And maybe after we're both feeling better, we can go visit Drew's grave."

Walter looks completely taken aback by my offer. "What? Really? Are you sure?"

I look Walter straight in the eyes. "One hundred percent, like Cap always says."

Cap chuckles. "Looks like my Oscarisms, as I've come to call them, are starting to rub off on you after all, kid. Maybe there's hope for you yet."

I roll my eyes back at Captain Cowboy before I notice another absence. "What happened to Black?"

Captain Cowboy's good cheer immediately fizzles out. "The police arrested him when they reached the top floor. Surprisingly, he didn't put up a fight, probably because he'd gotten injured by the Meteor Monsters. He's back in jail now and this time, I hope, he doesn't escape or get help from the outside to escape."

I can't say I am surprised to hear that. Given Black's crimes, I think jailtime is a little lenient myself, but I am not the judge, so I guess my opinion on the matter ... doesn't matter.

That was a pun.

Maybe I really am turning into Cap's younger, cooler clone.

That horrifying thought is mercifully pushed out of my mind when Dakota says, "So in the end, everything worked out. Big brother is alive, nearly everyone else survived, the Meteor Monsters are gone for good, and the city is safe."

"Not just the city, Dakota," says Captain Cowboy. He gives me an approving look. "Toby here saved the whole world. He even tried to give his life to do it. Like a true hero."

I try not to flush. "Thanks, Cap. Everyone, really. I appreciate it. I was thinking of all of y'all in my final moments. Glad I get to see everyone again."

Dakota purses her lips and looks from me to Captain Cowboy and back again. I can just tell she has a burning question on her mind, one she really wants to ask but is afraid of how it might be perceived.

And if it's the same question I am thinking about, then I definitely won't be offended if she asks us.

"So ..." says Dakota slowly. She looks at me. "Are you going to go back to being Cap's sidekick, Toby?"

"Why wouldn't he?" says Walter. "Sure, the doctors probably need to sign off on his release, but Toby looks like he's pretty much fully recovered already. And since Wyldfyre is considered the Hero of Oklahoma City now, it would be kind of weird if he didn't get back to his superhero work."

Captain Cowboy smiles at me. "I'd definitely be happy to take you back on as soon as you feel ready to return to work, Toby."

Everyone looks excited about the prospect of me coming back to work as Wyldfyre ... which makes me feel bad for *not* being as excited.

Because I have the strongest feeling that I might not be able to.

Paintbrush, of course, catches my silence before anyone else. "Toby? Is there something wrong?"

I take a deep breath. "I need to test something. Mandy, Cap, would you help me out of bed, please?"

Fortunately, neither Captain Cowboy nor Paintbrush question why I need the help. They both just come over to the bed, take one arm each, and gently help me rise to my feet. I'm glad I asked for the help because as soon as my bare feet touch the cold floor, my legs nearly give out underneath me, forcing Cap and Paintbrush to redouble their support of my arms.

"Whoa, there, Toby!" says Captain Cowboy. "You all right, bud? Almost fell there."

"I'll be fine, Cap," I say. I hesitate. "Although I might need you and Mandy to let go now. I'll lean on the bed for support."

They both let go of me and step away, puzzled expressions on their faces. Neither of them seem to know what I am going to try next, which is fine because it's more for my benefit than theirs.

Leaning on the bed frame for support, I raise one hand into the air and shout my silly catchphrase:

"Fire up!"

37

Nothing happens.

I don't feel the familiar sensation of heat and warmth explode from my body like normal. In fact, I don't feel any heat at all, not even the slightest embers stirring in my soul.

When I focus on my body, I feel ... empty.

Almost as if I am missing a part of myself.

Dakota blinks at me. "Big brother, why didn't you transform into Wyldfyre? You said your catchphrase. Was it just a joke or something?"

Captain Cowboy frowns seriously. "Oh. I get it now."

Paintbrush nods. "Same. I don't want to, but I do."

Both Mom and Dad exchange knowing looks, as if they received the same memo as Cap and Paintbrush. Only Dakota and Walter look confused. Well, Dakota looks confused. Walter looks mostly angry.

"What?" says Walter, looking at the adults in annoyance. "What is wrong with Toby? And why aren't any of you telling us?"

I take a deep breath and put a hand on my scarred chest. "There's nothing wrong with me, Walt. That's exactly the problem. I'm just a normal human again."

Walter whips his head toward me, a look of total disbelief on his features. "Wait. Do you mean that you don't ... you aren't ..."

I nod. "That's right. I don't have my powers anymore. Which means I am not Wyldfyre anymore, too."

Dakota practically jumps out of her shoes in shock. "What? You aren't Wyldfyre anymore? How is that possible? I thought you were always going to be Wyldfyre."

I shake my head, slowly lowering my hand to my side. "When Despair and I split in half, we each got half of my Core. So when I blew up the meteor, I didn't just destroy the Cores of the Meteor Monsters. I also destroyed my own Core, which was the source of my powers this whole time."

Walter furrows his brow. "But how did you destroy your own Core without destroying yourself? Did you perform, like, midair surgery on yourself at the last minute or something like that?"

I resist the urge to laugh at Walter's crazy suggestion. "No. What I think happened is that I overloaded my Core, or my half-Core, probably, when I blew up the meteor. I really went all out, using up all of my fire, which might have been too much for it. So when the meteor exploded, so did my half-Core. As for how I survived that, maybe the shards of my half-Core still maintained enough power to protect me until Paintbrush and the others found me."

Walter frowns. "Is that even possible?"

I spread my arms wide, finally trusting my legs to support me, which they do, albeit weakly. "I'm still alive, so yes, I guess it is."

Dakota scratches the side of her face. "But if you don't have your powers anymore, then does that mean you can't be Captain Cowboy's sidekick anymore?"

Captain Cowboy shrugs. "Technically, you don't *need* powers to be a superhero. I don't have any and look at how well I am doing."

I bite my lower lip and sit back down on the bed just to give my legs a chance to rest. "Yeah, but it does make it easier. I still have all of my training and fighting skills, but if I am going to be your sidekick again, I will have to rethink my whole fighting style because it was based on the fact that I was basically immortal and unkillable."

"That's doable," says Captain Cowboy. "But I will understand if you want time to think about it or do something else. You've been through a lot lately, so it wouldn't be fair of me to force you to make a choice now."

"What about Mandy?" says Dakota, looking at Paintbrush again. "Are you staying with Cap as his sidekick, too? You still have your powers."

Paintbrush shakes her head. "No. I've decided I am going to go to nursing school and become a nurse, starting with classes this fall."

I am not surprised to hear that. She'd already told me that she'd been accepted into nursing school, though I have to admit it's still a little disappointing. Having a superhero girlfriend was pretty cool, but I didn't fall in love with her because she was a superhero, so this won't change our relationship much."

Mom smiles at Paintbrush. "Not a bad career choice. Although there's nothing wrong with being a superhero, either."

Mom flashes another, more seductive smile at Cap, who smiles right back at her with a big goofy grin. I forgot how much I hate it when adults flirt with each other in front of me. Makes me want to gag, even if I am happy they are together.

I sigh. "I will think about it. I just need time to think about my future. What I want and all that."

"Understandable," says Captain Cowboy with a nod. "Like I said, take all the time you need. Anyway, who's ready for some Hideaway Pizza? I can go pick us up a few pizzas to celebrate if anyone's interested."

Everyone expresses interest in Captain Cowboy's generous offer, including me. That cold breakfast definitely didn't fill me up. I feel hungry enough to eat two whole horses and then some.

But while everyone else chats excitedly about the pizza and about going to tell the others about my survival, I stare up at the ceiling of my room, trying to puzzle out not only my own feelings about losing my powers, but also my own future.

38

Surprisingly, I was released from the hospital that very same day a few hours after I woke up. The doctors taking care of me did run a couple of tests but said I was in good shape to go home. They did warn me against overexerting myself and told me to rest, but I wasn't planning to hit the streets of OKC and start knocking some criminals around or anything.

But I get it. That's how medical people are. That's how Mom is and probably how Paintbrush will be once she's done with nursing school.

I spend the next few weeks at Captain Cowboy's home near Nichols Hills, which is where my family moved in after he and Mom got married. I do get a few visitors, like Gary and Granny, but I mostly stay to myself and to my family.

Which is good, because Captain Cowboy says every journalist and news organization in OKC—and even some beyond—want to talk to me. Evidently, news of the destruction of the Meteor Monsters, along with rumors about Wyldfyre's apparent 'death,' has gone viral online. None of these people actually *know* I am Wyldfyre, of course, but everyone knows Wyldfyre works for Captain Cowboy, so asking him for news about me makes sense. Cap jokes that he does feel a little jealous that everyone wants to talk to me instead of him, but I don't think even Cap wants *this* much media attention.

Also, both the governor of Oklahoma and the mayor of OKC want to throw a big celebration to capitalize on the destruction of the Meteor Monsters. The governor even declared the day I destroyed the meteor 'Wyldfyre Day' in honor of my achievements, but I keep ignoring their requests to meet. Even the President of the United States himself keeps reaching out to me but I ignore him, too. That might be rude, but I really don't want to talk to anyone right now until I decide what I want to do with myself.

So I spend the next few weeks mostly resting and recovering. Well, aside from a couple of visits to the graves of Drew and Pietro, but those were on the down low. Walter did tell me that he's thinking of becoming a sidekick himself, though, which would definitely be interesting (though only after he does his time in juvenile detention, although I understand that his actions in the Logikill incident got his time in jail cut by a few years).

And, of course, drawing in my sketchbook.

Might seem weird to be back to doing the same thing that basically got us in that mess, but I am still an artist at heart and something about losing my powers brought back my artistic creativity.

But I don't draw supervillains or monsters this time.

Instead, I draw pictures of Captain Cowboy's house, the wildlife I see out the windows, cars and people walking on the streets, images of my own family members ... pretty much anything that catches my interest.

The way I see it, sketching helps me think. I figure if I can see what I am sketching, it will tell me what I am interested in and what I should do with my life next. A little corny, maybe, but I've learned that a little corniness isn't always a bad thing.

Thus, three weeks after waking from my coma, I find myself sketching one thing more than anything else. Not a real person or object ... well, not one that is real anymore, anyway.

But I keep coming back to it over and over again, more than any other subject.

Although I don't tell anyone else about it until one day, I hear a knock at the door to my room and I look up from my sketchbook on my desk and say, "Yes?"

The door cracks open and Captain Cowboy's smiling face pokes through. "Hey there, Toby! Thought you would be in here. Whatcha drawing?"

I put a hand over my sketchbook. "It's a secret. What do you want?"

Captain Cowboy opens the door more fully, giving me a knowing look. "No need to hide your drawing from me. I know what you are drawing."

I frown. "You do? Have you been spying on me or something?"

Captain Cowboy shakes his head. "Don't need to. I just know you. And I know what you've been thinking about these past few weeks."

I hesitate. Damn, Cap is good. "All right. So you know what I want to do with my future."

Cap nods and leans against the door frame. "I can guess, but I respect you enough to let you tell me, partner."

I take a deep breath. "Okay, but don't laugh when I show you, all right?"

Cap smiles. "Why'd I ever laugh at your drawings?"

I resist the urge to remind Cap that he has, in fact, reacted less than positively to my drawings in the past. Instead, I lift up my sketchbook and flip it around so he can see what I've drawn. "Was this what you were expecting?"

Cap tilts his head to the side. A slight smile tugs at the corner of his mouth. "Mostly. What're you calling it? The Rebirth of Wyldfyre or something cheesy like that?"

I scowl as I lower my sketchbook, with a brand new sketch of my Wyldfyre costume, onto the desk. "It's just Wyldfyre. A new costume for when I return to work with you. It won't have my powers, but I figure with your resources, we should be able to get it designed and made. We can even make replicas of my tapena and bow and arrows, though I'll have to be more careful with them so I don't lose them seeing as I can't just summon them on the spot anymore."

Cap nods. "Sounds like you've really thought this through, Toby. Can I assume this means you want to be a superhero now?"

I nod. "Yeah. I've thought about it and have decided that this is what I want to do. I'll keep drawing, of course, but I feel like the world needs superheroes more than it needs artists at the moment."

Cap shrugs. "The world needs both, honestly, but is that the whole reason why you've decided to become my sidekick again?"

I frown and sigh. "No. I'm also doing it because … I love helping people."

Cap blinks. "That's it?"

I raise my hands defensively. "What's wrong with that? Isn't that what superheroes are supposed to do?"

Cap laughs and takes his hat off his head, scratching his head. "Nothing wrong with that! I'm just surprised to hear you, of all people, say that. I remember when you were a selfish little brat who hated everything and was so mopey and angsty all the time. You've grown into quite the man, if I do say so myself."

I smile at Captain Cowboy. "I had a good teacher. And maybe, just maybe, I grew up a little bit in the process, too."

Captain Cowboy mocks a surprised look. "Toby? Growing up? Perish the thought."

I roll my eyes. "Har, har, Cap. Your sense of humor is amazing."

"Thanks," says Captain Cowboy with a mischievous smile. "I like to think that it is, too. Anyway, why don't you show me that drawing up close and explain all your thoughts about it? That way, we can order it from a superhero costume company and hopefully get the real thing in ASAP."

I smile again and, standing up, walk over to Cap and immediately start explaining my thought process behind each part of the design to him. Cap nods and gives me his thoughts every now and then but otherwise listens very closely to what I have to say.

And now, for the first time in a very long time, I have a lot of hope for my future.

I have a girlfriend, a new family, a dream job, and way more friends than I ever thought I would have.

I'll miss my powers for sure, but I won't let my lack of powers stop me from being Wyldfyre, the Hero of Oklahoma City.

Because it's not powers that make you a real hero.

It's what you do that makes you a hero.

THE END OF MAKE YOUR OWN SUPERVILLAIN ...
AND THE BEGINNING OF THE MERGE, LAUNCHING SPRING 2025!

NOTES FROM THE AUTHOR

Dear reader,

Thank you for reading *Sloth*! I hope you enjoyed this book. Writing the final book in a series, especially one as long as Make Your Own Supervillain, is both fun yet challenging. I hope I gave a satisfactory conclusion to the adventures of Wyldfyre, Captain Cowboy, and all the others. This is their final adventure for now, but I am certainly not opposed to revisiting Oklahoma City and its superheroes again in a future series or book.

In the meantime, however, the very end of the last chapter hinted, rather ominously, at the coming of The Merge.

That, of course, is my next epic multiverse crossover trilogy! But whereas previous crossover trilogies have focused on bringing together my many different superheroes from across my multiverse, this one focuses on a completely new character in a new world that is (seemingly) unrelated to any I have written previously.

Meet Justin Justice Wright, who lives in New Gold City, Texas with his parents and siblings. After a harrowing encounter with a gang of bullies, Justin steals his dad's super technology, known as the Gate System, to become the superhero Paradigm, who, using his father's mysterious Gates, can transform into superheroes like Bolt, Winter, Wyldfyre, and others, complete with their powers and costumes.

What seems like a simple superhero adventure quickly turns into a mind-boggling adventure into the nature of reality itself as Justin discovers the true origin behind the creation of his universe ... and the woman who is determined to make sure that neither Justin nor anyone else understand the truth.

Sounds interesting? Then you will definitely want to keep an eye out for The Merge #1: Unity, launching spring 2025 on Amazon. Preorder your copy HERE!

See ya,

Lucas Flint, October 2024, Sherman, Texas

Also By Lucas Flint

The Superhero's Son:
The Superhero's Test
The Superhero's Team
The Superhero's Summit
The Superhero's Powers
The Superhero's Origin
The Superhero's World
The Superhero's Vision
The Superhero's World
The Superhero's End

The Young Neos:
Brothers
Powers
Counterparts
Dimensions
Heroes

Minimum Wage Sidekick:
First Job
First Date
First Offer
First Magic
First Mentor

LUCAS FLINT

First War

The Supervillain's Kids:
Bait & Switch
Tag Team
Blood Gems
Prison Break

The Legacy Superhero:
A Superhero's Legacy
A Superhero's Death
A Superhero's Revenge
A Superhero's Assault

Dimension Heroes:
Crossover
Team Up
Amalgamation

Lightning Bolt:
The Superhero's Return
The Superhero's Glitch
The Superhero's Cure
The Superhero's Strike
The Superhero's Clone

Capes Online:
The Player Blackout
The Player Plague
The Player Revolt
The Player Hunter
The Player Glitch
The Player Flag

SLOTH

The Player Legion

Capes & Masks:
First Knight
First Storm
First Hero
First Movie

Tournament of Heroes:
Clash of the Heroes
Prophecy of the Heroes
Fate of the Heroes

Ashley Jason:
Ashley Jason and the Superhero Academy
Ashley Jason and the Lost Hero
Ashley Jason and the Dragon King
Ashley Jason and the Final Exam

VR Hero:
Reset
Trial
Frameup
Order
Future

Heroes of the Multiverse:
Across the Worlds
Across the Rift
Across the Multiverse

Make Your Own Supervillain:
Gluttony

Pride

Envy

Wrath

Greed

Lust

Sloth

Fake Superhero:

Fake Hero

Fake Comic

Fake Chess

Available wherever books are sold!

About the Author

Lucas Flint writes superhero fiction. He is the author of The Superhero's Son, Minimum Wage Sidekick, The Legacy Superhero, and Capes Online, among others. He lives in Sherman, Texas with his wife and daughter.

Find links to books, social media, updates on newest releases, and more by going to his website at www.lucasflint.com.

Milton Keynes UK
Ingram Content Group UK Ltd.
UKHW042007281024
450365UK00003B/231